Honoré de Balzac

Bureaucracy

Or, a civil service reformer

Honoré de Balzac

Bureaucracy
Or, a civil service reformer

ISBN/EAN: 9783337295615

Printed in Europe, USA, Canada, Australia, Japan

Cover: Foto ©Andreas Hilbeck / pixelio.de

More available books at **www.hansebooks.com**

HONORÉ DE BALZAC

TRANSLATED BY

KATHARINE PRESCOTT WORMELEY

BUREAUCRACY

OR

A CIVIL SERVICE REFORMER

ROBERTS BROTHERS

3 SOMERSET STREET

BOSTON

1889

CONTENTS.

BUREAUCRACY.

❖

I.

THE RABOURDIN HOUSEHOLD.

In Paris, where men of thought and study bear a certain likeness to one another, living as they do in a common centre, you must have met with several resembling Monsieur Rabourdin, whose acquaintance we are about to make at a moment when he is head of a bureau in one of our most important ministries. At this period he was forty years old, with gray hair of so pleasing a shade that women might at a pinch fall in love with it for it softened a somewhat melancholy countenance, blue eyes full of fire, a skin that was still fair, though rather ruddy and touched here and there with strong red marks; a forehead and nose *à la* Louis XV., a serious mouth, a tall figure, thin, or perhaps wasted, like that of a man just recovering from illness, and finally, a bearing that was midway between the indolence of a mere idler and the thoughtfulness of a busy man. If this portrait serves to depict his character, a sketch of

1

the man's dress will bring it still further into relief. Rabourdin wore habitually a blue surtout, a white cravat, a waistcoat crossed *à la* Robespierre, black trousers without straps, gray silk stockings and low shoes. Well-shaved, and with his stomach warmed by a cup of coffee, he left home at eight in the morning with the regularity of clock-work, always passing along the same streets on his way to the ministry: so neat was he, so formal, so starched that he might have been taken for an Englishman on the road to his embassy.

From these general signs you will readily discern a family man, harassed by vexations in his own household, worried by annoyances at the ministry, yet philosopher enough to take life as he found it; an honest man, loving his country and serving it, not concealing from himself the obstacles in the way of those who seek to do right; prudent, because he knew men; exquisitely courteous with women, of whom he asked nothing, — a man full of acquirements, affable with his inferiors, holding his equals at a great distance, and dignified towards his superiors. At the epoch of which we write, you would have noticed in him the coldly resigned air of one who has buried the illusions of his youth and renounced every secret ambition; you would have recognized a discouraged, but not disgusted man, one who still clings to his first projects, — more perhaps to employ his faculties than in the hope of a doubtful success. He was not decorated with any order, and always accused himself of weakness for having worn that of the *Fleur-de-lis* in the early days of the Restoration.

The life of this man was marked by certain mysterious peculiarities. He had never known his father; his mother, a woman to whom luxury was everything, always elegantly dressed, always on pleasure bent, whose beauty seemed to him miraculous and whom he very seldom saw, left him little at her death; but she had given him that too common and incomplete education which produces so much ambition and so little ability. A few days before his mother's death, when he was just sixteen, he left the Lycée Napoleon to enter as supernumerary a government office, where an unknown protector had provided him with a place. At twenty-two years of age Rabourdin became under-head-clerk; at twenty-five, head-clerk, or, as it was termed, head of the bureau. From that day the hand that assisted the young man to start in life was never felt again in his career, except as to a single circumstance; it led him, poor and friendless, to the house of a Monsieur Leprince, formerly an auctioneer, a widower said to be extremely rich, and father of an only daughter. Xavier Rabourdin fell desperately in love with Mademoiselle Célestine Leprince, then seventeen years of age, who had all the matrimonial claims of a dowry of two hundred thousand francs. Carefully educated by an artistic mother, who transmitted her own talents to her daughter, this young lady was fitted to attract distinguished men. Tall, handsome, and finely-formed, she was a good musician, drew and painted, spoke several languages, and even knew something of science, — a dangerous advantage, which requires a woman to avoid carefully all appearance of pedantry. Blinded by mistaken tenderness, the mother gave the daughter false ideas as to her probable future; to the maternal eyes a duke or an ambassador, a marshal of France or a minister of State, could alone give her Célestine her due place in society. The young lady had, moreover, the manners, language, and habits of the great world. Her dress was richer and more elegant than was suitable for an unmarried girl; a husband could give her nothing more than she now had, except happiness. Besides all such indulgences, the foolish spoiling of the mother, who died a year after the girl's marriage, made a husband's task all the more difficult. What coolness and composure of mind were needed to rule such a woman! Commonplace suitors held back in fear. Xavier Rabourdin, without parents and without fortune other than his situation under government, was proposed to Célestine by her father. She resisted for a long time; not that she had any personal objection to her suitor, who was young, handsome, and much in love, but she

shrank from the plain name of Madame Rabourdin.
Monsieur Leprince assured his daughter that Xavier
was of the stock that statesmen came of. Célestine
answered that a man named Rabourdin would never be
anything under the government of the Bourbons, etc.
Forced back to his intrenchments, the father made the
serious mistake of telling his daughter that her future
husband was certain of becoming Rabourdin *de something or other* before he reached the age of admission
to the Chamber. Xavier was soon to be appointed
Master of petitions, and general secretary at his ministry. From these lower steps of the ladder the young
man would certainly rise to the higher ranks of the
administration, possessed of a fortune and a name bequeathed to him in a certain will of which he, Monsieur
Leprince, was cognizant. On this the marriage took
place.

Rabourdin and his wife believed in the mysterious
protector to whom the auctioneer alluded. Led away
by such hopes and by the natural extravagance of happy
love, Monsieur and Madame Rabourdin spent nearly
one hundred thousand francs of their capital in the first
five years of married life. By the end of this time
Célestine, alarmed at the non-advancement of her
husband, insisted on investing the remaining hundred
thousand francs of her dowry in landed property,
which returned only a slender income; but her future

inheritance from her father would amply repay all present privations with perfect comfort and ease of life. When the worthy auctioneer saw his son-in-law disappointed of the hopes they had placed on the nameless protector, he tried, for the sake of his daughter, to repair the secret loss by risking part of his fortune in a speculation which had favorable chances of success. But the poor man became involved in one of the liquidations of the house of Nucingen, and died of grief, leaving nothing behind him but a dozen fine pictures which adorned his daughter's salon, and a few old-fashioned pieces of furniture, which she put in the garret.

Eight years of fruitless expectation made Madame Rabourdin at last understand that the paternal protector of her husband must have died, and that his will, if it ever existed, was lost or destroyed. Two years before her father's death the place of chief of division, which became vacant, was given, over her husband's head, to a certain Monsieur de la Billardière, related to a deputy of the Right who was made minister in 1823. It was enough to drive Rabourdin out of the service; but how could he give up his salary of eight thousand francs and perquisites, when they constituted three fourths of his income and his household was accustomed to spend them? Besides, if he had patience for a few more years he would then be entitled to a pension. What a fall was this for a woman whose high expectations at the opening of her life were more or less warranted, and one who was admitted on all sides to be a superior woman.

Madame Rabourdin had justified the expectations formed of Mademoiselle Leprince; she possessed the elements of that apparent superiority which pleases the world; her liberal education enabled her to speak to every one in his or her own language; her talents were real; she showed an independent and elevated mind; her conversation charmed as much by its variety and ease as by the oddness and originality of her ideas. Such qualities, useful and appropriate in a sovereign or an ambassadress, were of little service to a household compelled to jog in the common round. Those who have the gift of speaking well desire an audience; they like to talk, even if they sometimes weary others. To satisfy the requirements of her mind Madame Rabourdin took a weekly reception-day and went a great deal into society to obtain the consideration her self-love was accustomed to enjoy. Those who know Parisian life will readily understand how a woman of her temperament suffered, and was martyrized at heart by the scantiness of her pecuniary means. No matter what foolish declarations people make about money, they one and all, if they live in Paris, must grovel before accounts, do homage to figures, and kiss the forked hoof of the golden calf. What a problem was hers! twelve thousand francs a year to defray the costs of a household consisting of father, mother, two children, a chambermaid and cook, living on the second floor of a house in the rue Duphot, in an apartment costing two thousand francs a year. Deduct the dress and the carriages of Madame before you estimate the gross expenses of the family, for dress precedes everything; then see what remains for the education of the children (a girl of eight and a boy of nine, whose maintenance must cost at least two thousand francs besides) and you will find that Madame Rabourdin could barely afford to give her husband thirty francs a month. That is the position of half the husbands in Paris, under penalty of being thought monsters.

Thus it was that this woman who believed herself destined to shine in the world was condemned to use her mind and her faculties in a sordid struggle, fighting hand to hand with an account-book. Already, terrible sacrifice of pride! she had dismissed her man-servant, not long after the death of her father. Most women grow weary of this daily struggle; they complain but they usually end by giving up to fate and taking what comes to them; Célestine's ambition, far from lessening, only increased through difficulties, and led her, when she found she could not conquer them, to sweep them aside. To her mind this complicated tangle of the affairs of life was a Gordian knot impossible to untie and which genius ought to cut. Far from accepting the pettiness of middle-class existence, she was angry at the delay which kept the great things of life from her grasp, — blaming fate as deceptive. Célestine sincerely believed herself a superior woman. Perhaps she was right; perhaps she would have been great under great circumstances; perhaps she was not in her right place. Let us remember there are as many varieties of woman as there are of man, all of which society fashions to meet its needs. Now in the social order, as in Nature's order, there are more young shoots than there are trees, more spawn than full-grown fish, and many great capacities (Athanase Granson, for instance) which die withered for want of moisture, like seeds on stony ground. There are, unquestionably, household women, accomplished women, ornamental women, women who are exclusively wives, or mothers, or sweethearts, women purely spiritual or purely material; just as there are soldiers, artists, artisans, mathematicians, poets, merchants, men who understand money, or agriculture, or government, and nothing else. Besides all this, the eccentricity of events leads to endless cross-purposes; many are called and few are chosen is the law of earth as of heaven. Madame Rabourdin conceived herself fully capable of directing a statesman, inspiring an artist, helping an inventor and pushing his interests, or of devoting her powers to the financial politics of a Nucingen, and playing a brilliant part in the great world. Perhaps she was only endeavoring to excuse to her own mind a hatred for the laundry lists and the duty of overlooking the housekeeping bills, together with the petty economies and cares of a small establishment. She was superior only in those things where it gave her pleasure to be so. Feeling as keenly as she did the thorns of a position which can only be likened to that of Saint-Laurence on his gridiron, is it any wonder that she sometimes cried out? So, in her paroxysms of thwarted ambition, in the moments when her wounded vanity gave her terrible shooting pains, Célestine turned upon Xavier Rabourdin. Was it not her husband's duty to give her a suitable position in the world? If she were a man she would have had the energy to make a rapid fortune for the sake of rendering an adored wife happy! She reproached him for being too honest a man. In the mouth of some women this accusation is a charge of imbecility. She sketched out for him certain brilliant plans in which she took no account of the hindrances imposed by men and things; then, like all women under the influence of vehement feeling, she became in thought as Machiavellian as Gondreville, and more unprincipled than Maxime de Trailles. At such times Célestine's mind took a wide range, and she imagined herself at the summit of her ideas.

When these fine visions first began Rabourdin, who saw the practical side, was cool. Célestine, much grieved, thought her husband narrow-minded, timid, unsympathetic; and she acquired, insensibly, a wholly false opinion of the companion of her life. In the first place, she often extinguished him by the brilliancy of her arguments. Her ideas came to her in flashes, and she sometimes stopped him short when he began an explanation, because she did not choose to lose the slightest sparkle of her own mind. From the earliest days of their marriage Célestine, feeling herself beloved and admired by her husband, treated him without ceremony; she put herself above conjugal laws and the rules of private courtesy by expecting love to pardon all her little wrong-doings; and, as she never in any way corrected herself, she was always in the ascendant. In such a situation the man holds to the wife very much the position of a child to a teacher when the latter cannot or will not recognize that the mind he has ruled in childhood is becoming mature. Like Madame de Staël, who exclaimed in a room full of people, addressing, as we may say, a greater man than herself, "Do you know you have really said something very profound!" Madame Rabourdin said of her husband: "He certainly has a good deal of sense at times." Her disparaging opinion of him gradually appeared in her behavior through almost imperceptible motions. Her attitude

and manners expressed a want of respect. Without
being aware of it she injured her husband in the eyes of
, others ; for in all countries society, before making up
its mind about a man, listens for what his wife thinks
of him, and obtains from her what the Genevese term
" pre-advice."

When Rabourdin became aware of the mistakes
which love had led him to commit it was too late, —
the groove had been cut; he suffered and was silent.
Like other men in whom sentiments and ideas are
of equal strength, whose souls are noble and their
brains well balanced, he was the defender of his wife
before the tribunal of his own judgment; he told himself that nature doomed her to a disappointed life
through his fault, *his;* she was like a thoroughbred English horse, a racer harnessed to a cart full of stones ;
she it was who suffered ; and he blamed himself. His
wife, by dint of constant repetition, had inoculated him
with her own belief in herself. Ideas are contagious in
a household ; the ninth thermidor, like so many other
portentous events, was the result of female influence.
Thus, goaded by Célestine's ambition, Rabourdin had
long considered the means of satisfying it, though he
hid his hopes, so as to spare her the tortures of uncertainty. The man was firmly resolved to make his way
in the administration by bringing a strong light to bear
upon it. He intended to bring about one of those revo-

lutions which send a man to the head of either one
party or another in society; but being incapable of so
doing in his own interests, he merely pondered useful
thoughts and dreamed of triumphs won for his country
by noble means. His ideas were both generous and
ambitious; few officials have not conceived the like;
but among officials as among artists there are more
miscarriages than births; which is tantamount to
Buffon's saying that "Genius is patience."

Placed in a position where he could study French
administration and observe its mechanism, Rabourdin
worked in the circle where his thought revolved, which,
we may remark parenthetically, is the secret of much
human accomplishment; and his labor culminated finally in the invention of a new system for the Civil Service of government. Knowing the people with whom
he had to do, he maintained the machine as it then
worked, as it still works and will continue to work; for
everybody fears to remodel it, though no one, according
to Rabourdin, ought to be unwilling to simplify it. In his
opinion, the problem to be resolved lay in a better use
of the same forces. His plan, in its simplest form, was
to revise taxation and lower it in a way that should not
diminish the revenues of the State, and to obtain, from
a budget equal to the budgets which now excite such
rabid discussion, results that should be two-fold greater
than the present results. Long practical experience

had taught Rabourdin that perfection is brought about
in all things by changes in the direction of simplicity.
To economize is to simplify. To simplify means to
suppress unnecessary machinery; removals naturally
follow. His system, therefore, depended on the weed-
ing out of officials and the establishment of a new order
of administrative offices. No doubt the hatred which
all reformers incur takes its rise here. Removals required by this perfecting process, always ill-understood,
threaten the well-being of those on whom a change in
their condition is thus forced. What rendered Rabourdin
really great was that he was able to restrain the enthusiasm that possesses all reformers, and to patiently seek
out a slow evolving medium for all changes so as to
avoid shocks, leaving time and experience to prove the
excellence of each reform. The grandeur of the result
anticipated might make us doubt its possibility if we
lose sight of this essential point in our rapid analysis
of his system. It is, therefore, not unimportant to
show through his own self-communings, however incomplete they be, the point of view from which he looked at
the administrative horizon. This tale, which is evolved
from the very heart of the Civil Service, may also serve
to show some of the evils of our present social customs.

Xavier Rabourdin, deeply impressed by the trials and
poverty which he witnessed in the lives of the government clerks, endeavored to ascertain the cause of their

growing deterioration. He found it in those petty partial revolutions, the eddies, as it were, of the storm of 1789, which the historians of great social movements neglect to inquire into, although as a matter of fact it is they which have made our manners and customs what they now are.

Formerly, under the monarchy, the bureaucratic armies did not exist. The clerks, few in number, were under the orders of a prime minister who communicated with the sovereign; thus they directly served the king. The superiors of these zealous servants were simply called head-clerks. In those branches of administration which the king did not himself direct, such for instance as the *fermes* (the public domains throughout the country on which a revenue was levied), the clerks were to their superior what the clerks of a business-house are to their employer; they learned a science which would one day advance them to prosperity. Thus, all points of the circumference were fastened to the centre and derived their life from it. The result was devotion and confidence. Since 1789 the State, call it the Nation if you like, has replaced the sovereign. Instead of looking directly to the chief magistrate of this nation, the clerks have become, in spite of our fine patriotic ideas, the subsidiaries of the government; their superiors are blown about by the winds of a power called "the administration," and do not know from day to day where they may be on the morrow. As the routine of public business must go on, a certain number of indispensable clerks are kept in their places, though they hold these places on sufferance, anxious as they are to retain them. Bureaucracy, a gigantic power set in motion by dwarfs, was generated in this way. Though Napoleon, by subordinating all things and all men to his will, retarded for a time the influence of bureaucracy (that ponderous curtain hung between the service to be done and the man who orders it), it was permanently organized under the constitutional government, which was, inevitably, the friend of all mediocrities, the lover of authentic documents and accounts, and as meddlesome as an old tradeswoman. Delighted to see the various ministers constantly struggling against the four hundred petty minds of the Elected of the Chamber, with their ten or a dozen ambitious and dishonest leaders, the Civil Service officials hastened to make themselves essential to the warfare by adding their quota of assistance under the form of written action; they created a power of inertia and named it "Report." Let us explain the Report.

When the kings of France took to themselves ministers, which first happened under Louis XV., they made them render reports on all important questions, instead of holding, as formerly, grand councils of state with the nobles. Under the constitutional government, the ministers of the various departments were insensibly led by their bureaus to imitate this practice of kings. Their time being taken up in defending themselves before the two Chambers and the court, they let themselves be guided by the leading-strings of the Report. Nothing important was ever brought before the government that a minister did not say, even when the case was urgent, "I have called for a report." The Report thus became, both as to the matter concerned and for the minister himself, the same as a report to the Chamber of Deputies on a question of laws, — namely, a disquisition in which the reasons for and against are stated with more or less partiality. No real result is attained; the minister, like the Chamber, is fully as well prepared before as after the report is rendered. A determination, in whatever matter, is reached in an instant. Do what we will, the moment comes when the decision must be made. The greater the array of reasons for and against, the less sound will be the judgment. The finest things of which France can boast have been accomplished without reports and where decisions were prompt and spontaneous. The dominant law of a statesman is to apply precise formulas to all cases, after the manner of judges and physicians.

Rabourdin, who said to himself: "A minister should have decision, should know public affairs and direct their course," saw "Report" rampant throughout France, from the colonel to the marshal, from the commissary of police to the king, from the prefects to the ministers of state, from the Chamber to the courts. After 1818 everything was discussed, compared, and weighed, either in speech or writing; public business took a literary form. France went to ruin in spite of this array of documents; dissertations stood in place of action; a million of reports were written every year; bureaucracy was enthroned! Records, statistics, documents, failing which France would have been ruined, circumlocution, without which there could be no advance, increased, multiplied, and grew majestic. From that day forth bureaucracy used to its own profit the mistrust that stands between receipts and expenditures; it degraded the administration for the benefit of the administrators; in short, it spun those lilliputian threads which have chained France to Parisian centralization, — as if from 1500 to 1800 France had undertaken nothing for want of thirty thousand government clerks! In fastening upon public offices, like a mistletoe on a pear-tree, these officials indemnified themselves amply, and in the following manner.

The ministers, compelled to obey the princes or the Chambers who impose upon them the distribution of the public moneys, and forced to retain the workers in office, proceeded to diminish salaries and increase the number of those workers, thinking that if more persons were employed by government the stronger the government would be. And yet the contrary law is an axiom written on the universe ; there is no vigor except where there are few active principles. Events proved in July, 1830, the error of the materialism of the Restoration. To plant a government in the hearts of a nation it is necessary to bind *interests* to it, not *men*. The government-clerks being led to detest the administrations which lessened both their salaries and their importance, treated them as a courtesan treats an aged lover, and gave them mere work for money ; a state of things which would have seemed as intolerable to the administration as to the clerks, had the two parties dared to feel each other's pulse, or had the higher salaries not succeeded in stifling the voices of the lower. Thus wholly and solely occupied in retaining his place, drawing his pay, and securing a pension, the government official thought everything permissible that conduced to these results. This state of things led to servility on the part of the clerks and to endless intrigues within the various departments, where the humbler clerks struggled vainly against degenerate members of the aristocracy, who sought positions in the government bureaus for their ruined sons.

Superior men could scarcely bring themselves to tread these tortuous ways, to stoop, and cringe, and creep through the mire of these cloacas, where the presence of a fine mind only alarmed the other denizens. The ambitious man of genius grows old in obtaining his triple crown; he does not follow in the steps of Sixtus the Fifth merely to become head of a bureau. No one comes or stays in the government offices but idlers, incapables, or fools. Thus the mediocrity of French administration has slowly come about. Bureaucracy, made up entirely of petty minds, stands as an obstacle to the prosperity of the nation; delays for seven years, by its machinery, the project of a canal which would have stimulated the production of a province; is afraid of everything, prolongs procrastination, and perpetuates the abuses which in turn perpetuate and consolidate itself. Bureaucracy holds all things and the administration itself in leading strings; it stifles men of talent who are bold enough to be independent of it or to enlighten it on its own follies. About the time of which we write the pension list had just been issued, and on it Rabourdin saw the name of an underling in office rated for a larger sum than the old colonels, maimed and wounded for their country. In that fact lies the whole history of bureaucracy.

Another evil, brought about by modern customs, which Rabourdin counted among the causes of this secret demoralization, was the fact that there is no real subordination in the administration in Paris; complete equality reigns between the head of an important division and the humblest copying-clerk; one is as powerful as the other in an arena outside of which each lords it in his own way. Education, equally distributed through the masses, brings the son of a porter into a government office to decide the fate of some man of merit or some landed proprietor whose door-bell his father may have answered. The last comer is therefore on equal terms with the oldest veteran in the service. A wealthy supernumerary splashes his superior as he drives his tilbury to Longchamps and points with his whip to the poor father of a family, remarking to the pretty woman at his side, " That's my chief." The Liberals call this state of things PROGRESS; Rabourdin thought it ANARCHY at the heart of power. He saw how it resulted in restless intrigues, like those of a harem between eunuchs and women and imbecile sultans, or the petty troubles of nuns full of underhand vexations, or college tyrannies, or diplomatic manœuvrings fit to terrify an ambassador, all put in motion to obtain a fee or an increase of salary; it was like the hopping of fleas harnessed to pasteboard cars, the spitefulness of slaves, often visited on the minister himself. With all this were the really useful men, the workers, victims of such parasites; men sincerely devoted to their country, who stood vigorously out from the background of the other incapables, yet who were often forced to succumb through unworthy trickery.

All the higher offices were gained through parliamentary influence, royalty had nothing now to do with them, and the subordinate clerks became, after a time, merely the running-gear of the machine; the most important consideration with them being to keep the wheels well greased. This fatal conviction entering some of the best minds smothered many statements conscientiously written on the secret evils of the national government; lowered the courage of many hearts, and corrupted sterling honesty, weary of injustice and won to indifference by deteriorating annoyances. A clerk in the employ of the Rothchilds corresponds with all England; another, in a government office, may communicate with all the prefects; but where the one learns the way to make his fortune, the other loses time and health and life to no avail. An undermining evil lies here. Certainly a nation does not seem threatened with immediate dissolution because an able clerk is sent away and a middling sort of man replaces him. Unfortunately for the welfare of nations individual men never seem essential to their existence. But in the long run when the belittling process is fully carried out nations will disappear. Every one who seeks instruction on this point can look at Venice, Madrid, Amsterdam, Stockholm, Rome; all places which were formerly resplendent with mighty powers and are now destroyed by the infiltrating littleness which gradually attained the highest eminence. When the day of struggle came, all was found rotten, the State succumbed to a weak attack. To worship the fool who succeeds, and not to grieve over the fall of an able man is the result of our melancholy education, of our manners and customs which drive men of intellect into disgust, and genius to despair.

What a difficult undertaking is the rehabilitation of the Civil Service while the liberal cries aloud in his newspapers that the salaries of clerks are a standing theft, calls the items of the budget a cluster of leeches, and every year demands why the nation should be saddled with a thousand million of taxes. In Monsieur Rabourdin's eyes the clerk in relation to the budget was very much what the gambler is to the game; that which he wins he puts back again. All remuneration implies something furnished. To pay a man a thousand francs a year and demand his whole time was surely to organize theft and poverty. A galley-slave costs nearly as much, and does less. But to expect a man whom the State remunerated with twelve thousand francs a year to devote himself to his country was a profitable contract for both sides, fit to allure all capacities.

These reflections had led Rabourdin to desire the recasting of the clerical official staff. To employ fewer men, to double or treble salaries, and do away with pensions, to choose only young clerks (as did Napoleon,

Louis XIV., Richelieu, and Ximenes), but to keep them long and train them for the higher offices and greatest honors, these were the chief features of a reform which if carried out would be as beneficial to the State as to the clerks themselves. It is difficult to recount in detail, chapter by chapter, a plan which embraced the whole budget and continued down through the minutest details of administration in order to keep the whole synthetical; but perhaps a slight sketch of the principal reforms will suffice for those who understand such matters, as well as for those who are wholly ignorant of the administrative system. Though the historian's position is rather hazardous in reproducing a plan which may be thought the politics of a chimney-corner, it is, nevertheless, necessary to sketch it so as to explain the author of it by his own work. Were the recital of his efforts omitted, the reader would not believe the narrator's word if he merely delared the talent and the courage of this official.

Rabourdin's plan divided the government into three ministries, or departments. He thought that if the France of former days possessed brains strong enough to comprehend in one system both foreign and domestic affairs, the France of to-day was not likely to be without its Mazarin, its Suger, its Sully, its de Choiseul, or its Colbert to direct even vast administrative departments. Besides, constitutionally speaking, three ministers will agree better than seven; and, in the restricted number there is less chance for mistaken choice; moreover, it might be that the kingdom would some day escape from those perpetual ministerial oscillations which interfered with all plans of foreign policy and prevented all ameliorations of home rule. In Austria, where many diverse united nations present so many conflicting interests to be conciliated and carried forward under one crown, two statesmen alone bear the burden of public affairs and are not overwhelmed by it. Was France less prolific of political capacities than Germany? The rather silly game of what are called "constitutional institutions" carried beyond bounds has ended, as everybody knows, in requiring a great many offices to satisfy the multifarious ambition of the middle classes. It seemed to Rabourdin, in the first place, natural to unite the ministry of war with the ministry of the navy. To his thinking the navy was one of the current expenses of the war department, like the artillery, cavalry, infantry, and commissariat. Surely it was an absurdity to give separate administrations to admirals and marshals when both were employed to one end, namely, the defense of the nation, the overthrow of an enemy, and the security of the national possessions. The ministry of the interior ought in like manner to combine the departments of commerce, police, and finances, or it belied its own name. To the ministry of foreign affairs belonged the administration of justice, the household of the king, and all that concerned arts, sciences, and *belles lettres*. All patronage ought to flow directly from the sovereign. Such ministries necessitated the supremacy of a council. Each required the work of two hundred officials, and no more, in its central administration offices, where Rabourdin proposed that they should live, as in former days under the monarchy. Taking the sum of twelve thousand francs a year for each official as an average, he estimated seven millions as the cost of the whole body of such officials, which actually stood at twenty in the budget.

By thus reducing the ministers to three heads he suppressed departments which had come to be useless, together with the enormous costs of their maintenance in Paris. He proved that an arrondissement could be managed by ten men; a prefecture by a dozen at the most; which reduced the entire civil service force throughout France to five thousand men, exclusive of the departments of war and justice. Under this plan the clerks of the courts were charged with the system of loans, and the ministry of the interior with that of registration and the management of domains. Thus Rabourdin united in one centre all divisions that were allied in nature. The mortgage system, inheritance, and registration did not pass outside of their own sphere of action and only required three additional clerks in the justice courts and three in the royal courts. The steady application of this principle brought Rabourdin to reforms in the finance system. He merged the collection of revenue into one channel, taxing consumption in bulk instead of taxing property. According to his ideas, consumption was the sole thing properly taxable in times of peace. Land-taxes should always be held in reserve in case of war; for then only could the State justly demand sacrifices from the soil, which was in danger; but in times of peace it was a serious political fault to burden it beyond a certain limit; otherwise it could never be depended on in great emergencies. Thus a loan should be put on the market when the country was tranquil, for at such times it could be placed at par, instead of at fifty per cent loss as in bad times; in war times resort should be had to a land-tax.

" The invasion of 1814 and 1815," Rabourdin would say to his friends, " founded in France and practically explained an institution which neither Law nor Napoleon had been able to establish, — I mean *Credit*."

Unfortunately, Xavier considered the true principles of this admirable machine of civil service very little understood at the period when he began his labor of reform in 1820. His scheme levied a toll on consumption by means of direct taxation and suppressed the whole machinery of indirect taxation. The levying of the taxes was simplified by a single classification of a great number of articles. This did away with the more harassing customs at the gates of the cities, and obtained the largest revenues from the remainder, by lessening the enormous expense of collecting them. To lighten the burden of taxation is not, in matters of finance, to diminish the taxes, but to assess them better; if lightened, you increase the volume of business by giving it freer play; the individual pays less and the State receives more. This reform, which may seem immense, rests on very simple machinery. Rabourdin regarded the tax on personal property as the most trustworthy representative of general consumption. Individual fortunes are usually revealed in France by rentals, by the number of servants, horses, carriages, and luxuries, the costs of which are all to the interest of the public treasury. Houses and what they contain vary comparatively but little, and are not liable to disappear. After pointing out the means of making a tax-list on personal property which should be more impartial than the existing list, Rabourdin assessed the sums to be brought into the treasury by indirect taxation as so much per cent on each individual share. A tax is a levy of money on things or persons under disguises that are more or less specious. These disguises, excellent when the object is to extort money, become ridiculous in the present day, when the class on which the taxes weigh the heaviest knows why the State imposes them and by what machinery they are given back. In fact the budget is not a strong-box to hold what is put into it, but a watering-pot; the more it takes in and the more it pours out the better for the prosperity of the country. Therefore, supposing there are six millions of tax-payers in easy circumstances (Rabourdin proved their existence, including the rich) is it not better to make them pay a duty on the consumption of wine, which would not be more offensive than that on doors and windows and would return a hundred millions, rather than harass them by taxing the thing itself. By this system of taxation, each individual tax-payer pays less in reality, while the State receives more, and consumers profit by a vast reduction in the price of things which the State releases from its perpetual and harassing interference. Rabourdin's scheme retained a tax on the cultivation of vineyards, so as to protect that industry from the too great abundance of its own products. Then, to reach the consumption of the poorer tax-payers, the licenses of retail dealers were taxed according to the population of the neighborhoods in which they lived.

In this way, the State would receive without cost or vexatious hindrances an enormous revenue under three forms; namely, a duty on wine, on the cultivation of vineyards, and on licenses, where now an irritating array of taxes existed as a burden on itself and its officials. Taxation was thus imposed upon the rich without overburdening the poor. To give another example. Suppose a share assessed to each person of one or two francs for the consumption of salt and you obtain ten or a dozen millions; the modern *gabelle* disappears, the poor breathe freer, agriculture is relieved, the State receives as much, and no tax-payer complains. All persons, whether they belong to the industrial classes or to the capitalists, will see at once the benefits of a tax so assessed when they discover how commerce increases, and life is ameliorated in the country districts. In short, the State will see from year to year the number of her well-to-do tax-payers increasing. By doing away with the machinery of indirect taxation, which is very costly (a State, as it were, within the State), both the public finances and the individual tax-payer are greatly benefited, not to speak of the saving in costs of collecting.

The whole subject is indeed less a question of finance than a question of government. The State should possess nothing of its own, neither forests, nor mines, nor public works. That it should be the owner of domains was, in Rabourdin's opinion, an administrative contradiction. The State cannot turn its possessions to profit and it deprives itself of taxes; it thus loses two forms of production. As to the manufactories of the government, they are just as unreasonable in the sphere of industry. The State obtains products at a higher cost than those of commerce, produces them more slowly, and loses its tax upon the industry, the maintenance of which it, in turn, reduces. Can it be thought a proper method of governing a country to manufacture instead of promoting manufactures? to possess property instead of creating more possessions and more diverse ones? In Rabourdin's system the State exacted no money security; he allowed only mortgage securities; and for this reason : Either the State holds the security in specie, and that embarrasses business and the movement of money; or it invests it at a higher rate than the State itself pays, and that is a contemptible robbery; or else it loses on the transaction, and that is folly; moreover, if it is obliged at any time to dispose of a mass of these securities it gives rise in certain cases to terrible bankruptcy.

The territorial tax did not entirely disappear in Rabourdin's plan, — he kept a minute portion of it as a point of departure in case of war; but the productions of the soil were freed, and industry, finding raw material at a low price, could compete with foreign nations without the deceptive help of customs. The rich carried on the administration of the provinces without compensation except that of receiving a peerage under certain conditions. Magistrates, learned bodies, officers of the lower grades found their services honorably rewarded;

no man employed by government failed to obtain great consideration through the value and extent of his labors and the excellence of his salary; every one was able to provide for his own future and France was delivered from the cancer of pensions. As a result Rabourdin's scheme exhibited only seven hundred millions of expenditures and twelve hundred millions of receipts. A saving of five hundred millions annually had far more virtue than the accumulation of a sinking fund whose dangers were plainly to be seen. In that fund the State, according to Rabourdin, became a stock-holder, just as it persisted in being a land-holder and a manufacturer. To bring about these reforms without too roughly jarring the existing state of things or incurring a Saint-Bartholomew of clerks, Rabourdin considered that an evolution of twenty years would be required.

Such were the thoughts maturing in Rabourdin's mind ever since his promised place had been given to Monsieur de la Billardière, a man of sheer incapacity. This plan, so vast apparently yet so simple in point of fact, which did away with so many large staffs and so many little offices all equally useless, required for its presentation to the public mind close calculations, precise statistics, and self-evident proof. Rabourdin had long studied the budget under its double aspect of ways and means and of expenditure. Many a night he had lain awake unknown to his wife. But so far he had only dared to conceive the plan and fit it prospectively to the administrative skeleton; all of which counted for nothing, — he must gain the ear of a minister capable of appreciating his ideas. Rabourdin's success depended on the tranquil condition of political affairs, which up to this time were still unsettled. He had not considered the government as permanently secure until three hundred deputies at least had the courage to form a compact majority systematically ministerial. An administration founded on that basis had come into power since Rabourdin had finished his elaborate plan. At this time the luxury of peace under the Bourbons had eclipsed the warlike luxury of the days when France shone like a vast encampment, prodigal and magnificent because it was victorious. After the Spanish campaign, the administration seemed to enter upon an era of tranquillity in which some good might be accomplished; and three months before the opening of our story a new reign had begun without any apparent opposition; for the liberalism of the Left had welcomed Charles X. with as much enthusiasm as the Right. Even clear-sighted and suspicious persons were misled. The moment seemed propitious for Rabourdin. What could better conduce to the stability of the government than to propose and carry through a reform whose beneficial results were to be so vast?

Never had Rabourdin seemed so anxious and preoccupied as he now did in the mornings as he walked from his house to the ministry, or at half-past four in the afternoon, when he returned.   Madame Rabourdin, on her part, disconsolate over her wasted life, weary of secretly working to obtain a few luxuries of dress, never appeared so bitterly discontented as now ; but, like any wife who is really attached to her husband, she considered it unworthy of a superior woman to condescend to the shameful devices by which the wives of some officials eke out the insufficiency of their husband's salary. This feeling made her refuse all intercourse with Madame Colleville, then very intimate with François Keller, whose parties eclipsed those of the rue Duphot.   Nevertheless, she mistook the quietude of the political thinker and the preoccupation of the intrepid worker for the apathetic torpor of an official broken down by the dulness of routine, vanquished by that most hateful of all miseries, the mediocrity that simply earns a living ; and she groaned at being married to a man without energy.

Thus it was that about this period in their lives she resolved to take the making of her husband's fortune on herself; to thrust him at any cost into a higher sphere, and to hide from him the secret springs of her machinations.   She carried into all her plans the independence of ideas which characterized her, and was proud to think that she could rise above other women by sharing

none of their petty prejudices and by keeping herself
untrammelled by the restraints which society imposes.
In her anger she resolved to fight fools with their own
weapons, and to make herself a fool if need be. She
saw things coming to a crisis. The time was favorable.
Monsieur de la Billardière, attacked by a dangerous
illness, was likely to die in a few days. If Rabourdin
succeeded him, his talents (for Célestine did vouchsafe
him an administrative gift) would be so thoroughly
appreciated that the office of Master of petitions, formerly promised, would now be given to him; she fancied she saw him king's commissioner, presenting bills
to the Chambers and defending them; then indeed she
could help him; she would even be, if needful, his secretary; she would sit up all night to do the work! All
this to drive in the Bois in a pretty carriage, to equal
Madame Delphine de Nucingen, to raise her salon to
the level of Madame Colleville's, to be invited to the
great ministerial solemnities, to win listeners and make
them talk of her as " Madame Rabourdin *de* something
or other" (she had not yet determined on the estate),
just as they did of Madame Firmiani, Madame d'Espard,
Madame d'Aiglemont, Madame de Carigliano, and thus
efface forever the odious name of Rabourdin.

These secret schemes brought some changes into the
household. Madame Rabourdin began to walk with a
firm step in the path of *debt.* She set up a manservant,

and put him in livery of brown cloth with red pipings, she renewed parts of her furniture, hung new papers on the walls, adorned her salon with plants and flowers, always fresh, and crowded it with knick-knacks that were then in vogue; then she, who had always shown scruples as to her personal expenses, did not hesitate to put her dress in keeping with the rank to which she aspired, the profits of which were discounted in several of the shops where she equipped herself for war. To make her "Wednesdays" fashionable she gave a dinner on Fridays, the guests being expected to pay their return visit and take a cup of tea on the following Wednesday. She chose her guests cleverly among influential deputies or other persons of note who, sooner or later, might advance her interests. In short, she gathered an agreeable and befitting circle about her. People amused themselves at her house; they said so at least, which is quite enough to attract society in Paris. Rabourdin was so absorbed in completing his great and serious work that he took no notice of the sudden reappearance of luxury in the bosom of his family.

Thus the wife and the husband were besieging the same fortress, working on parallel lines, but without each other's knowledge.

II.

MONSIEUR DES LUPEAULX.

At the ministry to which Rabourdin belonged there flourished, as general-secretary, a certain Monsieur Clément Chardin des Lupeaulx, one of those men whom the tide of political events sends to the surface for a few years, then engulfs on a stormy night, but whom we find again on a distant shore, tossed up like the carcass of a wrecked ship which still seems to have life in her. We ask ourselves if that derelict could ever have held goodly merchandize or served a high emprize, co-operated in some defence, held up the trappings of a throne, or borne away the corpse of a monarchy. At this particular time Clément des Lupeaulx (the " Lupeaulx " absorbed the " Chardin) " had reached his culminating period. In the most illustrious lives as in the most obscure, in animals as in secretary-generals, there is a zenith and there is a nadir, a period when the fur is magnificent, the fortune dazzling. In the nomenclature which we derive from fabulists, des Lupeaulx belonged to the species Bertrand, and was always in search of Ratons. As he is one of the principal actors in this drama he deserves a description, all the more precise because the revolution of July has suppressed his office, eminently useful as it was, to a constitutional ministry.

Moralists usually employ their weapons against obtrusive abominations. In their eyes, crime belongs to the assizes or the police-courts ; but the socially refined evils escape their ken ; the adroitness that triumphs under shield of the Code is above them or beneath them ; they have neither eye-glass nor telescope ; they want good stout horrors easily visible. With their eyes fixed on the carnivora, they pay no attention to the reptiles ; happily, they abandon to the writers of comedy the shading and colorings of a Chardin des Lupeaulx. Vain and egotistical, supple and proud, libertine and gourmand, grasping from the pressure of debt, discreet as a tomb out of which nought issues to contradict the epitaph intended for the passer's eye, bold and fearless when soliciting, good-natured and witty in all acceptations of the word, a timely jester, full of tact, knowing how to compromise others by a glance or a nudge, shrinking from no mudhole, but gracefully leaping it, intrepid Voltairean, yet punctual at mass if a fashionable company could be met in Saint Thomas Aquinas, — such a man as this secretary-general resembled, in one way or another, all the mediocrities who form the kernel of the political world.

Knowing in the science of human nature, he assumed the character of a listener, and none was ever more attentive. Not to awaken suspicion he was flattering *ad nauseam*, insinuatiug as a perfume, and cajoling as a woman.

Des Lupeaulx was just forty years old. His youth had long been a vexation to him, for he felt that the making of his career depended on his becoming a deputy. How had he reached his present position? may be asked. By very simple means. He began by taking charge of certain delicate missions which can be given neither to a man who respects himself nor to a man who does not respect himself, but are confided to grave and enigmatic individuals who can be acknowledged or disavowed at will. His business was that of being always compromised; but his fortunes were pushed as much by defeat as by success. He well understood that under the Restoration, a period of continual compromises between men, between things, between accomplished facts and other facts looming on the horizon, it was all-important for the ruling powers to have a household drudge. Observe in a family some old charwoman who can make beds, sweep the floors, carry away the dirty linen, who knows where the silver is kept, how the creditors should be pacified, what persons should be let in and who must be kept out of the house, and such a creature, even if she has all the vices, and is dirty, decrepit, and toothless, or puts into the lottery and steals thirty sous a day for her stake, and you will find the masters like her from habit, talk and consult in her hearing upon even critical matters; she comes and goes, suggests resources, gets on the scent of secrets, brings the rouge or the shawl at the right moment, lets herself be scolded and pushed downstairs, and the next morning reappears smiling with an excellent bouillon. No matter how high a statesman may stand, he is certain to have some household drudge, before whom he is weak, undecided, disputatious with fate, self-questioning, self-answering, and buckling for the fight. Such a familiar is like the soft wood of savages, which, when rubbed against the hard wood, strikes fire. Sometimes great geniuses illumine themselves in this way. Napoleon lived with Berthier, Richelieu with Père Joseph; des Lupeaulx was the familiar of everybody? He continued friends with fallen ministers and made himself their intermediary with their successors, diffusing thus the perfume of the last flattery and the first compliment. He well understood how to arrange all the little matters which a statesman has no leisure to attend to. He saw necessities as they arose; he obeyed well; he could gloss a base act with a jest and get the whole value of it; and he chose for the services he thus rendered those that the recipients were not likely to forget.

Thus, when it was necessary to cross the ditch be-

tween the Empire and the Restoration, at a time when
every one was looking about for planks, and the curs
of the Empire were howling their devotion right and
left, des Lupeaulx borrowed large sums from the usurers and crossed the frontier. Risking all to win all, he
bought up Louis XVIII.'s most pressing debts, and was
the first to settle nearly three millions of them at
twenty per cent—for he was lucky enough to be backed
by Gobseck in 1814 and 1815. It is true that Messrs.
Gobseck, Werdet, and Gigonnet swallowed the profits,
but des Lupeaulx had agreed that they should have
them ; he was not playing for a stake ; he challenged the
bank, as it were, knowing very well that the king was
·not a man to forget this debt of honor. Des Lupeaulx
was not mistaken ; he was appointed Master of petitions, Knight of the order of Saint Louis, and officer of
the Legion of honor. Once on the ladder of political
success, his clever mind looked about for the means
to maintain his foothold ; for in the fortified city into
which he had wormed himself, generals do not long
keep useless mouths. So to his general trade of household drudge and go-between he added that of gratuitous
consultation on the secret maladies of power.

After discovering in the so-called superior men of
the Restoration their utter inferiority in comparison
with the events which had brought them to the front,
he overcame their political mediocrity by putting into

their mouths, at a crisis, the word of command for which men of real talent were listening. It must not be thought that this word was the outcome of his own mind. Were it so, des Lupeaulx would have been a man of genius, whereas he was only a man of talent. He went everywhere, collected opinions, sounded consciences, and caught all the tones they gave out. He gathered knowledge like a true and indefatigable political bee. This walking Bayle dictionary did not act, however, like that famous lexicon; he did not report all opinions without drawing his own conclusions; he had the talent of a fly which drops plumb upon the best bit of meat in the middle of a kitchen. In this way he came to be regarded as an indispensable helper to statesmen. A belief in his capacity had taken such deep root in all minds that the more ambitious public men felt it was necessary to compromise des Lupeaulx in some way to prevent his rising higher; they made up to him for his subordinate public position by their secret confidence.

Nevertheless, feeling that such men were dependent on him, this gleaner of ideas exacted certain dues. He received a salary on the staff of the National Guard, where he held a sinecure which was paid for by the city of Paris; he was government commissioner to a secret society; and filled a position of superintendence in the royal household. His two official posts which appeared on the budget were those of secretary-general to his ministry and Master of petitions. What he now wanted was to be made commander of the Legion of honor, gentleman of the bed-chamber, count, and deputy. To be elected deputy it was necessary to pay taxes to the amount of a thousand francs; and the miserable homestead of the des Lupeaulx was rated at only five hundred. Where could he get money to build a mansion and surround it with sufficient domain to throw dust in the eyes of a constituency? Though he dined out every day, and was lodged for the last nine years at the cost of the State, and driven about in the minister's equipage, des Lupeaulx possessed absolutely nothing, at the time when our tale opens, but thirty thousand francs of debt — undisputed property. A marriage might float him and pump the waters of debt out of his bark; but a good marriage depended on his advancement, and his advancement required that he should be a deputy. Searching about him for the means of breaking through this vicious circle, he could think of nothing better than some immense service to render or some delicate intrigue to carry through for persons in power. Alas! conspiracies were out of date; the Bourbons were apparently on good terms with all parties; and, unfortunately, for the last few years the government had been so thoroughly held up to the light of day by the silly discussions of the Left, whose aim seemed to be to make government of any kind impossible in France, that no good strokes of business could be made. The last were tried in Spain, and what an outcry they excited !

In addition to all this, des Lupeaulx complicated matters by believing in the friendship of his minister, to whom he had the imprudence to express the wish to sit on the ministerial benches. The minister guessed the real meaning of the desire, which simply was that des Lupeaulx wanted to strengthen a precarious position, so that he might throw off all dependence on his chief. The harrier turned against the huntsman ; the minister gave him cuts with the whip and caresses, alternately, and set up rivals to him. But des Lupeaulx behaved like an adroit courtier with all competitors ; he laid traps into which they fell, and then he did prompt justice upon them. The more he felt himself in danger the more anxious he became for an irremovable position ; yet he was compelled to play low ; one moment's indiscretion, and he might lose everything. A pen-stroke might demolish his civilian epaulets, his place at court, his sinecure, his two offices and their advantages ; in all, six salaries retained under fire of the law against pluralists. Sometimes he threatened his minister as a mistress threatens her lover ; telling him he was about to marry a rich widow. At such times the minister petted and cajoled des Lupeaulx. After one

of these reconciliations he received the formal promise
of a place in the Academy of Belles-lettres on the first
vacancy. "It would pay," he said, "the keep of a
horse." His position, so far as it went, was a good
one, and Clément Chardin des Lupeaulx flourished in it
like a tree planted in good soil. He could satisfy his
vices, his caprices, his virtues and his defects.

 The following were the toils of his life. He was
obliged to choose, among five or six daily invitations,
the house where he could be sure of the best dinner.
Every morning he went to his minister's morning
reception to amuse that official and his wife, and to
pet their children. Then he worked an hour or two;
that is to say, he lay back in a comfortable chair and
read the newspapers, dictated the meaning of a letter,
received visitors when the minister was not present,
explained the work in a general way, caught or shed a
few drops of the holy-water of the court, looked over
the petitions with an eyeglass, or wrote his name on the
margin, — a signature which meant " I think it absurd;
do what you like about it." Every body knew that when
des Lupeaulx was interested in any person or in any
thing he attended to the matter personally. He allowed
the head-clerks to converse privately about affairs of
delicacy, but he listened to their gossip. From time
to time he went to the Tuileries to get his cue. And
he always waited for the minister's return from the

Chamber, if in session, to hear from him what intrigue or manœuvre he was to set about. This official sybarite dressed, dined, and visited a dozen or fifteen salons between eight at night and three in the morning. At the opera he talked with journalists, for he stood high in their favor; a perpetual exchange of little services went on between them; he poured into their ears his misleading news and swallowed theirs; he prevented them from attacking this or that minister on such or such a matter, on the plea that it would cause real pain to their wives or their mistresses.

"Say that his bill is worth nothing, and prove it if you can, but do not say that Mariette danced badly. The devil! have n't we all played our little plays; and which of us knows what will become of him in times like these? You may be minister yourself to-morrow, you who are spicing the cakes of the 'Constitutionel' to-day."

Sometimes, in return, he helped editors, or got rid of obstacles to the performances of some play; gave gratuities and good dinners at the right moment, or promised his services to bring some affair to a happy conclusion. Moreover, he really liked literature and the arts; he collected autographs, obtained splendid albums *gratis*, and possessed sketches, engravings, and pictures. He did a great deal of good to artists by simply not injuring them and by furthering their wishes on certain occasions when their self-love wanted some rather costly gratification. Consequently, he was much liked in the world of actors and actresses, journalists and artists. For one thing, they had the same vices and the same indolence as himself. Men who could all say such witty things in their cups or in company with a *danseuse*, how could they help being friends? If des Lupeaulx had not been a general-secretary he would certainly have been a journalist. Thus, in that fifteen years' struggle in which the harlequin sabre of epigram opened a breach by which insurrection entered the citadel, des Lupeaulx never received so much as a scratch.

As the young fry of clerks looked at this man playing bowls in the gardens of the ministry with the minister's children, they cracked their brains to guess the secret of his influence and the nature of his services; while, on the other hand, the aristocrats in all the various ministries looked upon him as a dangerous Mephistopheles, courted him, and gave him back with usury the flatteries he bestowed in the higher sphere. As difficult to decipher as a hieroglyphic inscription to the clerks, the vocation of the secretary and his usefulness were as plain as the rule of three to the self-interested. This lesser Prince de Wagram of the administration, to whom the duty of gathering opinions and ideas and making verbal reports thereon was entrusted, knew all the secrets of parliamentary politics; dragged in the lukewarm, fetched, carried, and buried propositions, said the *yes* and *no* that the ministers dared not say for themselves. Compelled to receive the first fire and the first blows of despair or wrath, he laughed or bemoaned himself with the minister, as the case might be. Mysterious link by which many interests were in some way connected with the Tuileries, and safe as a confessor, he sometimes knew everything and sometimes nothing; and, in addition to all these functions came that of. saying for the minister those things that a minister cannot say of himself. In short, with this political Hephæstion the minister might dare to be himself; to take off his wig and his false teeth, lay aside his scruples, put on his slippers, unbutton his conscience, and give way to his trickery. However, it was not all a bed of roses for des Lupeaulx; he flattered and advised his master, forced to flatter in order to advise, to advise while flattering, and disguise the advice under the flattery. All politicians who follow this trade have bilious faces; and their constant habit of giving affirmative nods acquiescing in what is said to them, or seeming to do so, gives a certain peculiar turn to their heads. They agree indifferently with whatever is said before them. Their talk is full of " buts," " notwithstandings," " for myself I should," " were I in your place" (they often say " in your place "), — phrases, however, which pave the way to opposition.

In person, Clément des Lupeaulx had the remains of a handsome man ; five feet six inches tall, tolerably stout, complexion flushed with good living, powdered head, delicate spectacles, and a worn-out air ; the natural skin blond, as shown by the hand, puffy like that of an old woman, rather too square, and with short nails — the hand of a satrap. His foot was elegant. After five o'clock in the afternoon des Lupeaulx was always to be seen in open-worked silk stockings, low shoes, black trousers, cashmere waistcoat, cambric handkerchief (without perfume), gold chain, blue coat of the shade called " king's blue," with brass buttons and a string of orders. In the morning he wore creaking boots and gray trousers, and the short close surtout coat of the politician. His general appearance early in the day was that of a sharp lawyer rather than that of a ministerial officer. Eyes glazed by the constant use of spectacles made him plainer than he really was, if by chance he took those appendages off. To real judges of character, as well as to upright men who are at ease only with honest natures, des Lupeaulx was intolerable. To them, his gracious manners only draped his lies ; his amiable protestations and hackneyed courtesies, new to the foolish and ignorant, too plainly showed their texture to an observing mind. Such

4

minds considered him a rotten plank, on which no foot should trust itself.

No sooner had the beautiful Madame Rabourdin decided to interfere in her husband's administrative advancement than she fathomed Clément des Lupeaulx's true character, and studied him thoughtfully to discover whether in this thin strip of deal there were ligneous fibres strong enough to let her lightly trip across it from the bureau to the department, from a salary of eight thousand a year to twelve thousand. The clever woman believed she could play her own game with this political roué; and Monsieur des Lupeaulx was partly the cause of the unusual expenditures which now began and were continued in the Rabourdin household.

The rue Duphot, built up under the Empire, is remarkable for several houses with handsome exteriors, the apartments of which are skilfully laid out. That of the Rabourdins was particularly well arranged, — a domestic advantage which has much to do with the nobleness of private lives. A pretty and rather wide antechamber, lighted from the courtyard, led to the grand salon, the windows of which looked on the street. To the right of the salon were Rabourdin's study and bedroom, and behind them the dining-room, which was entered from the antechamber; to the left was Madame's bedroom and dressing-room, and behind them her daughter's little bedroom. On reception days the

door of Rabourdin's study and that of his wife's bedroom were thrown open. The rooms were thus spacious
enough to contain a select company, without the absurdity which attends many middle-class entertainments,
where unusual preparations are made at the expense of
the daily comfort, and consequently give the effect of
exceptional effort. The salon had lately been rehung
in gold-colored silk with carmelite touches. Madame's
bedroom was draped in a fabric of true blue and furnished in a rococo manner. Rabourdin's study had in-
herited the late hangings of the salon, carefully cleaned,
and was adorned by the fine pictures once belonging to
Monsieur Leprince. The daughter of the late auctioneer had utilized in her dining-room certain exquisite
Turkish rugs which her father had bought at a bargain ;
panelling them on the walls in ebony, the cost of which
has since become exorbitant. Elegant buffets made by
Boulle, also purchased by the auctioneer, furnished the
sides of the room, at the end of which sparkled the
brass arabesques inlaid in tortoise-shell of the first tall
clock that reappeared in the nineteenth century to claim
honor for the masterpieces of the seventeenth. Flowers
perfumed these rooms so full of good taste and of exquisite things, where each detail was a work of art well
placed and well surrounded, and where Madame Rabourdin, dressed with that natural simplicity which
artists alone attain, gave the impression of a woman

accustomed to such elegancies, though she never spoke
of them, but allowed the charms of her mind to complete
the effect produced upon her guests by these delightful
surroundings.	Thanks to her father, Célestine was
able to make society talk of her as soon as the rococo
became fashionable.

Accustomed as des Lupeaulx was to false as well as
real magnificence in all their stages, he was, neverthe-
less, surprised at Madame Rabourdin's home.	The
charm it exercised over this Parisian Asmodeus can be
explained by a comparison.	A traveller wearied with
the rich aspects of Italy, Brazil, or India, returns to his
own land and finds on his way a delightful little lake,
like the Lac d'Orta at the foot of Monte Rosa, with an
island resting on the calm waters, bewitchingly simple ;
a scene of nature and yet adorned ; solitary, but well
surrounded with choice plantations and foliage and
statues of fine effect.	Beyond lies a vista of shores both
wild and cultivated ; tumultuous grandeur towers above,
but in itself all the proportions are human.	The world
that the traveller has lately viewed is here in miniature,
modest and pure ; his soul, refreshed, bids him remain
where a charm of melody and poesy surrounds him
with harmony and awaken ideas within his mind.	Such
a scene represents both life and a monastery.

A few days earlier the beautiful Madame Firmiani,
one of the charming women of the faubourg Saint-

Germain who visited and liked Madame Rabourdin, had said to des Lupeaulx (invited expressly to hear the remark), " Why do you not call on Madame —? " with a motion towards Célestine ; " she gives delightful parties, and her dinners, above all, are — better than mine."

Des Lupeaulx allowed himself to be drawn into an engagement by the handsome Madame Rabourdin, who, for the first time, turned her eyes on him as she spoke. He had, accordingly, gone to the rue Duphot, and that tells the tale. Woman has but one trick, cries Figaro, but that's infallible. After dining once at the house of this unimportant official, des Lupeaulx made up his mind to dine there often. Thanks to the perfectly proper and becoming advances of the beautiful woman, whom her rival, Madame Colleville, called the Célimène of the rue Duphot, he had dined there every Friday for the last month, and returned of his own accord for a cup of tea on Wednesdays.

Within a few days Madame Rabourdin, having watched him narrowly and knowingly, believed she had found on the secretarial plank a spot where she might safely set her foot. She was no longer doubtful of success. Her inward joy can be realized only in the families of government officials where for three or four years prosperity has been counted on through some appointment, long expected and long sought. How many troubles to be allayed! how many entreaties and pledges given to the ministerial divinities! how many visits of self-interest paid! At last, thanks to her boldness, Madame Rabourdin heard the hour strike when she was to have twenty thousand francs a year instead of eight thousand.

"And I shall have managed well," she said to herself. "I have had to make a little outlay; but these are times when hidden merit is overlooked, whereas if a man keeps himself well in sight before the world, cultivates social relations and extends them, he succeeds. After all, ministers and their friends interest themselves only in the people they see; but Rabourdin knows nothing of the world! If I had not cajoled those three deputies they might have wanted La Billardière's place themselves; whereas, now that I have invited them here, they will be ashamed to do so and will become our supporters instead of rivals. I have rather played the coquette, but — it is delightful that the first nonsense with which one fools a man sufficed."

The day on which a serious and unlooked-for struggle about this appointment began, after a ministerial dinner which preceded one of those receptions which ministers regard as public, des Lupeaulx was standing beside the fireplace near the minister's wife. While taking his coffee he once more included Madame Rabourdin among the seven or eight really superior women in Paris. Several times already he had staked Madame Rabourdin very much as Corporal Trim staked his cap.

"Don't say that too often, my dear friend, or you will injure her," said the minister's wife, half-laughing.

Women never like to hear praise of other women; they keep silence themselves to lessen its effect.

"Poor La Billardière is dying," remarked his Excellency the minister; "that place falls to Rabourdin, one of our most able men, and to whom our predecessors did not behave well, though one of them actually owed his position in the prefecture of police under the Empire to a certain great personage who was interested in Rabourdin. But, my dear friend, you are still young enough to be loved by a pretty woman for yourself—"

"If La Billardière's place is given to Rabourdin I may be believed when I praise the superiority of his wife," replied des Lupeaulx, piqued by the minister's sarcasm; "but if Madame la Comtesse would be willing to judge for herself—"

"You want me to invite her to my next ball, don't you? Your clever woman will meet a knot of other women who only come here to laugh at us, and when they hear 'Madame Rabourdin' announced—"

"But Madame Firmiani is announced at the Foreign Office parties?"

"Ah, but she was born a Cadignan!" said the newly

created count, with a savage look at his general-secretary, for neither he nor his wife were noble.

The persons present thought important matters were being talked over, and the solicitors for favors and appointments kept at a little distance. When des Lupeaulx left the room the countess said to her husband, "I think des Lupeaulx is in love."

"For the first time in his life, then," he replied, shrugging his shoulders, as much as to inform his wife that des Lupeaulx did not concern himself with such nonsense.

Just then the minister saw a deputy of the Right Centre enter the room, and he left his wife abruptly to cajole an undecided vote. But the deputy, under the blow of a sudden and unexpected disaster, wanted to make sure of a protector and he had come to announce privately that in a few days he should be compelled to resign. Thus forewarned, the minister would be able to open his batteries for the new election before those of the opposition.

The minister, or to speak correctly, des Lupeaulx had invited to dinner on this occasion one of those irremovable officials who, as we have said, are to be found in every ministry; an individual much embarrassed by his own person, who, in his desire to maintain a dignified appearance, was standing erect and rigid on his two legs, held well together like the Greek hermæ. This functionary waited near the fireplace to thank the secretary, whose abrupt and unexpected departure from the room disconcerted him at the moment when he was about to turn a compliment. This official was the cashier of the ministry, the only clerk who did not tremble when the government changed hands.

At the time of which we write, the Chamber did not meddle shabbily with the budget, as it does in the deplorable days in which we now live; it did not contemptibly reduce ministerial emoluments, nor save, as they say in the kitchen, the candle-ends; on the contrary, it granted to each minister taking charge of a public department an indemnity, called an "outfit." It costs, alas, as much to enter on the duties of a minister as to retire from them; indeed, the entrance involves expenses of all kinds which it is quite impossible to inventory. This indemnity amounted to the pretty little sum of twenty-five thousand francs. When the appointment of a new minister was gazetted in the "Moniteur," and the greater or lesser officials, clustering round the stoves or before the fireplaces and shaking in their shoes, asked themselves: "What will he do? will he increase the number of clerks? will he dismiss two to make room for three?" the cashier tranquilly took out twenty-five clean bank-bills and pinned them together with a satisfied expression on his beadle face. The next day he mounted the private staircase and had himself ushered into the minister's presence by the lackeys,

who considered the money and the keeper of money,
the contents and the container, the idea and the form,
as one and the same power. The cashier caught the
ministerial pair at the dawn of official delight, when
the newly appointed statesman is benign and affable.
To the minister's inquiry as to what brings him there, he
replies with the bank-notes, — informing his Excellency
that he hastens to pay him the customary indemnity.
Moreover, he explains the matter to the minister's wife,
who never fails to draw freely upon the fund, and sometimes takes all, for the " outfit " is looked upon as a
household affair. The cashier then proceeds to turn
a compliment, and to slip in a few politic phrases :
" If his Excellency would deign to retain him ; if, satisfied with his purely mechanical services, he would," etc.
As a man who brings twenty-five thousand francs is
always a worthy official, the cashier is sure not to leave
without his confirmation to the post from which he has
seen a succession of ministers come and go during a
period of, perhaps, twenty-five years. His next step is
to place himself at the orders of Madame ; he brings the
monthly thirteen thousand francs whenever wanted ; he
advances or delays the payment as requested, and thus
manages to obtain, as they said in the monasteries,
a voice in the chapter.

Formerly book-keeper at the Treasury, when that
establishment kept its books by double entry, the Sieur

Saillard was compensated for the loss of that position by his appointment as cashier of a ministry. He was a bulky, fat man, very strong in the matter of book-keeping, and very weak in everything else; round as a round O, simple as how-do-you-do, — a man who came to his office with measured steps, like those of an elephant, and returned with the same measured tread to the place Royale, where he lived on the ground-floor of an old mansion belonging to him. He usually had a companion on the way in the person of Monsieur Isidore Baudoyer, head of a bureau in Monsieur de la Billardière's division, consequently one of Rabourdin's colleagues. Baudoyer was married to Elisabeth Saillard, the cashier's only daughter, and had hired, very naturally, the apartments above those of his father-in-law. No one at the ministry had the slightest doubt that Saillard was a blockhead, but neither had any one ever found out how far his stupidity could go; it was too compact to be examined; it did not ring hollow; it absorbed everything and gave nothing out. Bixiou (a clerk of whom more anon) caricatured the cashier by drawing a head in a wig at the top of an egg, and two little legs at the other end, with this inscription: "Born to pay out and take in without blundering. A little less luck, and he might have been lackey to the bank of France; a little more ambition, and he could have been honorably discharged."

At the moment of which we are now writing, the minister was looking at his cashier very much as we gaze at a window or a cornice, without supposing that either can hear us, or fathom our secret thoughts.

"I am all the more anxious that we should settle everything with the prefect in the quietest way, because des Lupeaulx has designs upon the place for himself," said the minister, continuing his talk with the deputy; "his paltry little estate is in your arrondissement; we don't want him as deputy."

"He has neither years nor rentals enough to be eligible," said the deputy.

"That may be; but you know how it was decided for Casimir Périer as to age; and as to worldly possessions, des Lupeaulx does possess something, — not much, it is true; but the law does not take into account increase, which he may very well obtain; commissions have wide margins for the deputies of the Centre, you know, and we cannot openly oppose the good-will that is shown to this dear friend."

"But where could he get the money?"

"How did Manuel manage to become the owner of a house in Paris?" cried the minister.

The cashier listened and heard, but reluctantly and against his will. These rapid remarks, murmured as they were, struck his ear by one of those acoustic rebounds which are very little studied. As he heard these political confidences, however, a keen alarm took possession of his soul. He was one of those simple-minded beings, who are shocked at listening to anything they are not intended to hear, or entering where they are not invited, and seeming bold when they are really timid, inquisitive where they are truly discreet. The cashier accordingly began to glide along the carpet and edge himself away, so that the minister saw him at a distance when he first took notice of him. Saillard was a ministerial henchman absolutely incapable of indiscretion; even if the minister had known that he had overheard a secret he had only to whisper " motus " in his ear to be sure it was perfectly safe. The cashier, however, took advantage of an influx of office-seekers, to slip out and get into his hackney-coach (hired by the hour for these costly entertainments), and return to his home in the place Royale.

III.

THE TEREDOS NAVALIS, OTHERWISE CALLED SHIP-WORM.

WHILE old Saillard was driving across Paris his son-in-law, Isidore Baudoyer, and his daughter Elisabeth, Baudoyer's wife, were playing a virtuous game of boston with their confessor, the Abbé Gaudron, in company with a few neighbors and a certain Martin Falleix, a brass-founder in the faubourg Saint-Antoine, to whom Saillard had loaned the necessary money to establish a business. This Falleix, a respectable Auvergnat who had come to seek his fortune in Paris with his smelting-pot on his back, had found immediate employment with the firm of Brézac, collectors of metals and other relics from old *châteaux* in the provinces. About twenty-seven years of age, and spoiled, like others, by success, Martin Falleix had had the luck to become the active agent of Monsieur Saillard, the sleeping-partner in the working out of a discovery made by Falleix in smelting (patent of invention and gold medal granted at the exposition of 1825). Madame Baudoyer, whose only daughter was treading — to use an expression of old Saillard's — on the tail of her twelve years, laid claim to Falleix, a thickset, swarthy, active young fellow, of shrewd principles, whose education she was superintending. The said education, according to her ideas, consisted in teaching him to play boston, to hold his cards properly, and not to let others see his game ; to shave himself regularly before he came to the house, and to wash his hands with good cleansing soap; not to swear, to speak her kind of French, to wear boots instead of shoes, cotton shirts instead of sacking, and to brush up his hair instead of plastering it flat. During the preceding week Elisabeth had finally succeeded in persuading Falleix to give up wearing a pair of enormous flat earrings resembling hoops.

"You go too far, Madame Baudoyer," he said, seeing her satisfaction at the final sacrifice ; " you order me about too much. You make me clean my teeth, which loosens them ; presently you will want me to brush my nails and curl my hair, which won't do at all in our business ; we don't like dandies."

Elisabeth Baudoyer, *née* Saillard, is one of those persons who escape portraiture through their utter commonness ; yet who ought to be sketched, because they are specimens of that second-rate Parisian *bourgeoisie* which occupies a place above the well-to-do artisan and below the upper middle classes, — a tribe whose virtues are well-nigh vices, whose defects are never kindly, but whose habits and manners, dull and insipid though they be, are not without a certain originality. Something pinched and puny about Elisabeth Saillard was painful to the eye. Her figure, scarcely over four feet in height, was so thin that the waist measured less than twenty inches. Her small features, which clustered close about the nose, gave her face a vague resemblance to a weazel's snout. Though she was past thirty years old she looked scarcely more than sixteen. Her eyes, of a porcelain blue, over-weighted by heavy eyelids which fell nearly straight from the arch of the eyebrows, had little light in them. Everything about her appearance was commonplace: witness her flaxen hair, tending to whiteness; her flat forehead, from which the light did not reflect; and her dull complexion, with gray, almost leaden, tones. The lower part of the face, more triangular than oval, ended irregularly the otherwise irregular outline of her face. Her voice had a rather pretty range of intonation, from sharp to sweet. Elisabeth was a perfect specimen of the second-rate little *bourgeoise* who lectures her husband behind the curtains; obtains no credit for her virtues; is ambitious without intelligent object, and solely through the development of her domestic selfishness. Had she lived in the country she would have bought up adjacent land; being, as she was, connected with the administration, she was determined to push her way.

If we relate the life of her father and mother, we shall show the sort of woman she was by a picture of her childhood and youth.

Monsieur Saillard married the daughter of an upholsterer keeping shop under the arcades of the Market. Limited means compelled Monsieur and Madame Saillard at their start in life to bear constant privation. After thirty-three years of married life, and twenty-nine years of toil in a government office, the property of "the Saillards" — their circle of acquaintance called them so — consisted of sixty thousand francs entrusted to Falleix, the house in the place Royale, bought for forty thousand in 1804, and thirty-six thousand francs given in dowry to their daughter Elisabeth. Out of this capital about fifty thousand came to them by the will of the widow Bidault, Madame Saillard's mother. Saillard's salary from the government had always been four thousand five hundred francs a year, and no more; his situation was a blind alley that led nowhere, and had tempted no one to supersede him. These ninety thousand francs, put together sou by sou, were the fruit therefore of a sordid economy unintelligently employed. In fact, the Saillards did not know how better to manage their savings than to carry them, five thousand francs at a time, to their notary, Monsieur Sorbier, Cardot's predecessor, and let him invest them at five per cent in first mortgages, with the wife's rights reserved in case the borrower was married! In 1804 Madame Saillard obtained a government office for the sale of stamped papers, a circumstance which brought a servant into the household for the first time. At the time of which we write, the house, which was worth a hundred thousand francs, brought in a rental of eight thousand. Falleix paid seven per cent for the sixty thousand invested in the foundry, besides an equal division of profits. The Saillards were therefore enjoying an income of not less than seventeen thousand francs a year. The whole ambition of the good man now centred on obtaining the cross of the Legion and his retiring pension.

Elisabeth, the only child, had toiled steadily from infancy in a home where the customs of life were rigid and the ideas simple. A new hat for Saillard was a matter of deliberation; the time a coat could last was estimated and discussed; umbrellas were carefully hung up by means of a brass buckle. Since 1804 no repairs of any kind had been done to the house. The Saillards kept the ground-floor in precisely the state in which their predecessor left it. The gilding of the pier-glasses was rubbed off; the paint on the cornices was hardly visible through the layers of dust that time had collected. The fine large rooms still retained certain sculptured marble mantel-pieces and ceilings, worthy of Versailles, together with the old

furniture of the widow Bidault. The latter consisted
of a curious mixture of walnut armchairs, disjointed,
and covered with tapestry; rosewood bureaus; round
tables on single pedestals, with brass railings and
cracked marble tops; one superb Boulle secretary,
the value of which style had not yet been recognized;
in short, a chaos of bargains picked up by the worthy
widow, — pictures bought for the sake of the frames,
china services of a composite order; to wit, a magnificent Japanese dessert set, and all the rest porcelains
of various makes, unmatched silver plate, old glass, fine
damask, and a four-post bedstead, hung with curtains
and garnished with plumes.

Amid these curious relics, Madame Saillard always
sat on a sofa of modern mahogany, near a fireplace full
of ashes and without fire, on the mantel-shelf of which
stood a clock, some antique bronzes, candelabra with
paper flowers but no candles, for the careful housewife
lighted the room with a tall tallow candle always gutter-
ing down into the flat brass candlestick which held it.
Madame Saillard's face, despite its wrinkles, was expressive of obstinacy and severity, narrowness of ideas,
an uprightness that might be called quadrangular, a
religion without piety, straightforward, candid avarice,
and the peace of a quiet conscience. You may see in
certain Flemish pictures the wives of burgomasters cut
out by nature on this same pattern and wonderfully

reproduced on canvas; but these dames wear fine robes of velvet and precious stuffs, whereas Madame Saillard possessed no robes, only that venerable garment called in Touraine and Picardy *cottes*, elsewhere petticoats, or skirts pleated behind and on each side, with other skirts hanging over them. Her bust was inclosed in what was called a *casaquin*, another obsolete name for a short gown or jacket. She continued to wear a cap with starched wings, and shoes with high heels. Though she was now fifty-seven years old, and her lifetime of vigorous household work ought now to be rewarded with well-earned repose, she was incessantly employed in knitting her husband's stockings and her own, and those of an uncle, just as her countrywomen knit them, moving about the room, talking, pacing up and down the garden, or looking round the kitchen to watch what was going on.

The Saillards' avarice, which was really imposed on them in the first instance by dire necessity, was now a second nature. When the cashier got back from the office, he laid aside his coat, and went to work in the large garden, shut off from the courtyard by an iron railing, and which the family reserved to itself. For years Elisabeth, the daughter, went to market every morning with her mother, and the two did all the work of the house. The mother cooked well, especially a duck with turnips; but, according to Saillard, no one could equal

Elisabeth in hashing the remains of a leg of mutton with onions. " You might eat your boots with those onions and not know it," he remarked. As soon as Elisabeth knew how to hold a needle, her mother made her mend the household linen and her father's coats. Always at work, like a servant, she never went out alone. Though living close by the boulevard du Temple, where Franconi, La Gaîté, and l'Ambigu-Comique were within a stone's throw, and, further on, the Porte-Saint-Martin, Elisabeth had never seen a comedy. When she asked to "see. what it was like" (with the Abbé Gaudron's permission, be it understood), Monsieur Baudoyer took her — for the glory of the thing, and to show her the finest that was to be seen — to the Opera, where they were playing "The Chinese Laborer." Elisabeth thought "the comedy" as wearisome as the plague of flies, and never wished to see another. On Sundays, after walking four times to and fro between the place Royale and Saint-Paul's church (for her mother made her practise the precepts and the duties of religion), her parents took her to the pavement in front of the Café Turc, where they sat on chairs placed between a railing and the wall. The Saillards always made haste to reach the place early so as to choose the best seats, and found much entertainment in watching the passers-by. In those days the Café Turc was the rendezvous of the fashionable society of the

Marais, the faubourg Saint-Antoine, and the circumjacent regions.

Elisabeth never wore anything but cotton gowns in summer and merino in winter, which she made herself. Her mother gave her twenty francs a month for her expenses, but her father, who was very fond of her, mitigated this rigorous treatment with a few presents. She never read what the Abbé Gaudron, vicar of Saint-Paul's and the family director, called profane books. This discipline had borne fruit. Forced to employ her feelings on some passion or other, Elizabeth became eager after gain. Though she was not lacking in sense or perspicacity, religious theories, and her complete ignorance of higher emotions had encircled all her faculties with an iron band; they were exercised solely on the commonest things of life; spent in few directions they were able to concentrate themselves on a matter in hand. Repressed by religious devotion, her natural intelligence exercised itself within the limits marked out by cases of conscience, which form a mine of subtleties among which self-interest selects its subterfuges. Like those saintly personages in whom religion does not stifle ambition, Elisabeth was capable of requiring others to do a blamable action that she might reap the fruits; and she would have been, like them again, implacable as to her dues and dissembling in her actions. Once offended, she watched her adversaries with the perfidious patience of a cat, and was capable of bringing about some cold and complete vengeance, and then laying it to the account of God. Until her marriage the Saillards lived without other society than that of the Abbé Gaudron, a priest from Auvergne appointed vicar of Saint-Paul's after the restoration of Catholic worship. Besides this ecclesiastic, who was a friend of the late Madame Bidault, a paternal uncle of Madame Saillard, an old paper-dealer retired from business ever since the year II. of the Republic, and now sixty-nine years old, came to see them on Sundays only, because on that day no government business went on.

This little old man, with a livid face blazoned by the red nose of a tippler and lighted by two gleaming vulture eyes, allowed his gray hair to hang loose under a three-cornered hat, wore breeches with straps that extended beyond the buckles, cotton stockings of mottled thread knitted by his niece, whom he always called " the little Saillard," stout shoes with silver buckles, and a surtout coat of mixed colors. He looked very much like those verger-beadle-bell-ringing-grave-digging-parish-clerks who are taken to be caricatures until we see them performing their various functions. On the present occasion he had come on foot to dine with the Saillards, intending to return in the same way to the rue Greneta, where he lived on the third floor of an old house. His business was that of discounting commercial paper in the quartier Saint-Martin, where he was known by the nickname of "Gigonnet," from the nervous, convulsive movement with which he lifted his legs in walking, like a cat. Monsieur Bidault began this business in the year II. in partnership with a Dutchman named Werbrust, a friend of Gobseck.

Some time later Saillard made the acquaintance of Monsieur and Madame Transon, wholesale dealers in pottery, with an establishment in the rue de Lesdiguières, who took an interest in Elisabeth and introduced young Isidore Baudoyer to the family with the intention of marrying her. Gigonnet approved of the match, for he had long employed a certain Mitral, uncle of the young man, as clerk. Monsieur and Madame Baudoyer, father and mother of Isidore, highly respectable leather-dressers in the rue Censier, had slowly made a moderate fortune out of a small trade. After marrying their only son, on whom they settled fifty thousand francs, they determined to live in the country, and had lately removed to the neighborhood of Île-d'Adam, where after a time they were joined by Mitral. They frequently came to Paris, however, where they kept a corner in the house in the rue Censier which they gave to Isidore on his marriage. The elder Baudoyers had an income of about three thousand francs left to live upon after establishing their son.

Mitral was a being with a sinister wig, a face the color of Seine water, lighted by a pair of Spanish-tobacco-colored eyes, cold as a well-rope, always smelling a rat, and close-mouthed about his property. He probably made his fortune in his own hole and corner, just as Werbrust and Gigonnet made theirs in the quartier Saint-Martin.

Though the Saillards' circle of acquaintance increased, neither their ideas nor their manners and customs changed. The saint's-days of father, mother, daughter, son-in-law, and grandchild were carefully observed, also the anniversaries of birth and marriage, Easter, Christmas, New Year's day, and Epiphany. These festivals were preceded by great domestic sweepings and a universal clearing up of the house, which added an element of usefulness to the ceremonies. When the festival day came, the presents were offered with much pomp and an accompaniment of flowers, — silk stockings or a fur cap for old Saillard; gold earrings and articles of plate for Elisabeth or her husband, for whom, little by little, the parents were accumulating a whole silver service; silk petticoats for Madame Saillard, who laid the stuff by and never made it up. The recipient of these gifts was placed in an armchair and asked by those present for a certain length of time, "Guess what we have for you!" Then came a splendid dinner, lasting at least five hours, to which were invited the Abbé Gaudron,

Falleix, Rabourdin, Monsieur Godard, under-head-clerk to Monsieur Baudoyer, Monsieur Bataille, captain of the company of the National Guard to which Saillard and his son-in-law belonged. Monsieur Cardot, who was invariably asked, did as Rabourdin did, namely, accepted one invitation out of six. The company sang at dessert, shook hands and embraced with enthusiasm, wishing each other all manner of happiness ; the presents were exhibited and the opinion of the guests asked about them. The day Saillard received his fur cap he wore it during the dessert, to the satisfaction of all present. At night, mere ordinary acquaintances were bidden, and dancing went on till very late, formerly to the music of one violin, but for the last six years Monsieur Godard, who was a great flute player, contributed the piercing tones of a flageolet to the festivity. The cook, Madame Baudoyer's nurse, and old Catherine, Madame Saillard's woman-servant, together with the porter or his wife, stood looking on at the door of the salon. The servants. always received three francs on these occasions to buy themselves wine or coffee.

This little circle looked upon Saillard and Baudoyer as transcendent beings ; they were government officers ; they had risen by their own merits ; they worked, it was said, with the minister himself ; they owed their fortune to their talents ; they were politicians. Baudoyer was considered the more able of the two ; his

position as head of a bureau presupposed labor that
was more intricate and arduous than that of a cashier.
Moreover, Isidore, though the son of a leather-dresser,
had had the genius to study and to cast aside his
father's business and find a career in politics, which had
led him to a post of eminence. In short, silent and
uncommunicative as he was, he was looked upon as a
deep thinker, and perhaps, said the admiring circle, he
would some day become deputy of the eighth arrondissement. As Gigonnet listened to such remarks as these,
he pressed his already pinched lips closer together, and
threw a glance at his great-niece, Elisabeth.

In person, Isidore was a tall, stout man of thirty-
seven, who perspired freely, and whose head looked as
if he had water on the brain. This enormous head,
covered with chestnut hair cropped close, was joined to
the neck by rolls of flesh which overhung the collar of
his coat. He had the arms of Hercules, hands worthy
of Domitian, a stomach which sobriety held within the
limits of the majestic, to use a saying of Brillat-Sava-
rin. His face was a good deal like that of the Emperor
Alexander. The Tartar type was in the little eyes and
the flattened nose slightly turned up, in the frigid lips
and the short chin. The forehead was low and narrow.
Though his temperament was lymphatic, the devout
Isidore was under the influence of a conjugal passion
which time did not lessen.

In spite, however, of his resemblance to the hand-some Russian Emperor and the terrible Domitian, Isidore Baudoyer was nothing more than a political office-holder, of little ability as head of his department, a cut-and-dried routine man, who concealed the fact that he was a flabby cipher by so ponderous a person-ality that no scalpel could cut deep enough to let the operator see into him. His severe studies, in which he had shown the patience and sagacity of an ox, and his square head, deceived his parents, who firmly believed him an extraordinary man. Pedantic and hypercritical, meddlesome and fault-finding, he was a terror to the clerks under him, whom he worried in their work, en-forcing the rules rigorously, and arriving himself with such terrible punctuality that not one of them dared to be a moment late. Baudoyer wore a blue coat with gilt buttons, a chamois waistcoat, gray trousers and cravats of various colors. His feet were large and ill-shod. From the chain of his watch depended an enormous bunch of old trinkets, among which in 1824 he still wore "American beads," which were much the fashion in the year VII.

In the bosom of this family, bound together by the force of religious ties, by the inflexibility of its customs, by one solitary emotion, that of avarice, a passion which was now as it were its compass, Elisabeth was forced to commune with herself, instead of imparting her ideas to

those around her, for she felt herself without equals in
mind who could comprehend her. Though facts compelled her to judge her husband, her religious duty led
her to keep up as best she could a favorable opinion of
him; she showed him marked respect; honored him
as the father of her child, her husband, the temporal
power, as the vicar of Saint-Paul's told her. She would
have thought it a mortal sin to make a single gesture,
or give a single glance, or say a single word which
would reveal to others her real opinion of the imbecile
Baudoyer. She even professed to obey passively all his
wishes. But her ears were receptive of many things;
she thought them over, weighed and compared them in
the solitude of her own mind, and judged so soberly of
men and events that at the time when our history begins she was the hidden oracle of the two functionaries,
her husband and father, who had, unconsciously, come
to do nothing whatever without consulting her. Old
Saillard would say, innocently, "Is n't she clever, that
Elisabeth of mine?" But Baudoyer, too great a fool
not to be puffed up by the false reputation the quartier
Saint-Antoine bestowed upon him, denied his wife's
cleverness all the while that he was making use of it.

Elisabeth had long felt sure that her uncle Bidault,
otherwise called Gigonnet, was rich and handled vast
sums of money. Enlightened by self-interest, she
had come to understand Monsieur des Lupeaulx far

better than the minister understood him. Finding
herself married to a fool, she never allowed herself
to think that life might have gone better with her,
she only imagined the possibility of better things without expecting or wishing to attain them. All her best
affections found their vocation in her love for her daughter, to whom she spared the pains and privations she
had borne in her own childhood; she believed that in
this affection she had her full share in the world of
feeling. Solely for her daughter's sake she had per-
suaded her father to take the important step of going into partnership with Falleix. Falleix had been
brought to the Saillards' house by old Bidault, who
lent him money on his merchandise. Falleix thought
his old countryman extortionate, and complained to the
Saillards that Gigonnet demanded eighteen per cent
from an Auvergnat. Madame Saillard ventured to
remonstrate with her uncle.

"It is just because he is an Auvergnat that I take
only eighteen per cent," said Gigonnet, when she spoke
to him.

Falleix, who had made a discovery at the age of
twenty-eight, and communicated it to Saillard, seemed
to carry his heart in his hand (an expression of old
Saillard's), and also seemed likely to make a great
fortune. Elisabeth determined to husband him for
her daughter and train him herself, having, as she

calculated, seven years to do it in. Martin Falleix felt and showed the deepest respect for Madame Baudoyer, whose superior qualities he was able to recognize. If he were fated to make millions he would always belong to her family, where he had found a home. The little Baudoyer girl was already trained to bring him his tea and to take his hat.

On the evening of which we write, Monsieur Saillard, returning from the ministry, found a game of boston in full blast; Elisabeth was advising Falleix how to play; Madame Saillard was knitting in the chimney-corner and overlooking the cards of the vicar; Monsieur Baudoyer, motionless as a mile-stone, was employing his mental capacity in calculating how the cards were placed, and sat opposite to Mitral, who had come up from Île-d'Adam for the Christmas holidays. No one moved as the cashier entered, and for some minutes he walked up and down the room, his fat face contracted with unaccustomed thought.

"He is always so when he dines at the ministry," remarked Madame Saillard; "happily, it is only twice a year, or he'd die of it. Saillard was never made to be in the government — Well, now, I do hope, Saillard," she continued in a loud tone, "that you are not going to keep on those silk breeches and that handsome coat. Go and take them off; don't wear them at home, my man."

"Your father has something on his mind," said Baudoyer to his wife, when the cashier was in his bedroom, undressing without any fire.

"Perhaps Monsieur de la Billardière is dead," said Elisabeth, simply; "and as he is anxious you should have the place, it worries him."

"Can I be useful in any way?" said the vicar of Saint-Paul's; "if so, pray use my services. I have the honor to be known to Madame la Dauphine. These are days when public offices should be given only to faithful men, whose religious principles are not to be shaken."

"Dear me!" said Falleix, "do men of merit need protectors and influence to get places in the government service? I am glad I am an iron-master; my customers know where to find a good article — "

"Monsieur," interrupted Baudoyer, "the government is the government; never attack it in this house."

"You speak like the 'Constitutionnel,' said the vicar.

"The 'Constitutionnel' never says anything different from that," replied Baudoyer, who never read it.

The cashier believed his son-in-law to be as superior in talent to Rabourdin as God was greater than Saint-Crépin, to use his own expression; but the good man coveted this appointment in a straight-

forward, honest way. Influenced by the feeling which
leads all officials to seek promotion, — a violent, unre-
flecting, almost brutal passion, — he desired success,
just as he desired the cross of the Legion of honor,
without doing anything against his conscience to obtain
it, and solely, as he believed, on the strength of his
son-in-law's merits. To his thinking, a man who had
patiently spent twenty-five years in a government office
behind an iron railing had sacrificed himself to his
country and deserved the cross. But all that he dreamed
of doing to promote his son-in-law's appointment in
La Billardière's place was to say a word to his Excellency's wife when he took her the month's salary.

"Well, Saillard, you look as if you had lost all
your friends! Do speak; do, pray, tell us something," cried his wife when he came back into the
room.

Saillard, after making a little sign to his daughter,
turned on his heel to keep himself from talking politics before strangers. When Monsieur Mitral and
the vicar had departed, Saillard rolled back the card-
table and sat down in an armchair in the attitude he
always assumed when about to tell some office-gossip,
— a series of movements which answered the purpose
of the three knocks given at the Théâtre-Français.
After binding his wife, daughter, and son-in-law to
the deepest secrecy, — for, however petty the gossip,

their places, as he thought, depended on their discretion, — he related the incomprehensible enigma of the resignation of a deputy, the very legitimate desire of the general-secretary to get elected to the place, and the secret opposition of the minister to this wish of a man who was one of his firmest supporters and most zealous workers. This, of course, brought down an avalanche of suppositions, flooded with the sapient arguments of the two officials, who sent back and forth to each other a wearisome flood of nonsense. Elisabeth quietly asked three questions : —

" If Monsieur des Lupeaulx is on our side, will Monsieur Baudoyer be appointed in Monsieur de la Billardière's place? "

" Heavens ! I should think so," cried the cashier.

" My uncle Bidault and Monsieur Gobseck helped him in 1814," thought she. " Is he in debt? " she asked, aloud.

" Yes, " cried the cashier with a hissing and prolonged sound on the last letter; " his salary was attached, but some of the higher powers released it by a bill at sight."

" Where is the des Lupeaulx estate? "

" Why, don't you know? in the part of the country where your grandfather and your great-uncle Bidault belong, in the arrondissement of the deputy who wants to resign."

When her colossus of a husband had gone to bed, Elisabeth leaned over him, and though he always treated her remarks as women's nonsense, she said, "Perhaps you will really get Monsieur de la Billardière's place."

"There you go with your imaginations!" said Baudoyer; "leave Monsieur Gaudron to speak to the Dauphine and don't meddle with politics."

At eleven o'clock, when all were asleep in the place Royale, Monsieur des Lupeaulx was leaving the Opera for the rue Duphot. This particular Wednesday was one of Madame Rabourdin's most brilliant evenings. Many of her customary guests came in from the theatres and swelled the company already assembled, among whom were several celebrities, such as: Canalis the poet, Schinner the painter, Dr. Bianchon, Lucien de Rubempré, Octave de Camps, the Comte de Granville, the Vicomte de Fontaine, du Bruel the vaudevillist, Andoche Finot the journalist, Derville, one of the best heads in the law courts, the Comte du Châtelet, deputy, du Tillet, banker, and several elegant young men, such as Paul de Manerville and the Vicomte de Portenduère. Célestine was pouring out tea when the general-secretary entered. Her dress that evening was very becoming; she wore a black velvet robe without ornament of any kind, a black gauze scarf, her hair smoothly bound about her head and raised in a heavy braided mass, with long curls à *l'Anglaise* falling on either side her face. The charms which particularly distinguished this woman were the Italian ease of her artistic nature, her ready comprehension, and the grace with which she welcomed and promoted the least appearance of a wish on the part of others. Nature had given her an elegant, slender figure, which could sway lightly at a word, black eyes of oriental shape, able, like those of the Chinese women, to see out of their corners. She well knew how to manage a soft, insinuating voice, which threw a tender charm into every word, even such as she merely chanced to utter ; her feet were like those we see in portraits where the painter boldly lies and flatters his sitter in the only way which does not compromise anatomy. Her complexion, a little yellow by day, like that of most brunettes, was dazzling at night under the wax candles, which brought out the brilliancy of her black hair and eyes. Her slender and well-defined outlines reminded an artist of the Venus of the Middle Ages rendered by Jean Goujon, the illustrious sculptor of Diane de Poitiers.

Des Lupeaulx stopped in the doorway, and leaned against the woodwork. This ferret of ideas did not deny himself the pleasure of spying upon sentiment, and this woman interested him more than any of the others to whom he had attached himself. Des Lupeaulx had reached an age when men assert pretensions in regard to women. The first white hairs lead to the latest passions, all the more violent because they are astride of vanishing powers and dawning weakness. The age of forty is the age of folly, — an age when man wants to be loved for himself; whereas at twenty-five life is so full that he has no wants. At twenty-five he overflows with vigor and wastes it with impunity, but at forty he learns that to use it in that way is to abuse it. The thoughts that came into des Lupeaulx's mind at this moment were melancholy ones. The nerves of the old beau relaxed; the agreeable smile, which served as a mask and made the character of his countenance, faded; the real man appeared, and he was horrible. Rabourdin caught sight of him and thought, " What has happened to him? can he be disgraced in any way?" The general-secretary was, however, only thinking how the pretty Madame Colleville, whose intentions were exactly those of Madame Rabourdin, had summarily abandoned him when it suited her to do so. Rabourdin caught the sham statesman's eyes fixed on his wife, and he recorded the look in his memory. He was too keen an observer not to understand des Lupeaulx to the bottom, and he deeply despised him ; but, as with most busy men, his feelings and sentiments seldom came to the surface. Absorption in a beloved work is practically equivalent to the cleverest dissimulation, and thus it was that the opinions and ideas of Rabourdin were a sealed book to des Lupeaulx. The former was sorry to see the man in his house, but he was never willing to oppose his wife's wishes. At this particular moment, while he talked confidentially with a supernumerary of his office who was destined, later, to play an unconscious part in a political intrigue resulting from the death of La Billardière, he watched, though half-abstractedly, his wife and des Lupeaulx.

Here we must explain, as much for foreigners as for our own grandchildren, what a supernumerary in a government office in Paris means.

The supernumerary is to the administration what a choir-boy is to a church, what the company's child is to the regiment, what the figurante is to a theatre; something artless, naïve, innocent, a being blinded by illusions. Without illusions what would become of any of us? They give strength to bear the *res angusta domi* of arts and the beginnings of all science by inspiring us with faith. Illusion is illimitable faith. Now the supernumerary has faith in the administration; he never thinks it cold, cruel, and hard, as it really is. There are two kinds of supernumeraries, or hangers-on, — one poor, the other rich. The poor one is rich in hope and wants a place, the rich one is poor in spirit and wants nothing. A wealthy family is not so foolish as to put its able men into the administration. It confides an unfledged scion to some head-clerk, or gives him in charge of a director who initiates him into what Bilboquet, that profound philosopher, called the high comedy of government; he is spared all the horrors of drudgery and is finally appointed to some important office. The rich supernumerary never alarms the other clerks; they know he does not endanger their interests, for he seeks only the highest posts in the administration. About the period of which we write many families were saying to themselves: "What can we do with our sons?" The army no longer offered a chance for fortune. Special careers, such as civil and military engineering, the navy, mining, and the professorial chair were all fenced about by strict regulations or to be obtained only by competition; whereas in the civil service the revolving wheel which turned clerks into prefects, subprefects, assessors, and collectors, like the figures in a magic lantern, was subjected to no such rules and entailed no drudgery. Through this easy gap emerged into life the rich supernumeraries who drove their tilburys, dressed well, and wore moustachios, all of them as impudent as parvenus. Journalists were apt to persecute the tribe, who were cousins, nephews, brothers, or other relatives of some minister, some deputy, or an influential peer. The humbler clerks regarded them as a means of influence.

The poor supernumerary, on the other hand, who

is the only real worker, is almost always the son of
some former clerk's widow, who lives on a meagre
pension and sacrifices herself to support her son until
he can get a place as copying-clerk, and then dies
leaving him no nearer the head of his department
than writer of deeds, order-clerk, or, possibly, under-
head-clerk.   Living always in some locality where
rents are low, this humble supernumerary starts early
from home.   For him the Eastern question relates
only to the morning skies.   To go on foot and not
get muddied, to save his clothes, and allow for the
time he may lose in standing under shelter during a
shower, are the preoccupations of his mind.   The
street pavements, the flagging of the quays and the
boulevards, when first laid down, were a boon to
him.   If, for some extraordinary reason, you happen
to be in the streets of Paris at half-past seven or
eight o'clock of a winter's morning, and see through
piercing cold or fog or rain a timid, pale young man
loom up, cigarless, take notice of his pockets. You
will be sure to see the outline of a roll which his
mother has given him to stay his stomach between
breakfast and dinner. The guilelessness of the supernumerary does not last long. A youth enlightened by gleams of Parisian life soon measures the
frightful distance that separates him from a head-
clerkship, a distance which no mathematician, neither

Archimedes, nor Leibnitz, nor Laplace has ever reck-
oned, the distance that exists between 0 and the
figure 1. He begins to perceive the impossibilities of
his career; he hears talk of favoritism; he discovers
the intrigues of officials; he sees the questionable
means by which his superiors have pushed their way,
—one has married a young woman who made a false
step; another, the natural daughter of a minister;
this one shouldered the responsibility of another's
fault; that one, full of talent, risks his health in doing, with the perseverance of a mole, prodigies of
work which the man of influence feels incapable of
doing for himself, though he takes the credit. Everything is known in a government office. The incapable
man has a wife with a clear head, who has pushed
him along and got him nominated for deputy; if he
has not talent enough for an office, he cabals in the
Chamber. The wife of another has a statesman at
her feet. A third is the hidden informant of a powerful journalist. Often the disgusted and hopeless
supernumerary sends in his resignation. About three
fourths of his class leave the government employ without ever obtaining an appointment, and their number
is winnowed down to either those young men who are
foolish or obstinate enough to say to themselves, "I
have been here three years, and I must end sooner or
later by getting a place," or to those who are con-

scious of a vocation for the work. Undoubtedly the position of supernumerary in a government office is precisely what the novitiate is in a religious order, — a trial. It is a rough trial. The State discovers how many of them can bear hunger, thirst, and penury without breaking down, how many can toil without revolting against it; it learns which temperaments can bear up under the horrible experience — or if you like, the disease — of government official life. From this point of view the apprenticeship of the supernumerary, instead of being an infamous device of the government to obtain labor *gratis*, becomes a useful institution.

The young man with whom Rabourdin was talking was a poor supernumerary named Sébastien de la Roche, who had picked his way on the points of his toes, without incurring the least splash upon his boots, from the rue du Roi-Doré in the Marais. He talked of his mamma, and dared not raise his eyes to Madame Rabourdin, whose house appeared to him as gorgeous as the Louvre. He was careful to show his gloves, well cleaned with india-rubber, as little as he could. His poor mother had put five francs in his pocket in case it became absolutely necessary that he should play cards; but she enjoined him to take nothing, to remain standing, and to be very careful not to knock over a lamp or the bric-à-brac from an étagère. His dress was all of the strictest black. His fair face, his eyes, of a fine shade of green with golden reflections, were in keeping with a handsome head of auburn hair. The poor lad looked furtively at Madame Rabourdin, whispering to himself, " How beautiful ! " and was likely to dream of that fairy when he went to bed.

Rabourdin had noted a vocation for his work in the lad, and as he himself took the whole service seriously, he felt a lively interest in him. He guessed the poverty of his mother's home, kept together on a widow's pension of seven hundred francs a year — for the education of the son, who was just out of college, had absorbed all her savings. He therefore treated the youth almost paternally ; often endeavored to get him some fee from the Council, or paid it from his own pocket. He overwhelmed Sébastien with work, trained him, and allowed him to do the work of du Bruel's place, for which that vaudevillist, otherwise known as Cursy, paid him three hundred francs out of his salary. In the minds of Madame de la Roche and her son, Rabourdin was at once a great man, a tyrant, and an angel. On him all the poor fellow's hopes of getting an appointment depended, and the lad's devotion to his chief was boundless. He dined once a fortnight in the rue Duphot ; but always at a family dinner, invited by Rabourdin himself ; Madame asked him to evening parties only when she wanted partners.

At that moment Rabourdin was scolding poor Sébastien, the only human being who was in the secret of his immense labors. The youth copied and recopied the famous " statement," written on a hundred and fifty folio sheets, besides the corroborative documents, and the summing up (contained in one page), with the estimates bracketed, the captions in a running hand, and the sub-titles in a round one. Full of enthusiasm, in spite of his merely mechanical participation in the great idea, the lad of twenty would rewrite whole pages for a single blot, and made it his glory to touch up the writing, regarding it as the element of a noble undertaking. Sébastien had that afternoon committed the great imprudence of carrying into the general office, for the purpose of copying, a paper which contained the most dangerous facts to make known prematurely, namely, a memorandum relating to the officials in the central offices of all the ministries, with facts concerning their fortunes, actual and prospective, together with the individual enterprises of each outside of his government employment.

All government clerks in Paris who are not endowed, like Rabourdin, with patriotic ambition or other marked capacity, usually add the profits of some industry to the salary of their office, in order to eke out a living. A number do as Monsieur Saillard did, — put their money into a business carried on by others, and spend their evenings in keeping the books of their associates. Many clerks are married to milliners, licensed tobacco dealers, women who have charge of the public lotteries or reading-rooms. Some, like the husband of Madame Colleville, Célestine's rival, play in the orchestra of a theatre; others like du Bruel, write vaudevilles, comic operas, melodramas, or act as prompters behind the scenes. We may mention among them Messrs. Planard, Sewrin, etc. · Pigault-Lebrun, Piis, Duvicquet, in their day, were in government employ. Monsieur Scribe's head-librarian was a clerk in the Treasury.

Besides such information as this, Rabourdin's memorandum contained an inquiry into the moral and physical capacities and faculties necessary in those who were to examine the intelligence, aptitude for labor, and sound health of the applicants for government service, — three indispensable qualities in men who are to bear the burden of public affairs and should do their business well and quickly. But this careful study, the result of ten years' observation and experience, and of a long acquaintance with men and things obtained by intercourse with the various functionaries in the different ministries, would assuredly have, to those who did not see its purport and connection, an air of treachery and police espial. If a single page of these papers were to fall under the eye of those concerned, Monsieur Rabourdin was lost. Sébastien, who admired his chief without reservation, and who was, as yet, wholly ignorant of the evils of bureaucracy, had the follies of guilelessness as well as its grace. Blamed on a former occasion for carrying away these papers, he now bravely acknowledged his fault to its fullest extent; he related how he had put away both the memorandum and the copy carefully in a box in the office where no one would ever find them. Tears rolled from his eyes as he realized the greatness of his offence.

"Come, come!" said Rabourdin, kindly. "Don't be so imprudent again, but never mind now. Go to the office very early to-morrow morning; here is the key of a small safe which is in my roller secretary; it shuts with a combination lock. You can open it with the word 'sky;' put the memorandum and your copy into it and shut it carefully."

This proof of confidence dried the poor fellow's tears. Rabourdin advised him to take a cup of tea and some cakes.

"Mamma forbids me to drink tea, on account of my chest," said Sébastien.

"Well, then, my dear child," said the imposing Madame Rabourdin, who wished to appear gracious, "here are some sandwiches and cream; come and sit by me."

She made Sébastien sit down beside her, and the lad's heart rose in his throat as he felt the robe of this divinity brush the sleeve of his coat. Just then the beautiful woman caught sight of Monsieur des Lupeaulx standing in the doorway. She smiled, and not waiting till he came to her, she went to him.

"Why do you stay there as if you were sulking?" she asked.

"I am not sulking," he returned; "I came to announce some good news, but the thought has overtaken me that it will only add to your severity towards me. I fancy myself six months hence almost a stranger to you. Yes, you are too clever, and I too experienced,—too blasé, if you like,—for either of us to deceive the other. Your end is attained without its costing you more than a few smiles and gracious words."

"Deceive each other! what can you mean?" she cried, in a hurt tone.

"Yes; Monsieur de la Billardière is dying, and from what the minister told me this evening I judge that your husband will be appointed in his place."

He thereupon related what he called his scene at the ministry and the jealousy of the countess, repeating her remarks about the invitation he had asked her to send to Madame Rabourdin.

"Monsieur des Lupeaulx," said Madame Rabourdin, with dignity, "permit me to tell you that my husband is the oldest head-clerk as well as the most capable man in the division; also that the appointment

of La Billardière over his head made much talk in the
service, and that my husband has stayed on for the last
year expecting this promotion, for which he has really
no competitor and no rival."

" That is true."

" Well, then," she resumed, smiling and showing
her handsome teeth, " how can you suppose that the
friendship I feel for you is marred by a thought of
self-interest? Why should you think me capable of
that?"

Des Lupeaulx made a gesture of admiring denial.

" Ah!" she continued, " the heart of woman will
always remain a secret for even the cleverest of men.
Yes, I welcomed you to my house with the greatest
pleasure; and there was, I admit, a motive of self-
interest behind my pleasure—"

" Ah!"

" You have a career before you," she whispered in
his ear, " a future without limit; you will be deputy,
minister!" (What happiness for an ambitious man
when such things as these are warbled in his ear by the
sweet voice of a pretty woman!) " Oh, yes! I know
you better than you know yourself. Rabourdin is a
man who could be of immense service to you in such
a career; he could do the steady work while you were
in the Chamber. Just as you dream of the ministry, so I dream of seeing Rabourdin in the Council

of State, and general director. It is therefore my object to draw together two men who can never injure, but, on the contrary, must greatly help each other. Is n't that a woman's mission? If you are friends, you will both rise the faster, and it is surely high time that each of you made hay. I have burned my ships," she added, smiling. "But you are not as frank with me as I have been with you."

"You would not listen to me if I were," he replied, with a melancholy air, in spite of the deep inward satisfaction her remarks gave him. "What would such future promotions avail me, if you dismiss me now?"

"Before I listen to you," she replied, with native Parisian liveliness, "we must be able to understand each other."

And she left the old fop to go and speak with Madame de Chessel, a countess from the provinces, who seemed about to take leave.

"That is a very extraordinary woman," said des Lupeaulx to himself. "I don't know my own self when I am with her."

Accordingly, this man of no principle, who six years earlier had kept a ballet-girl, and who now, thanks to his position, made himself a seraglio with the pretty wives of the under-clerks, and lived in the world of journalists and actresses, became devotedly attentive all the evening to Célestine, and was the last to leave the house.

"At last!" thought Madame Rabourdin, as she undressed that night, "we have the place! Twelve thousand francs a year and perquisites, beside the rents of our farm at Grajeux,—nearly twenty thousand francs a year. It is not affluence, but at least it is n't poverty."

IV.

THREE-QUARTER LENGTH PORTRAITS OF CERTAIN GOVERNMENT OFFICIALS.

If it were possible for literature to use the microscope of the Leuwenhoëks, the Malpighis, and the Raspails (an attempt once made by Hoffmann, of Berlin), and if we could magnify and then picture the *teredos navalis,* in other words, those ship-worms which brought Holland within an inch of collapsing by honey-combing her dykes, we might have been able to give a more distinct idea of Messieurs Gigonnet, Baudoyer, Saillard, Gaudron, Falleix, Transon, Godard and company, borers and burrowers, who proved their undermining power in the thirtieth year of this century.

But now it is time to show another set of *teredos,* who burrowed and swarmed in the government offices where the principal scenes of our present study took place.

In Paris nearly all these government bureaus resemble each other. Into whatever ministry you penetrate to ask some slight favor, or to get redress for a trifling wrong, you will find the same dark corridors, ill-lighted stairways, doors with oval panes of glass like eyes, as at the theatre. In the first room as you enter you will find the office servant; in the second, the under-clerks; the private office of the second head-clerk is to the right or left, and further on is that of the head of the bureau. As to the important personage called, under the Empire, head of division, then, under the Restoration, director, and now by the former name, head or chief of division, he lives either above or below the offices of his three or four different bureaus.

Speaking in the administrative sense, a bureau consists of a man-servant, several supernumeraries (who do the work *gratis* for a certain number of years), various copying clerks, writers of bills and deeds, order clerks, principal clerks, second or under head-clerk, and head-clerk, otherwise called head or chief of the bureau. These denominational titles vary under some administrations; for instance, the order-clerks are sometimes called auditors, or again, book-keepers.

Paved like the corridor, and hung with a shabby paper, the first room, where the servant is stationed, is furnished with a stove, a large black table with inkstand, pens, and paper, and benches, but no mats on which to wipe the public feet. The clerk's office beyond is a large room, tolerably well lighted, but seldom floored with wood. Wooden floors and fireplaces are commonly kept sacred to heads of bureaus and divisions; and so are closets, wardrobes, mahogany tables, sofas and armchairs covered with red or green morocco, silk curtains, and other articles of administrative luxury. The clerk's office contents itself with a stove, the pipe of which goes into the chimney, if there be a chimney. The wall paper is plain and all of one color, usually green or brown. The tables are of black wood. The private characteristics of the several clerks often crop out in their method of settling themselves at their desks, — the chilly one has a wooden footstool under his feet; the man with a bilious temperament has a metal mat; the lymphatic being who dreads draughts constructs a fortification of boxes as a screen. The door of the under-head-clerk's office always stands open so that he may keep an eye to some extent on his subordinates.

Perhaps an exact description of Monsieur de la Billardière's division will suffice to give foreigners and provincials an idea of the internal manners and customs of a government office; the chief features of which are probably much the same in the civil service of all European governments.

In the first place, picture to yourself the man who is thus described in the Yearly Register:—

"CHIEF OF DIVISION. — Monsieur la baron Flamet de la Billardière (Athanase-Jean-François-Michel) formerly provost-marshal of the department of the Corrèze, gentleman in ordinary of the bed-chamber, president of the college of the department of the Dordogne, officer of the Legion of honor, knight of Saint Louis and of the foreign orders of Christ, Isabella, Saint Wladimir, etc., member of the Academy of Gers, and other learned bodies, vice-president of the Society of Belles-lettres, member of the Association of Saint-Joseph and of the Society of Prisons, one of the mayors of Paris, etc."

The personage who requires so much typographic space was at this time occupying an area five feet six in length by thirty-six inches in width in a bed, his head adorned with a cotton night-cap tied on by flame-colored ribbons; attended by Despleins, the King's surgeon, and young doctor Bianchon, flanked by two old female relatives, surrounded by phials of all kinds, bandages, appliances, and various mortuary instruments, and watched over by the curate of Saint-Roch, who was advising him to think of his salvation.

La Billardière's division occupied the upper floor of a magnificent mansion, in which the vast official ocean of a ministry was contained. A wide landing separated its two bureaus, the doors of which were duly labelled. The private offices and antechambers of the heads of the two bureaus, Monsieur Rabourdin and Monsieur Baudoyer, were below on the second floor, and beyond that of Monsieur Rabourdin were the antechamber, salon, and two offices of Monsieur de la Billardière.

·On the first floor, divided in two by an *entresol*, were the living-rooms and office of Monsieur Ernest de la Brière, an occult and powerful personage who must be described in a few words, for he well deserves a parenthesis. This young man held, during the whole time that this particular administration lasted, the position of private secretary to the minister. His apartment was connected by a secret door with the private office of his Excellency. A private secretary is to the minister himself what des Lupeaulx was to the ministry at large. The same difference existed between young La Brière and des Lupeaulx that there is between an aide-de-camp and a chief of staff. This ministerial apprentice decamps when his protector leaves office, returning sometimes when he returns. If the minister enjoys the royal favor when he falls, or still has parliamentary hopes, he takes his secretary with him into retirement only to bring him back on his return; otherwise he puts him to grass in some of the various administrative pastures, — for instance, in the Court of Exchequer, that wayside refuge where private secretaries wait for the storm to blow over. The young man is not precisely a government official; he is a political character, however; and sometimes his politics are limited to those of one man. When we think of the number of letters it is the private secretary's fate to open and read, besides all his other avocations, it is very evident that under a monarchical government his services would be well paid for. A drudge of this kind costs ten or twenty thousand francs a year; and he enjoys, moreover, the opera-boxes, the social invitations, and the carriages of the minister. The Emperor of Russia would be thankful to be able to pay fifty thousand a year to one of these amiable constitutional poodles, so gentle, so nicely curled, so caressing, so docile, always spick and span, — careful watch-dogs besides, and faithful to a degree! But the private secretary is a product of the representative government hot-house; he is propagated and developed there, and there only. Under a monarchy you will find none but courtiers and vassals, whereas under a constitutional government you may be flattered, served, and adulated by free men. In France ministers are better off than kings or women; they have some one who thoroughly understands them. Perhaps, indeed, the private secretary is to be pitied as much as women and white paper. They are nonentities who are made to bear all things. They are allowed no talent except hidden ones, which must be employed in the service of their ministers. A public show of talent would ruin them. The private secretary is therefore an intimate friend in the gift of government — However, let us return to the bureaus.

Three men-servants lived in peace in the Billardière division, to wit: a footman for the two bureaus, another for the service of the two chiefs, and a third for the director of the division himself. All three were lodged, warmed, and clothed by the State, and wore the well-known livery of the State, blue coat with red pipings for undress, and broad red, white, and blue braid for great occasions. La Billardière's man had the air of a gentleman-usher, an innovation which gave an aspect of dignity to the division.

Pillars of the ministry, experts in all manners and customs bureaucratic, well-warmed and clothed at the State's expense, growing rich by reason of their few wants, these lackeys saw completely through the government officials, collectively and individually. They had no better way of amusing their idle hours than by observing these personages and studying their peculiarities. They knew how far to trust the clerks with loans of money, doing their various commissions with absolute discretion; they pawned and took out of pawn, bought up bills when due, and lent money without interest, albeit no clerk ever borrowed of them without returning a "gratification." These servants without a master received a salary of nine hundred francs a year; new years' gifts and "gratifications" brought their emoluments to twelve hundred francs, and they made almost as much more by serving breakfasts to the clerks at the office.

The elder of these men, who was also the richest, waited upon the main body of the clerks. He was sixty years of age, with white hair cropped short like a brush; stout, thickset, and apoplectic about the neck, with a vulgar pimpled face, gray eyes, and a mouth like a furnace door; such was the profile portrait of Antoine, the oldest attendant at the ministry. He had brought his two nephews, Laurent and Gabriel, from Echelles in Savoie, — one to serve the heads of the bureaus, the other the director himself. All three came to open the offices and clean them, between seven and eight o'clock in the morning; at which time they read the newspapers and talked civil service politics from their point of view with the servants of other divisions, exchanging the bureaucratic gossip. In common with servants of modern houses who know their masters' private affairs thoroughly, they lived at the ministry like spiders at the centre of a web, where they felt the slightest jar of the fabric.

On a Thursday morning, the day after the ministerial reception and Madame Rabourdin's evening party, just as Antoine was trimming his beard and his nephews were assisting him in the antechamber of the division on the upper floor, they were surprised by the unexpected arrival of one of the clerks.

"That's Monsieur Dutocq," said Antoine, "I know him by that pickpocket step of his. He is always moving round on the sly, that man. He is on your back before you know it. Yesterday, contrary to his usual ways, he outstayed the last man in the office ; such a thing has n't happened three times since he has been at the ministry."

Here follows the portrait of Monsiur Dutocq, order-clerk in the Rabourdin bureau : Thirty-eight years old, oblong face and bilious skin, grizzled hair always cut close, low forehead, heavy eyebrows meeting together, a crooked nose and pinched lips ; tall, the right shoulder slightly higher than the left ; brown coat, black waist-coat, silk cravat, yellowish trousers, black woollen stockings, and shoes with flapping bows ; thus you behold him.   Idle and incapable, he hated Rabourdin, — naturally enough, for Rabourdin had no vice to flatter, and no bad or weak side on which Dutocq could make himself useful.   Far too noble to injure a clerk, the chief was also too clear-sighted to be deceived by any make-believe.   Dutocq kept his place therefore solely through Rabourdin's generosity, and was very certain that he could never be promoted if the latter succeeded La Billardière.   Though he knew himself incapable of important work, Dutocq was well aware that in a government office incapacity is no hindrance to advancement ; La Billardière's own appointment over the head of so capable a man as Rabourdin had been a striking and fatal example of this.   Wickedness combined with self-interest works with a power equivalent to that of intellect; evilly disposed and wholly self-interested, Dutocq had endeavored to strengthen his position by becoming a spy in all the offices. After 1816 he assumed a marked religious tone, foreseeing the favor which the fools of those days would bestow on those they indiscriminately called Jesuits. Belonging to that fraternity in spirit, though not admitted to its rites, Dutocq went from bureau to bureau, sounded consciences by recounting immoral jests, and then reported and paraphrased results to des Lupeaulx; the latter thus learned all the trivial events of the ministry, and often surprised the minister by his consummate knowledge of what was going on. He tolerated Dutocq under the idea that circumstances might some day make him useful, were it only to get him or some distinguished friend of his out of a scrape by a disgraceful marriage. The two understood each other well. Dutocq had succeeded Monsieur Poiret the elder, who had retired in 1814, and now lived in the pension Vauquer in the Latin quarter. Dutocq himself lived in a pension in the rue de Beaune, and spent his evenings in the Palais-Royal, sometimes going to the theatre, thanks to du Bruel, who gave him an author's ticket about once a week. And now, a word on du Bruel.

Though Sébastien did his work at the office for the small compensation we have mentioned, du Bruel was in the habit of coming there to advertise the fact that he was the under-head-clerk and to draw his salary. His real work was that of dramatic critic to a leading ministerial journal, in which he also wrote articles inspired by the ministers, — a very well understood, clearly defined, and quite unassailable position. Du Bruel was not lacking in those diplomatic little tricks which go so far to conciliate general good-will. He sent Madame Rabourdin an opera-box for a first representation, took her there in a carriage and brought her back, — an attention which evidently pleased her. Rabourdin, who was never exacting with his subordinates allowed du Bruel to go off to rehearsals, come to the office at his own hours, and work at his vaudevilles when there. Monsieur le Duc de Chaulieu, the minister, knew that du Bruel was writing a novel which was to be dedicated to himself. Dressed with the careless ease of a theatre man, du Bruel wore, in the morning, trousers strapped under his feet, shoes with gaiters, a waistcoat evidently vamped over, an olive surtout, and a black cravat. At night he played the gentleman in elegant clothes. He lived, for good reasons, in the same house as Florine, an actress for whom he wrote plays. Du Bruel, or to give him his pen name, Cursy, was working just now at a piece in five acts for the Français. Sébastien was devoted to the author, — who occasionally gave him tickets to the pit, — and applauded his pieces at the parts which du Bruel told him were of doubtful interest, with all the faith and enthusiasm of his years. In fact, the youth looked upon the play-wright as a great author, and it was to Sébastien that du Bruel said, the day after a first representation of a vaudeville produced, like all vaudevilles, by three collaborators, "The audience preferred the scenes written by two."

"Why don't you write alone?" asked Sébastien, naïvely.

There were good reasons why du Bruel did not write alone. He was the third of an author. A dramatic writer, as few people know, is made up of three individuals: first, the man with brains who invents the subject and maps out the structure, or *scenario*, of the vaudeville; second, the plodder, who works the piece into shape; and third, the toucher-up, who sets the songs to music, arranges the chorus and concerted pieces and fits them into their right place, and finally writes the puffs and the advertisements. Du Bruel was a plodder; at the office he read the newest books, extracted their wit, and laid it by for use in his dialogues. He was liked by his collaborators on account of his carefulness; the man with brains, sure of being understood, could cross his arms and feel that his ideas would be well rendered. The clerks in the office liked their companion well enough to attend a first performance of his plays in a body and applaud them, for he really deserved the title of a good fellow. His hand went readily to his pocket; ices and punch were bestowed without prodding, and he loaned fifty francs without asking them back. He owned a country-house at Aulnay, laid by his money, and had, besides the four thousand five hundred francs of his salary under government, twelve hundred francs pension from the civil list, and eight hundred from the three hundred thousand francs fund voted by the Chambers for encouragement of the Arts. Add to these diverse emoluments nine thousand francs earned by his quarters, thirds, and halves of plays in three different theatres and you will readily understand that such a man must be physically round, fat, and comfortable, with the face of a worthy capitalist. As to morals, he was the lover and the beloved of Tullia and felt himself preferred in heart to the brilliant Duc de Rhetoré, the lover in chief.

Dutocq had seen with great uneasiness what he called the liaison of des Lupeaulx with Madame Rabourdin, and his silent wrath on the subject was accumulating. He had too prying an eye not to have guessed that Rabourdin was engaged in some great work outside of his official labors, and he was provoked to feel that he knew nothing about it, whereas that little Sébastien was, wholly or in part, in the secret. Dutocq was intimate with Godard, under-head-clerk to Baudoyer, and

the high esteem in which Dutocq held Baudoyer was
the original cause of his acquaintance with Godard ; not
that Dutocq was sincere even in this ; but by praising
Baudoyer and saying nothing of Rabourdin he satisfied
his hatred after the fashion of little minds.

Joseph Godard, a cousin of Mitral on the mother's
side, made pretensions to the hand of Mademoiselle
Baudoyer, not perceiving that her mother was laying
siege to Falleix as a son-in-law. ˙He brought little
gifts to the young lady, artificial flowers, bonbons
on new-year's day and pretty boxes for her birthday.
Twenty-six years of age, a worker working without
purpose, steady as a girl, monotonous and apathetic,
holding cafés, cigars, and horsemanship in detestation,
going to bed regularly at ten o'clock and rising at
seven, gifted with some social talents, such as playing
quadrille music on the flute, which first brought him
into favor with the Saillards and the Baudoyers. He
was moreover a fifer in the National Guard, — to escape
his turn of sitting up all night in a barrack-room. Godard was devoted more especially to natural history. He
made collections of shells and minerals, knew how to
stuff birds, kept a mass of curiosities bought for nothing in his bedroom ; took possession of phials and
empty perfume bottles for his specimens ; pinned but-
terflies and beetles under glass, hung Chinese parasols
on the walls, together with dried fishskins. He lived

with his sister, an artificial-flower maker, in the rue de Richelieu. Though much admired by mammas this model young man was looked down upon by his sister's shop-girls, who had tried to inveigle him. Slim and lean, of medium height, with dark circles round his eyes, Joseph Godard took little care of his person; his clothes were ill-cut, his trousers bagged, he wore white stockings at all seasons of the year, a hat with a narrow brim and laced shoes. He was always complaining of his digestion. His principal vice was a mania for proposing rural parties during the summer season, excursions to Montmorency, picnics on the grass, and visits to creameries on the boulevard du Mont-Parnasse. For the last six months Dutocq had taken to visiting Mademoiselle Godard from time to time, with certain views of his own, hoping to discover in her establishment some female treasure.

Thus Baudoyer had a pair of henchmen in Dutocq and Godard. Monsieur Saillard, too innocent to judge rightly of Dutocq, was in the habit of paying him frequent little visits at the office. Young La Billardière, the director's son, placed as supernumerary with Baudoyer, made another member of the clique. The clever heads in the offices laughed much at this alliance of incapables. Bixiou nicknamed Baudoyer, Godard, and Dutocq a " Trinity without the Spirit," and little La Billardière the " Pascal Lamb."

"You are early this morning," said Antoine to Dutocq, laughing."

"So are you, Antoine," answered Dutocq; "you see, the newspapers do come earlier than you let us have them at the office."

"They did to-day, by chance," replied Antoine, not disconcerted; "they never come two days together at the same hour."

The two nephews looked at each other as if to say, in admiration of their uncle, "What cheek he has!"

"Though I make two sous by all his breakfasts," muttered Antoine, as he heard Monsieur Dutocq close the office door, "I'd give them up to get that man out of our division."

"Ah, Monsieur Sébastien, you are not the first here to-day," said Antoine, a quarter of an hour later, to the supernumerary.

"Who is here?" asked the poor lad, turning pale.

"Monsieur Dutocq," answered Laurent.

Virgin natures have, beyond all others, the inexplicable gift of second-sight, the reason of which lies perhaps in the purity of their nervous systems, which are, as it were, brand-new. Sébastien had long guessed Dutocq's hatred to his revered Rabourdin. So that when Laurent uttered his name a dreadful presentiment took possession of the lad's mind, and crying out, "I feared it!" he flew like an arrow into the corridor.

"There is going to be a row in the division," said Antoine, shaking his white head as he put on his livery. "It is very certain that Monsieur le baron is off to his account. Yes, Madame Gruget, the nurse, told me he could n't live through the day. What a stir there 'll be! oh! won't there! Go along, you fellows, and see if the stoves are drawing properly. Heavens and earth! our world is coming down about our ears."

"That poor young one," said Laurent, "had a sort of sunstroke when he heard that Jesuit of a Dutocq had got here before him."

"I have told him a dozen times, — for after all one ought to tell the truth to an honest clerk, and what I call an honest clerk is one like that little fellow who gives us *recta* his ten francs on new-year's day, — I have said to him again and again: The more you work the more they 'll make you work, and they won't promote you. He does n't listen to me; he tires himself out staying here till five o'clock, an hour after all the others have gone. Folly! he 'll never get on that way! The proof is that not a word has been said about giving him an appointment, though he has been here two years. It 's a shame! it makes my blood boil."

"Monsieur Rabourdin is very fond of Monsieur Sébastien," said Laurent.

"But Monsieur Rabourdin is n't a minister," retorted Antoine; "it will be a hot day when that happens, and the hens will have teeth ; he is too — but mum ! When I think that I carry salaries to those humbugs who stay away and do as they please, while that poor little La Roche works himself to death, I ask myself if God ever thinks of the civil service. And what do they give you, these pets of Monsieur le maréchal and Monsieur le duc? 'Thank you, my dear Antoine, thank you,' with a gracious nod ! Pack of sluggards ! go to work, or you 'll bring another revolution about your ears. Did n't see such goings-on under Monsieur Robert Lindet. I know, for I served my apprenticeship under Robert Lindet. The clerks had to work in his day ! You ought to have seen how they scratched paper here till midnight ; why, the stoves went out and nobody noticed it. It was all because the guillotine was there ! now-a-days they only mark 'em when they come in late !"

"Uncle Antoine," said Gabriel, "as you are so talkative this morning, just tell us what you think a clerk really ought to be."

"A government clerk," replied Antoine, gravely, "is a man who sits in a government office and writes. But there, there, what am I talking about? Without the clerks, where should we be, I 'd like to know? Go along and look after your stoves and mind you never say harm of a government clerk, you fellows. Gabriel, the stove in the large office draws like the devil ; you must turn the damper."

Antoine stationed himself at a corner of the landing whence he could see all the officials as they entered the porte-cochère; he knew every one at the ministry, and watched their behavior, observing narrowly the contrasts in their dress and appearance.

The first to arrive after Sébastien was a clerk of deeds in Rabourdin's office named Phellion, a respectable family-man. To the influence of his chief he owed a half-scholarship for each of his two sons in the College Henri IV.; while his daughter was being educated *gratis* at a boarding-school where his wife gave music lessons and he himself a course of history and one of geography in the evenings. He was about forty-five years of age, sergeant-major of his company in the National Guard, very compassionate in feeling and words, but wholly unable to give away a penny. Proud of his post, however, and satisfied with his lot, he applied himself faithfully to serve the government, believed he was useful to his country, and boasted of his indifference to politics, knowing none but those of the men in power. Monsieur Rabourdin pleased him highly whenever he asked him to stay half an hour longer to finish a piece of work. On such occasions he would say, when he reached home, " Public affairs detained me; when a man belongs to the government he is no longer master of himself." He compiled books of questions and answers on various studies for the use of young

ladies in boarding-schools. These little " solid trea-
tises," as he called them, were sold at the University
library under the name of " Historical and Geographi-
cal Catechisms." Feeling himself in duty bound to offer
a copy of each volume, bound in red morocco, to Madame Rabourdin, he always came in full dress to present
them, — breeches and silk stockings, and shoes with
gold buckles. Monsieur Phellion received his friends
on Thursday evenings, on which occasions the company
played *bouillote*, at five sous a game, and were regaled
with cakes and beer. He had never yet dared to invite
Monsieur Rabourdin to honor him with his presence,
though he would have regarded such an event as the
most distinguished of his life. He said if he could
leave one of his sons following in the steps of Monsieur Rabourdin he should die the happiest father in
the world.

One of his greatest pleasures was to explore the environs of Paris, which he did with a map. He knew
every inch of Arcueil, Bièvre, Fontenay-aux-Roses, and
Aulnay, so famous as the resort of great writers, and
hoped in time to know the whole western side of the
country around Paris. He intended to put his eldest
son into a government office and his second into the
École Polytechnique. He often said to the elder,
" When you have the honor to be a government clerk ; "
though he suspected him of a preference for the exact

sciences and did his best to repress it, mentally resolving to abandon the lad to his own devices if he persisted. When Rabourdin sent for him to come down and receive instructions about some particular piece of work, Phellion gave all his mind to it, — listening to every word the chief said, as a *dilettante* listens to an air at the Opera. Silent in the office, with his feet in the air resting on a wooden desk, and never moving them, he studied his task conscientiously. His official letters were written with the utmost gravity, and transmitted the commands of the minister in solemn phrases. Monsieur Phellion's face was that of a pensive ram, with little color and pitted by the small-pox; the lips were thick and the lower one pendent; the eyes light-blue, and his figure above the common height. Neat and clean as a master of history and geography in a young ladies' school ought to be, he wore fine linen, a pleated shirt-frill, a black cashmere waistcoat, left open and showing a pair of braces embroidered by his daughter, a diamond in the bosom of his shirt, a black coat, and blue trousers. In winter he added a nut-colored box-coat with three capes, and carried a loaded stick, necessitated, he said, by the profound solitude of the quarter in which he lived. He had given up taking snuff, and referred to this reform as a striking example of the empire a man could exercise over himself. Monsieur Phellion came slowly up the stairs, for he was afraid of

asthma, having what he called an "adipose chest."
He saluted Antoine with dignity.

The next to follow was a copying-clerk, who presented a strange contrast to the virtuous Phellion. Vimeux was a young man of twenty-five, with a salary of fifteen hundred francs, well-made and graceful, with a romantic face, and eyes, hair, beard, and eyebrows as black as jet, fine teeth, charming hands, and wearing a moustache so carefully trimmed that he seemed to have made it the business and occupation of his life. Vimeux had such aptitude for work that he despatched it much quicker than any of the other clerks. "He has a gift, that young man!" Phellion said of him when he saw him cross his legs and have nothing to do for the rest of the day, having got through his appointed task; "and see what a little dandy he is!" Vimeux breakfasted on a roll and a glass of water, dined for twenty sous at Katcomb's, and lodged in a furnished room, for which he paid twelve francs a month. His happiness, his sole pleasure in life, was dress. He ruined himself in miraculous waistcoats, in trousers that were tight, half-tight, pleated, or embroidered; in superfine boots, well-made coats which outlined his elegant figure; in bewitching collars, spotless gloves, and immaculate hats. A ring with a coat of arms adorned his hand, outside his glove, from which dangled a handsome cane; with these accessories he endeav-

ored to assume the air and manner of a wealthy
young man. After the office closed he appeared in
the great walk of the Tuileries, with a tooth-pick in
his mouth, as though he were a millionnaire who had
just dined. Always on the lookout for a woman, — an
Englishwoman, a foreigner of some kind, or a widow, —
who might fall in love with him, he practised the art
of twirling his cane and of flinging the sort of glance
which Bixiou told him was American. He smiled to
show his fine teeth; he wore no socks under his
boots, but he had his hair curled every day. Vimeux
was prepared, in accordance with fixed principles, to
marry a hunch-back with six thousand a year, or a
woman of forty-five at eight thousand, or an Englishwoman for half that sum. Phellion, who delighted in
his neat hand-writing, and was full of compassion for
the fellow, read him lectures on the duty of giving
lessons in penmanship, — an honorable career, he said,
which would ameliorate existence and even render it
agreeable; he promised him a situation in a young
ladies' boarding-school. But Vimeux's head was so
full of his own idea that no human being could prevent him from having faith in his star. He continued
to lay himself out, like a salmon at a fishmonger's, in
spite of his empty stomach and the fact that he had
fruitlessly exhibited his enormous moustachios and his
fine clothes for over three years. As he owed Antoine

more than thirty francs for his breakfasts, he lowered his eyes every time he passed him; and yet he never failed at midday to ask the man to buy him a roll.

After trying to get a few reasonable ideas into this foolish head, Rabourdin had finally given up the attempt as hopeless. Adolphe (his name was Adolphe) had lately economized on dinners and lived entirely on bread and water, to buy a pair of spurs and a riding-whip. Jokes at the expense of this starving Amadis were made only in the spirit of mischievous fun which creates vaudevilles, for he was really a kind-hearted fellow and a good comrade, who harmed no one but himself. A standing joke in the two bureaus was the question whether he wore corsets, and bets depended on it. Vimeux was originally appointed to Baudoyer's bureau, but he manœuvred to get himself transferred to Rabourdin's, on account of Baudoyer's extreme severity in relation to what were called "the English," — a name given by the government clerks to their creditors. "English day" means the day on which the government offices are thrown open to the public. Certain then of finding their delinquent debtors, the creditors swarm in and torment them, asking when they intend to pay, and threatening to attach their salaries. The implacable Baudoyer compelled the clerks to remain at their desks and endure this torture. "It was their place not to make debts," he said; and he considered his severity as a duty which he owed to the public weal. Rabourdin, on the contrary, protected the clerks against their creditors, and turned the latter away, saying that the government bureaus were open for public business, not private. Much ridicule pursued Vimeux in both bureaus when the clank of his spurs resounded in the corridors and on the staircases. The wag of the ministry, Bixiou, sent round a paper, headed by a caricature of his victim on a pasteboard horse, asking for subscriptions to buy him a live charger. Monsieur Baudoyer was down for a bale of hay taken from his own forage allowance, and each of the clerks wrote his little epigram; Vimeux himself, good-natured fellow that he was, subscribed under the name of "Miss Fairfax."

Handsome clerks of the Vimeux style have their salaries on which to live, and their good looks by which to make their fortune. Devoted to masked balls during the carnival, they seek their luck there, though it often escapes them. Many end the weary round by marrying milliners, or old women, — sometimes, however, young ones who are charmed with their handsome persons, and with whom they set up a romance illustrated with stupid love letters, which, nevertheless, seem to answer their purpose.

Bixiou (pronounce it Bisiou) was a draughtsman, who ridiculed Dutocq as readily as he did Rabourdin, whom he nicknamed " the virtuous woman." Without doubt the cleverest man in the division or even at the ministry (but clever after the fashion of a monkey, without aim or sequence), Bixiou was so essentially useful to Baudoyer and Godard that they upheld and protected him in spite of his misconduct; for he did their work when they were incapable of doing it for themselves. Bixiou wanted either Godard's or du Bruel's place as under-head-clerk, but his conduct interfered with his promotion. Sometimes he sneered at the public service ; this was usually after he had made some happy hit, such as the publication of portraits in the famous Fualdès case (for which he drew faces hap-hazard), or his sketch of the debate on the Castaing affair. At other times, when possessed with a desire to get on, he really applied himself to work, though he would soon leave off to write a vaudeville, which was never finished. A thorough egoist, a spendthrift and a miser in one, — that is to say, spending his money solely on himself, — sharp, aggressive, and indiscreet, he did mischief for mischief's sake ; above all, he attacked the weak, respected nothing and believed in nothing, neither in France, nor in God, nor in art, nor in the Greeks, nor in the Turks, nor in the monarchy, — insulting and disparaging everything that he could not comprehend. He was the first to paint a black cap on Charles X.'s head on the five-franc coins. He mimicked Dr. Gall when lecturing, till he made the most starched of diplomatists burst their buttons. Famous for his practical jokes, he varied them with such elaborate care that he always obtained a victim. His great secret in this was the power of guessing the inmost wishes of others ; he knew the way to many a castle in the air, to the dreams about which a man may be. fooled because he wants to be ; and he made such men sit to him for hours.

Thus it happened that this close observer, who could display unrivalled tact in developing a joke or driving home a sarcasm, was unable to use the same power to make men further his fortunes and promote him. The person he most liked to annoy was young La Billardière, his nightmare, his detestation, whom he was nevertheless constantly wheedling so as the better to torment him on his weakest side. He wrote him love letters signed "Comtesse de M——" or "Marquise de B——"; took him to the Opera on gala days and presented him to some grisette under the clock, after calling everybody's attention to the young fool. He allied himself with Dutocq (whom he regarded as a solemn juggler) in his hatred to Rabourdin and his praise of Baudoyer, and did his best to support him. Jean-Jacques Bixiou was the grandson of a Parisian grocer. His father, who died a colonel, left him to the care of his grandmother, who married her head-clerk, named Descoings, after the death of her first husband, and died in 1822.   Finding himself without prospects on leaving college, he attempted painting, but in spite of his intimacy with Joseph Bridau, his life-long friend, he abandoned art to take up caricature, vignette designing, and drawing for books, which twenty years later went by the name of "illustration."   The influence of the Ducs de Maufrigneuse and de Rhétoré, whom he knew in the society of actresses, procured him his employment under government in 1819.   On good terms with des Lupeaulx, with whom in society he stood on an equality, and intimate with du Bruel, he was a living proof of Rabourdin's theory as to the steady deterioration of the administrative hierarchy in Paris through the personal importance which a government official may acquire outside of a government office. Short in stature but well-formed, with a delicate face remarkable for its vague likeness to Napoleon's, thin lips, a straight chin, chestnut whiskers, twenty-seven years old, fair-skinned, with a piercing voice and sparkling eye, — such was Bixiou; a man, all sense and all wit, who abandoned himself to a mad pursuit of pleasure of every description, which threw him into a constant round of dissipation.   Hunter of grisettes, smoker, jester, diner-out and frequenter of supper-parties, always tuned to the highest pitch, shining equally in the greenroom and at the balls given among the grisettes of the Allée des Veuves, he was just as surprisingly entertaining at table as at a picnic, as gay and lively at midnight on the streets as in the morning when he jumped out of bed, and yet at heart gloomy and melancholy, like most of the great comic players.

Launched into the world of actors and actresses, writers, artists, and certain women of uncertain means, he lived well, went to the theatres without paying, gambled at Frascati, and often won. Artist by nature and really profound, though by flashes only, he swayed to and fro in life like a swing, without thinking or caring of a time when the cord would break. The liveliness of his wit and the prodigal flow of his ideas made him acceptable to all persons who took pleasure in the lights of intellect; but none of his friends liked him. Incapable of checking a witty saying, he would scarify his two neighbors before a dinner was half over. In spite of his skin-deep gayety, a secret dissatisfaction with his social position could be detected in his speech; he aspired to something better, but the fatal demon hiding in his wit hindered him from acquiring the gravity which imposes on fools. He lived on the second floor of a house in the rue de Ponthieu, where he had three rooms delivered over to

the untidiness of a bachelor's establishment, in fact, a
regular bivouac. He often talked of leaving France and
seeking his fortune in America. No wizard could fore-
tell the future of this young man in whom all talents
were incomplete; who was incapable of perseverance,
intoxicated with pleasure, and who acted on the belief
that the world ended on the morrow.

In the matter of dress Bixiou had the merit of never
being ridiculous; he was perhaps the only official of
the ministry whose dress did not lead outsiders to say,
"That man is a government clerk!" He wore elegant
boots with black trousers strapped under them, a fancy
waistcoat, a becoming blue coat, collars that were the
never-ending gift of grisettes, one of Bandoni's hats,
and a pair of dark-colored kid gloves. His walk and
bearing, cavalier and simple both, were not without
grace. He knew all this, and when des Lupeaulx
summoned him for a piece of impertinence said and
done about Monsieur de la Billardière and threatened
him with dismissal, Bixiou replied, "You will take me
back because my clothes do credit to the ministry;"
and des Lupeaulx, unable to keep from laughing, let
the matter pass. The most harmless of Bixiou's jokes
perpetrated among the clerks was the one he played
off upon Godard, presenting him with a butterfly just
brought from China, which the worthy man keeps in his
collection and exhibits to this day, blissfully uncon-

scious that it is only painted paper. Bixiou had the patience to work up the little masterpiece for the sole purpose of hoaxing his superior.

The devil always puts a martyr near a Bixiou. Baudoyer's bureau held the martyr, a poor copying-clerk twenty-two years of age, with a salary of fifteen hundred francs, named Auguste-Jean-François Minard. Minard had married for love the daughter of a porter, an artificial-flower maker employed by Mademoiselle Godard. Zélie Lorrain, a pupil, in the first place, of the Conservatoire, then by turns a *danseuse*, a singer, and an actress, had thought of doing as so many of the working-women do ; but the fear of consequences kept her from vice. She was floating undecidedly along, when Minard appeared upon the scene with a definite proposal of marriage. Zélie earned five hundred francs a year, Minard had fifteen hundred. Believing that they could live on two thousand, they married without settlements, and started with the utmost economy. They went to live, like turtle-doves, near the barrière de Courcelles, in a little apartment at three hundred francs a year, with white cotton curtains to the windows, a Scotch paper costing fifteen sous a roll on the walls, brick floors well polished, walnut furniture in the parlor, and a tiny kitchen that was very clean. Zélie nursed her children herself when they came, cooked, made her flowers, and kept the house. There was something very touching in this happy and laborious mediocrity. Feeling that Minard truly loved her, Zélie loved him. Love begets love, — it is the *abyssus abyssum* of the Bible. The poor man left his bed in the morning before his wife was up, that he might fetch provisions. He carried the flowers she had finished, on his way to the bureau, and bought her materials on his way back; then, while waiting for dinner, he stamped out her leaves, trimmed the twigs, or rubbed her colors. Small, slim, and wiry, with crisp red hair, eyes of a light yellow, a skin of dazzling fairness, though blotched with red, the man had a sturdy courage that made no show. He knew the science of writing quite as well as Vimeux. At the office he kept in the background, doing his alloted task with the collected air of a man who thinks and suffers. His white eyelashes and lack of eyebrows induced the relentless Bixiou to name him " the white rabbit." Minard — the Rabourdin of a lower sphere — was filled with the desire of placing his Zélie in better circumstances, and his mind searched the ocean of the wants of luxury in hopes of finding an idea, of making some discovery or some improvement which would bring him a rapid fortune. His apparent dulness was really caused by the continual tension of his mind; he went over the history of Cephalic Oils and the Paste of Sultans, lucifer matches and portable gas, jointed sockets for hydrostatic lamps, — in short, all the infinitely

little inventions of material civilization which pay so
well. He bore Bixiou's jests as a busy man bears the
buzzing of an insect; he was not even annoyed by them.
In spite of his cleverness, Bixiou never perceived the
profound contempt which Minard felt for him. Minard
never dreamed of quarrelling, however, — regarding
it as a loss of time. After a while his composure
tired out his tormentor. He always breakfasted with
his wife, and ate nothing at the office. Once a month
he took Zélie to the theatre, with tickets bestowed by
du Bruel or Bixiou; for Bixiou was capable of anything, even of doing a kindness. Monsieur and Madame
Minard paid their visits in person on New-Year's day.
Those who saw them often asked how it was that a
woman could keep her husband in good clothes, wear
a Leghorn bonnet with flowers, embroidered muslin
dresses, silk mantles, prunella boots, handsome fichus,
a Chinese parasol, and drive home in a hackney-coach,
and yet be virtuous; while Madame Colleville and other
ladies of her kind could scarcely make both ends meet,
though they had double Madame Minard's means.

In the two bureaus were two clerks so devoted to
each other that their friendship became the butt of all
the rest. He of the bureau Baudoyer, named Colleville,
was chief-clerk, and would have been head of the bureau
long before if the Restoration had never happened. His
wife was as clever in her way as Madame Rabourdin in

hers. Colleville, who was son of a first violin at the opera, fell in love with the daughter of a celebrated *danseuse*. Flavie Minoret, one of those capable and charming Parisian women who know how to make their husbands happy and yet preserve their own liberty, made the Colleville home a rendezvous for all our best artists and orators. Colleville's humble position under government was forgotten there. Flavie's conduct gave such food for gossip, however, that Madame Rabourdin had declined all her invitations. The friend in Rabourdin's bureau to whom Colleville was so attached was named Thuillier. All who knew one knew the other. Thuillier, called " the handsome Thuillier," an ex-Lothario, led as idle a life as Colleville led a busy one. Colleville, government official in the mornings and first clarionet at the Opéra-Comique at night, worked hard to maintain his family, though he was not without influential friends. He was looked upon as a very shrewd man, — all the more, perhaps, because he hid his ambitions under a show of indifference. Apparently content with his lot and liking work, he found every one, even the chiefs, ready to protect his brave career. During the last few weeks Madame Colleville had made an evident change in the household, and seemed to be taking to piety. This gave rise to a vague report in the bureaus that she thought of securing some more powerful influence than that of François Keller, the famous orator, who had been one of her chief adorers, but who, so far, had failed to obtain a better place for her husband. Flavie had, about this time — and it was one of her mistakes — turned for help to des Lupeaulx.

Colleville had a passion for reading the horoscopes of famous men in the anagram of their names. He passed whole months in decomposing and recomposing words and fitting them to new meanings. *Un Corse la finira*," found within the words "*Révolution Française ;*" *Eh, c'est large nez*," in " *Charles Genest*," an abbé at the court of Louis XIV., whose huge nose is recorded by Saint-Simon as the delight of the Duc de Bourgogne (the exigencies of this last anagram required the substitution of a *z* for an *s*), — were a never-ending marvel to Colleville. Raising the anagram to the height of a science, he declared that the destiny of every man was written in the words or phrase given by the transposition of the letters of his names and titles ; and his patriotism struggled hard to suppress the fact — signal evidence for his theory — that in Horatio Nelson, *honor est a Nilo*. Ever since the accession of Charles X. he had bestowed much thought on the king's anagram. Thuillier, who was fond of making puns, declared that an anagram was nothing more than a pun on letters. The sight of Colleville, a man of real feeling, bound almost indissolubly to Thuillier, the model of an egoist, presented a difficult problem to the mind of an observer. The clerks in the offices explained it by saying, "Thuillier is rich, and the Colleville household costly." This friendship, however, now consolidated by time, was based on feelings and on facts which naturally explained it; an account of which may be found elsewhere (see "Les Petits Bourgeois"). We may remark in passing that though Madame Colleville was well known in the bureaus, the existence of Madame Thuillier was almost unknown there. Colleville, an active man, burdened with a family of children, was fat, round, and jolly, whereas Thuillier "the beau of the Empire" without apparent anxieties and always at leisure, was slender and thin, with a livid face and a melancholy air. "We never know," said Rabourdin, speaking of the two men, "whether our friendships are born of likeness or of contrast."

Unlike these Siamese twins, two other clerks, Chazelle and Paulmier, were forever squabbling. One smoked, the other took snuff, and the merits of their respective use of tobacco were the origin of ceaseless disputes. Chazelle's home, which was tyrannized over by a wife, furnished a subject of endless ridicule to Paulmier; whereas Paulmier, a bachelor, often half-starved like Vimeux, with ragged clothes and half-concealed penury was a fruitful source of ridicule to Chazelle. Both were beginning to show a protuberant stomach; Chazelle's, which was round and projecting, had the impertinence, so Bixiou said, to enter the room first; Paulmier's corporation spread to right and left. A favorite amusement with Bixiou was to measure them quarterly. The two clerks, by dint of quarrelling over the details of their lives, and washing much of their dirty linen at the office, had obtained the disrepute which they merited. " Do you take me for a Chazelle?" was a frequent saying that served to end many an annoying discussion.

Monsieur Poiret junior, called "junior" to distinguish him from his brother Monsieur Poiret senior (now living in the Maison Vauquer, where Poiret junior sometimes dined, intending to end his days in the same retreat), had spent thirty years in the Civil Service. Nature herself is not so fixed and unvarying in her evolutions as was Poiret junior in all the acts of his daily life; he always laid his things in precisely the same place, put his pen in the same rack, sat down in his seat at the same hour, warmed himself at the stove at the same moment of the day. His sole vanity consisted in wearing an infallible watch, timed daily at the Hôtel de Ville as he passed it on his way to the office. From six to eight o'clock in the morning he kept the books of a large shop in the rue Saint-Antoine, and from six to eight o'clock in the evening those of the Maison Camusot, in the rue des Bourdonnais. He thus earned three thousand francs a year, counting his salary from the government. In a few months his term of service would be up, when he would retire on a pension; he therefore showed the utmost indifference to the political intrigues of the bureaus. Like his elder brother, to whom retirement from active service had proved a fatal blow, he would probably grow an old man when he could no longer come from his home to the ministry, sit in the same chair and copy a certain number of pages. Poiret's eyes were dim, his glance weak and lifeless, his skin discolored and wrinkled, gray in tone and speckled with blueish dots; his nose flat, his lips drawn inward to the mouth, where a few defective teeth still lingered. His gray hair, flattened to the head by the pressure of his hat, gave him the look of an ecclesiastic, — a resemblance he would scarcely have liked, for he hated priests and clergy, though he could give no reasons for his anti-religious views. This antipathy, however, did not prevent him from being extremely attached to whatever administration happened to be in power. He never buttoned his old green coat, even on the coldest days, and he always wore shoes with ties, and black trousers.

No human life was ever lived so thoroughly by rule. Poiret kept all his receipted bills, even the most trifling, and all his account-books, wrapped in old shirts and put away according to their respective years from the time of his entrance at the ministry. Rough copies of his

letters were dated and put away in a box, ticketed
"My Correspondence." He dined at the same restau-
rant (the Sucking Calf in the place du Châtelet), and
sat in the same place, which the waiters kept for him.
He never gave five minutes more time to the shop in
the rue Saint Antoine than justly belonged to it, and at
half-past eight precisely he reached the Café David,
where he breakfasted and remained till eleven. There
he listened to political discussions, his arms crossed on
his cane, his chin in his right hand, never saying a
word. The *dame du comptoir*, the only woman to
whom he ever spoke with pleasure, was the sole confi-
dant of the little events of his life, for his seat was
close to her counter. He played dominoes, the only
game he was capable of understanding. When his
partners did not happen to be present, he usually went
to sleep with his back against the wainscot, holding a
newspaper in his hand, the wooden file resting on the
marble of his table. He was interested in the buildings
going up in Paris, and spent his Sundays in walking
about to examine them. He was often heard to say,
"I saw the Louvre emerge from its rubbish; I saw
the birth of the place du Châtelet, the quai aux Fleurs
and the Markets." He and his brother, both born at
Troyes, were sent in youth to serve their apprenticeship in a government office. Their mother made herself notorious by misconduct, and the two brothers had

the grief of hearing of her death in the hospital at Troyes, although they had frequently sent money for her support. This event led them both not only to abjure marriage, but to feel a horror of children; ill at ease with them, they feared them as others fear mad-men, and watched them with haggard eyes.

Since the day when he first came to Paris Poiret junior had never gone outside the city. He began at that time to keep a journal of his life, in which he noted down all the striking events of his day. Du Bruel told him that Lord Byron did the same thing. This likeness filled Poiret junior with delight, and led him to buy the works of Lord Byron, translated by Chastopalli, of which he did not understand a word. At the office he was often seen in a melancholy attitude, as though absorbed in thought, when in fact he was thinking of nothing at all. He did not know a single person in the house where he lived, and always carried the keys of his apartment about with him. On New-Year's day he went round and left his own cards on all the clerks of the division. Bixiou took it into his head on one of the hottest of dog-days to put a layer of lard under the lining of a certain old hat which Poiret junior (he was, by the bye, fifty-two years old) had worn for the last nine years. Bixiou, who had never seen any other hat on Poiret's head, dreamed of it and declared he tasted it in his food; he therefore resolved, in the interests of his digestion, to relieve the bureau of the sight of that amorphous old hat. Poiret junior left the office regularly at four o'clock. As he walked along, the sun's rays reflected from the pavements and walls produced a tropical heat; he felt that his head was inundated, — he, who never perspired! Feeling that he was ill, òr on the point of being so, instead of going as usual to the Sucking Calf he went home, drew out from his desk the journal of his life, and recorded the fact in the following manner : —

" To-day, July 3, 1823, overtaken by extraordinary perspiration, a sign, perhaps, of the sweating-sickness, a malady which prevails in Champagne. I am about to consult Doctor Haudry. The disease first appeared as I reached the highest part of the quai des Écoles."

Suddenly, having taken off his hat, he became aware that the mysterious sweat had some cause independent of his own person. He wiped his face, examined the hat, and could find nothing, for he did not venture to take out the lining. All this he noted in his journal : —

" Carried my hat to the Sieur Tournan, hat-maker in the rue Saint-Martin, for the reason that I suspect some unknown cause for this perspiration, which, in that case, might not be perspiration, but, possibly, the effect of something lately added, or formerly done, to my hat."

Monsieur Tournan at once informed his customer of the presence of a greasy substance, obtained by the trying-out of the fat of a pig or a sow. The next day Poiret appeared at the office with another hat, lent by Monsieur Tournan while a new one was making; but he did not sleep that night until he had added the following sentence to the preceding entries in his journal: "It is asserted that my hat contained lard, the fat of a pig."

This inexplicable fact occupied the intellect of Poiret junior for the space of two weeks; and he never knew how the phenomenon was produced. The clerks told him tales of showers of frogs, and other dog-day wonders, also the startling fact that an imprint of the head of Napoleon had been found in the root of a young elm, with other eccentricities of natural history. Vimeux informed him that one day his hat — his, Vimeux's — had stained his forehead black, and that hat-makers were in the habit of using drugs. After that Poiret paid many visits to Monsieur Tournan to inquire into his methods of manufacture.

In the Rabourdin bureau was a clerk who played the man of courage and audacity, professed the opinions of the Left centre, and rebelled against the tyrannies of Baudoyer as exercised upon what he called the unhappy slaves of that office. His name was Fleury. He boldly subscribed to an opposition newspaper, wore a gray hat with a broad brim, red bands on his blue trousers, a blue waistcoat with gilt buttons, and a surtout coat crossed over the breast like that of a quartermaster of gendarmerie. Though unyielding in his opinions, he continued to be employed in the service, all the while predicting a fatal end to a government which persisted in upholding religion. He openly avowed his sympathy for Napoleon, now that the death of that great man put an end to the laws enacted against "the partisans of the usurper." Fleury, ex-captain of a regiment of the line under the Emperor, a tall, dark, handsome fellow, was now, in addition to his civil-service post, box-keeper at the Cirque-Olympique. Bixiou never ventured on tormenting Fleury, for the rough trooper, who was a good shot and clever at fencing, seemed quite capable of extreme brutality if provoked. An ardent subscriber to "Victoires et Conquêtes," Fleury nevertheless refused to pay his subscription, though he kept and read the copies, alleging that they exceeded the number proposed in the prospectus. He adored Monsieur Rabourdin, who had saved him from dismissal, and was even heard to say that if any misfortune happened to the chief through anybody's fault he would kill that person. Dutocq meanly courted Fleury because he feared him. Fleury, crippled with debt, played many a trick on his creditors. Expert in legal matters, he never signed a promissory note; and had prudently attached his own salary under the names of fictitious creditors, so that he was able to draw nearly the whole of it himself. He played écarté, was the life of evening parties, tossed off glasses of champagne without wetting his lips, and knew all the songs of Béranger by heart. He was proud of his full, sonorous voice. His three great admirations were Napoleon, Bolivar, and Béranger. Foy, Lafitte, and Casimir Delavigne he only esteemed. Fleury, as you will have guessed already, was a Southerner, destined, no doubt, to become the responsible editor of a liberal journal.

Desroys, the mysterious clerk of the division, consorted with no one, talked little, and hid his private life so carefully that no one knew where he lived, nor who were his protectors, nor what were his means of subsistence. Looking about them for the causes of this reserve, some of his colleagues thought him a *carbonaro*, others an Orleanist; there were others again who doubted whether to call him a spy or a man of solid merit. Desroys was, however, simply and solely the son of a " Conventionel," who did not vote the king's death. Cold and prudent by temperament, he had judged the world and ended by relying on no one but himself. Republican in secret, an admirer of Paul-Louis Courier and a friend of Michel Chrestien, he looked to time and public intelligence to bring about the triumph of his opinions from end to end of Europe. He dreamed of a new Germany and a new Italy. His heart swelled with that dull, collective love which we must call humanitarianism, the eldest son of deceased philanthropy, and which is to the divine catholic charity what system is to art, or reasoning to deed. This conscientious puritan of freedom, this apostle of an impossible equality, regretted keenly that his poverty forced him to serve the government, and he made various efforts to find a place elsewhere. Tall, lean, lanky, and solemn in appearance, like a man who expects to be called some day to lay down his life for a cause, he lived on a page of Volney, studied Saint-Just, and employed himself on a vindication of Robespierre, whom he regarded as the successor of Jesus Christ.

The last of the individuals belonging to these bureaus who merits a sketch here is the little La Billardière. Having, to his great misfortune, lost his mother, and being under the protection of the minister, safe therefore from the tyrannies of Baudoyer, and received in all the ministerial salons, he was nevertheless detested by every one because of his impertinence and conceit. The two chiefs were polite to him, but the clerks held him at arm's length and prevented all companionship by means of the extreme and grotesque politeness which they bestowed upon him. A pretty youth of twenty-two, tall and slender, with the manners of an Englishman, a dandy in dress, curled and perfumed, gloved and booted in the latest fashion, and twirling an eyeglass, Benjamin de la Billardière thought himself a charming fellow and possessed all the vices of the great world with none of its graces. He was now looking forward impatiently to the death of his father, that he might succeed to the title of baron. His cards were printed " le Chevalier de la Billardière " and on the wall of his office hung, in a frame, his coat of arms (sable, two swords in saltire, on a chief azure three mullets argent; with the motto: *Toujours fidèle*). Possessed with a mania for talking heraldry, he once asked the young Vicomte de Portenduère why his arms were charged in a certain way, and drew down upon himself the happy answer, " I did not make them." He talked of his devotion to the monarchy and the attentions the Dauphine paid him. He stood very well with des Lupeaulx, whom he thought his friend, and they often breakfasted together. Bixiou posed as his mentor, and hoped to rid the division and France of the young fool by tempting him to excesses, and openly avowed that intention.

Such were the principal figures in La Billardière's division of the ministry, where also were other clerks of less account, who resembled more or less those that are represented here. It is difficult even for an observer to decide from the aspect of these strange personalities whether the goose-quill tribe were becoming idiots from the effects of their employment or whether they entered the service because they were natural born fools. Possibly the making of them lies at the door of Nature and of the government both. Nature, to a civil-service clerk is, in fact, the sphere of the office; his horizon is bounded on all sides by green boxes; to him, atmospheric changes are the air of the corridors, the masculine exhalations contained in rooms without ventilators, the odor of paper, pens, and ink; the soil he treads is a tiled pavement or a wooden floor, strewn with a curious litter and moistened by the attendant's watering-pot; his sky is the ceiling toward which he yawns; his element is dust. Several distinguished doctors have remonstrated against the influence of this second nature, both savage and civilized, on the moral being vegetating in those dreadful pens called bureaus, where the sun seldom penetrates, where thoughts are tied down to occupations like that of horses who turn a crank and who, poor beasts, yawn distressingly and die quickly. Rabourdin was, therefore, fully justified in seeking to reform their present condition, by lessening their numbers and giving to each a larger salary and far heavier work. Men are neither wearied nor bored when doing great things. Under the present system government loses fully four hours out of the nine which the clerks owe to the service, — hours wasted, as we shall see, in conversations, in gossip, in disputes, and, above all, in underhand intriguing. The reader must have haunted the bureaus of the ministerial departments before he can realize how much their petty and belittling life resembles that of seminaries. Wherever men live collectively this likeness is obvious; in regiments, in law-courts, you will find the elements of the school on a smaller or larger scale. The government clerks, forced to be together for nine hours of the day, looked upon their office as a sort of class-room where they had tasks to perform, where the head of the bureau was no other than a schoolmaster, and where the gratuities bestowed took the place of prizes given out to protégés, — a place, moreover, where they teased and hated each other, and yet felt a certain comradeship, colder than that of a regiment, which itself is less hearty than that of seminaries. As a man advances in life he grows more selfish; egoism develops, and relaxes all the secondary bonds of affection. A government office is, in short, a microcosm of society, with its oddities and hatreds, its envy and its cupidity, its determination to push on, no matter who goes under, its frivolous gossip which gives so many wounds, and its perpetual spying.

V.

THE MACHINE IN MOTION.

At this moment the division of Monsieur de la Billardière was in a state of unusual excitement, resulting very naturally from the event which was about to happen; for heads of divisions do not die every day, and there is no insurance office where the chances of life and death are calculated with more sagacity than in a government bureau. Self-interest stifles all compassion, as it does in children, but the government service adds hypocrisy to boot.

The clerks of the bureau Baudoyer arrived at eight o'clock in the morning, whereas those of the bureau Rabourdin seldom appeared till nine, — a circumstance which did not prevent the work in the latter office from being more rapidly dispatched than that of the former. Dutocq had important reasons for coming early on this particular morning. The previous evening he had furtively entered the little study where Sébastien was at work, and had seen him copying some papers for Rabourdin; he concealed himself until he saw Sébastien leave the premises without taking any papers away with

him.   Certain, therefore, of finding the rather volumi-
nous memorandum which he had seen, together with its
copy, in some corner of the study, he searched through
the boxes one after another until he finally came upon
the fatal list.   He carried it in hot haste to an auto-
graph-printing house, where he obtained two pressed
copies of the memorandum, showing, of course, Rabourdin's own writing.   Anxious not to arouse suspicion,
he had gone very early to the office and replaced both
the memorandum and Sébastien's copy in the box from
which he had taken them.   Sébastien, who was kept up
till after midnight at Madame Rabourdin's party, was,
in spite of his desire to get to the office early, preceded
by the spirit of hatred.   Hatred lived in the rue Saint-
Louis-Saint-Honoré, whereas love and devotion lived
far-off in the rue du Roi-Doré in the Marais.   This
slight delay was destined to affect Rabourdin's whole
career.

Sébastien opened his box eagerly, found the memorandum and his own unfinished copy all in order, and
locked them at once into the desk as Rabourdin had
directed.   The mornings are dark in these offices
towards the end of December, sometimes indeed the
lamps are lit till after ten o'clock; consequently Sébastien did not happen to notice the pressure of the copy-
ing-machine upon the paper.   But when, about half-
past nine o'clock, Rabourdin looked at his memorandum

he saw at once the effects of the copying process, and all the more readily because he was then considering whether these autographic presses could not be made to do the work of copying clerks.

"Did any one get to the office before you?" he asked.

"Yes," replied Sébastien, — "Monsieur Dutocq."

"Ah! well, he was punctual. Send Antoine to me."

Too noble to distress Sébastien uselessly by blaming him for a misfortune now beyond remedy, Rabourdin said no more. Antoine came. Rabourdin asked if any clerk had remained at the office after four o'clock the previous evening. The man replied that Monsieur Dutocq had worked there later than Monsieur de la Roche, who was usually the last to leave. Rabourdin dismissed him with a nod, and resumed the thread of his reflections.

"Twice I have prevented his dismissal," he said to himself, "and this is my reward."

This morning was to Rabourdin like the solemn hour in which great commanders decide upon a battle and weigh all chances. Knowing the spirit of official life better than any one, he well knew that it would never pardon, any more than a school or the galleys or the army pardon, what looked like espionage or tale-bearing. A man capable of informing against his comrades is disgraced, dishonored, despised; the ministers in such a case would disavow their own agents. Nothing was left to an official so placed but to send in his resignation and leave Paris; his honor is permanently stained; explanations are of no avail; no one will either ask for them or listen to them. A minister may do the same thing and be thought a great man, able to choose the right instruments; but a mere subordinate will be judged as a spy, no matter what may be his motives. While justly measuring the folly of such judgment, Rabourdin knew that it was all-powerful; and he knew, too, that he was crushed. More surprised than overwhelmed, he now sought for the best course to follow under the circumstances; and with such thoughts in his mind he was necessarily aloof from the excitement caused in the division by the death of Monsieur de la Billardière; in fact he did not hear of it until young La Brière, who was able to appreciate his sterling value, came to tell him. About ten o'clock, in the bureau Baudoyer, Bixiou was relating the last moments of the life of the director to Minard, Desroys, Monsieur Godard, whom he had called from his private office, and Dutocq, who had rushed in with private motives of his own. Colleville and Chazelle were absent.

Bixiou [standing with his back to the stove and holding up the sole of each boot alternately to dry at the open door]. This morning, at half-past seven, I went to inquire after our most worthy and respectable director, knight of the order of Christ, *et cœtera, et cœtera*. Yes, gentlemen, last night he was a being with twenty *et cœteras*, to-day he is nothing, not even a government clerk. I asked all particulars of his nurse. She told me that this morning at five o'clock he became uneasy about the royal family. He asked for the names of all the clerks who had called to inquire after him; and then he said: "Fill my snuff-box, give me the newspaper, bring my spectacles, and change my ribbon of the Legion of honor, — it is very dirty." I suppose you know he always wore his orders in bed. He was fully conscious, retained his senses and all his usual ideas. But, presto! ten minutes later the water rose, rose, rose and flooded his chest; he knew he was dying for he felt the cysts break. At that fatal moment he gave evident proof of his powerful mind and vast intellect. Ah, we never rightly appreciated him! 'We used to laugh at him and call him a booby — did n't you, Monsieur Godard?

GODARD. I? I always rated Monsieur de la Billardière's talents higher than the rest of you.

BIXIOU. You and he could understand each other!

GODARD. He was n't a bad man; he never harmed any one.

BIXIOU. To do harm you must do something, and he never did anything. If it was n't you who said he was a dolt, it must have been Minard.

Minard [shrugging his shoulders]. I!

Bixiou. Well, then, it was you, Dutocq! [Dutocq made a vehement gesture of denial.] Oh! very good, then it was nobody. Every one in this office knew his intellect was herculean. Well, you were right. He ended, as I have said, like the great man that he was.

Desroys [impatiently]. Pray what did he do that was so great? he had the weakness to confess himself.

Bixiou. Yes, monsieur, he received the holy sacraments. But do you know what he did in order to receive them? He put on his uniform as gentleman-in-ordinary of the Bedchamber, with all his orders, and had himself powdered; they tied his queue (that poor queue!) with a fresh ribbon. Now I say that none but a man of remarkable character would have his queue tied with a fresh ribbon just as he was dying. There are eight of us here, and I don't believe one among us is capable of such an act. But that's not all; he said, — for you know all celebrated men make a dying speech; he said, — stop now, what did he say? Ah! he said, "I must attire myself to meet the King of Heaven, — I, who have so often dressed in my best for audience with the kings of earth." That's how Monsieur de la Billardière departed this life. He took upon himself to justify the saying of Pythagoras, "No man is known until he dies."

Colleville [rushing in]. Gentlemen, great news!

All. We know it.

Colleville. I defy you to know it! I have been hunting for it ever since the accession of His Majesty to the thrones of France and of Navarre. Last night I succeeded! but with what labor! Madame Colleville asked me what was the matter.

Dutocq. Do you think we have time to bother ourselves with your intolerable anagrams when the worthy Monsieur de la Billardière has just expired?

Colleville. That's Bixiou's nonsense! I have just come from Monsieur de la Billardière's; he is still living, though they expect him to die soon. [Godard, indignant at the hoax, goes off grumbling.] Gentlemen! you would never guess what extraordinary events are revealed by the anagram of this sacramental sentence [he pulls out a paper and reads], *Charles dix, par la grâce de Dieu, roi de France et de Navarre.*

Godard [re-entering]. Tell what it is at once, and don't keep people waiting.

Colleville [triumphantly unfolding the rest of the paper]. Listen!

À H. V. il cedera ;
De S. C. l. d. partira ;
En nauf errera.
Decede à Gorix.

Every letter is there! [He repeats it.] *À Henri cinq cedera* (his crown of course); *de Saint-Cloud partira; en nauf* (that's an old French word for skiff, vessel, felucca, corvette, anything you like) *errera* —

DUTOCQ. What a tissue of absurdities! How can the King cede his crown to a Henri V., who, according to your nonsense must be his grandson, when Monseigneur le Dauphin is living. Are you prophesying the Dauphin's death?

BIXIOU. What's Gorix, pray? — the name of a cat?

COLLEVILLE [provoked]. It is the archæological and lapidarial abbreviation of the name of a town, my good friend; I looked it out in Malte-Brun: Goritz, in Latin Gorixia, situated in Bohemia or Hungary, or it may be Austria —

BIXIOU. Tyrol, the Basque provinces, or South America. Why don't you set it all to music and play it on the clarionet?

GODARD [shrugging his shoulders and departing]. What utter nonsense!

COLLEVILLE. Nonsense! nonsense indeed! It is a pity you don't take the trouble to study fatalism, the religion of the Emperor Napoleon.

GODARD [irritated at Colleville's tone]. Monsieur Colleville, let me tell you that Bonaparte may perhaps be styled Emperor by historians, but it is extremely out of place to refer to him as such in a government office.

Bixiou [laughing]. Get an anagram out of that, my dear fellow.

Colleville [angrily]. Let me tell you that if Napoleon Bonaparte had studied the letters of his name on the 14th of April, 1814, he might perhaps be Emperor still.

Bixiou. How do you make that out?

Colleville [solemnly]. Napoleon Bonaparte. — No, appear not at Elba !

Dutocq. You 'll lose your place for talking such nonsense.

Colleville. If my place is taken from me, François Keller will make it hot for your minister. [Dead silence.] I 'd have you to know, Master Dutocq, that all known anagrams have actually come to pass. Look here, — you, yourself, — don't you marry, for there 's " coqu " in your name.

Bixiou [interrupting]. And *d, t*, for de-testable.

Dutocq [without seeming angry]. I don't care, as long as it is only in my name. Why don't you ana-grammatize, or whatever you call it, *Xavier Rabour-din, chef du bureau ?*

Colleville. Bless you, so I have !

Bixiou [mending his pen]. And what did you make of it?

Colleville. It comes out as follows : *D'abord rêva bureaux, E-u,* — (you catch the meaning? *et eut* — and had) *E-u fin riche;* which signifies that after first belonging to the administration, he gave it up and got rich elsewhere. [Repeats.] *D'abord rêva bureaux, E-u fin riche.*

DUTOCQ. That *is* queer!

BIXIOU. Try Isidore Baudoyer.

COLLEVILLE [mysteriously]. I sha'n't tell the other anagrams to any one but Thuillier.

BIXIOU. I'll bet you a breakfast that I can tell that one myself.

COLLEVILLE. And I'll pay if you find it out.

BIXIOU. Then I shall breakfast at your expense; but you won't be angry, will you? Two such geniuses as you and I need never conflict. ' *Isidore Baudoyer* anagrams into *Ris d'aboyeur d'oie.*

COLLEVILLE [petrified with amazement]. You stole it from me!

BIXIOU [with dignity]. Monsieur Colleville, do me the honor to believe that I am rich enough in absurdity not to steal my neighbor's nonsense.

BAUDOYER [entering with a bundle of papers in his hand]. Gentlemen, I request you to shout a little louder; you bring this office into such high repute with the administration. My worthy coadjutor, Monsieur Clergeot, did me the honor just now to come and ask a question, and he heard the noise you are making [passes into Monsieur Godard's room].

Bixiou [in a low voice]. The watch-dog is very tame this morning; there 'll be a change of weather before night.

Dutocq [whispering to Bixiou]. I have something I want to say to you.

Bixiou [fingering Dutocq's waistcoat]. You 've a pretty waistcoat, that cost you nothing; is that what you want to say?

Dutocq. Nothing, indeed! I never paid so dear for anything in my life. That stuff cost six francs a yard in the best shop in the rue de la Paix, — a fine dead stuff, the very thing for deep mourning.

Bixiou. You know about engravings and such things, my dear fellow, but you are totally ignorant of the laws of etiquette. Well, no man can be a universal genius! Silk is positively not admissible in deep mourning. Don't you see I am wearing woollen? Monsieur Rabourdin, Monsieur Baudoyer, and the minister are all in woollen; so is the faubourg Saint-Germain. There 's no one here but Minard who does n't wear woollen; he 's afraid of being taken for a sheep. That 's the reason why he did n't put on mourning for Louis XVIII.

[During this conversation Baudoyer is sitting by the fire in Godard's room, and the two are conversing in a low voice.]

Baudoyer. Yes, the worthy man is dying. The two ministers are both with him. My father-in-law has been notified of the event. If you want to do me a signal service you will take a cab and go and let Madame Baudoyer know what is happening; for Monsieur Saillard can't leave his desk, nor I my office. Put yourself at my wife's orders; do whatever she wishes. She has, I believe, some ideas of her own, and wants to take certain steps simultaneously. [The two functionaries go out together.]

GODARD. Monsieur Bixiou, I am obliged to leave the office for the rest of the day. You will take my place.

BAUDOYER [to Bixiou, benignly]. Consult me, if there is any necessity.

BIXIOU. This time, La Billardière is really dead.

DUTOCQ [in Bixiou's ear]. Come outside a minute. [The two go into the corridor and gaze at each other like birds of ill-omen.]

DUTOCQ [whispering]. Listen. Now is the time for us to understand each other and push our way. What would you say to your being made head of the bureau, and I under you?

BIXIOU [shrugging his shoulders]. Come, come, don't talk nonsense!

DUTOCQ. If Baudoyer gets La Billardière's place Rabourdin won't stay on where he is. Between ourselves, Baudoyer is so incapable that if du Bruel and you don't help him he will certainly be dismissed in a couple of months. If I know arithmetic that will give three empty places for us three to fill —

Bixiou. Three places right under our noses, which will certainly be given to some bloated favorite, some spy, some pious fraud, — to Colleville perhaps, whose wife has ended where all pretty women end — in piety.

Dutocq. No, to *you*, my dear fellow, if you will only, for once in your life, use your wits logically. [He stopped as if to study the effect of his adverb in Bixiou's face.] Come, let us play fair.

Bixiou [stolidly]. Let me see your game.

Dutocq. I don't wish to be anything more than under-head-clerk. I know myself perfectly well, and I know I have n't the ability, like you, to be head of a bureau. Du Bruel can be director, and you the head of this bureau; he will leave you his place as soon as he has made his pile; and as for me, I shall swim with the tide comfortably, under your protection, till I can retire on a pension.

Bixiou. Sly dog! but how do you expect to carry out a plan which means forcing the minister's hand and ejecting a man of talent. Between ourselves, Rabourdin is the only man capable of taking charge of the division, and I might say of the ministry. Do you know that they talk of putting in over his head that solid lump of foolishness, that cube of idiocy, Baudoyer?

Dutocq [consequentially]. My dear fellow, I am in a position to rouse the whole division against Rabourdin. You know how devoted Fleury is to him? Well, I can make Fleury despise him.

Bixiou. Despised by Fleury!

Dutocq. Not a soul will stand by Rabourdin; the clerks will go in a body and complain of him to the minister, — not only in our division, but in all the divisions —

Bixiou. Forward, march! infantry, cavalry, artillery, and marines of the guard! You rave, my good fellow! And I, what part am I to take in the business?

Dutocq. You are to make a cutting caricature, — sharp enough to kill a man.

Bixiou. How much will you pay for it?

Dutocq. A hundred francs.

Bixiou [to himself]. Then there is something in it.

Dutocq [continuing]. You must represent Rabourdin dressed as a butcher (make it a good likeness), find analogies between a kitchen and a bureau, put a skewer in his hand, draw portraits of the principal clerks and stick their heads on fowls, put them in a monstrous coop labelled "Civil service executions;" make him cutting the throat of one, and supposed to take the others in turn. You can have geese and ducks with heads like ours, — you understand! Baudoyer, for instance, he'll make an excellent turkey-buzzard.

BIXIOU. *Ris d'aboyeur d'oie!* [He has watched Dutocq carefully for some time.] Did you think of that yourself?

DUTOCQ. Yes, I myself.

BIXIOU [to himself]. Do evil feelings bring men to the same result as talents? [Aloud] Well, I'll do it [Dutocq makes a motion of delight] — when [full stop] — I know where I am and what I can rely on. If you don't succeed I shall lose my place, and I must make a living. You are a curious kind of innocent still, my dear colleague.

DUTOCQ. Well, you need n't make the lithograph till success is proved.

BIXIOU. Why don't you come out and tell me the whole truth?

DUTOCQ. I must first see how the land lays in the bureau ; we will talk about it later [goes off].

BIXIOU [alone in the corridor]. That fish, for he's more a fish than a bird, that Dutocq has a good idea in his head — I'm sure I don't know where he stole it. If Baudoyer should succeed La Billardière it would be fun, more than fun — profit! [Returns to the office.] Gentlemen, I announce glorious changes ; papa La Billardière is dead, really dead, — no nonsense, word of honor! Godard is off on business for our excellent chief Baudoyer, successor presumptive to the deceased. [Minard, Desroys, and Colleville raise their heads in amazement; they all lay down their pens, and Colleville blows his nose.] Every one of us is to be promoted! Colleville will be under-head-clerk at the very least. Minard may have my place as chief clerk — why not? he is quite as dull as I am. Hey, Minard, if you should get twenty-five hundred francs a-year your little wife would be uncommonly pleased, and you could buy yourself a pair of boots now and then.

COLLEVILLE. But you don't get twenty-five hundred francs.

BIXIOU. Monsieur Dutocq gets that in Rabourdin's office; why should n't I get it this year? Monsieur Baudoyer gets it.

COLLEVILLE. Only through the influence of Monsieur Saillard. No other chief clerk gets that in any of the divisions.

PAULMIER. Bah! Has n't Monsieur Cochin three thousand? He succeeded Monsieur Vavasseur, who served ten years under the Empire at four thousand. His salary was dropped to three when the King first returned; then to two thousand five hundred before Vavasseur died. But Monsieur Cochin, who succeeded him, had influence enough to get the salary put back to three thousand.

COLLEVILLE. Monsieur Cochin signs E. A. L. Cochin (he is named Émile-Adolphe-Lucian), which, when ana-grammed, gives Cochineal. Now observe, he 's a partner in a druggist's business in the rue des Lombards, the Maison Matifat, which made its fortune by that identical colonial product.

BAUDOYER [entering]. Monsieur Chazelle, I see, is not here; you will be good enough to say I asked for him, gentlemen.

BIXIOU [who had hastily stuck a hat on Chazelle's chair when he heard Baudoyer's step]. Excuse me, Monsieur, but Chazelle has gone to the Rabourdins' to make an inquiry.

CHAZELLE [entering with his hat on his head, and not seeing Baudoyer]. La Billardière is done for, gentlemen! Rabourdin is head of the division and Master of petitions; he has n't stolen *his* promotion, that 's very certain.

BAUDOYER [to Chazelle]. You found that appointment in your second hat, I presume [points to the hat on the chair]. This is the third time within a month that you have come after nine o'clock. If you continue the practice you will get on — elsewhere. [To Bixiou, who is reading the newspaper.] My dear Monsieur Bixiou, do pray leave the newspapers to these gentlemen who are going to breakfast, and come into my office for your orders for the day. I don't know what Monsieur Rabourdin wants with Gabriel; he keeps him to do his private errands, I believe. I 've rung three times and can't get him. [Baudoyer and Bixiou retire into the private office.]

CHAZELLE. Damned unlucky!

PAULMIER [delighted to annoy Chazelle]. Why did n't you look about when you came into the room? You might have seen the elephant, and the hat too; they are big enough to be visible.

CHAZELLE [dismally]. Disgusting business! I don't see why we should be treated like slaves because the government gives us four francs and sixty-five centimes a day.

FLEURY [entering]. Down with Baudoyer! hurrah for Rabourdin! — that's the cry in the division.

CHAZELLE [getting more and more angry]. Baudoyer can turn me off if he likes, I sha'n't care. In Paris there are a thousand ways of earning five francs a day; why, I could earn that at the Palais de Justice, copying briefs for the lawyers.

PAULMIER [still prodding him]. It is very easy to say that; but a government place is a government place, and that plucky Colleville, who works like a galley-slave outside of this office, and who could earn, if he lost his appointment, much more than his salary, prefers to keep his place. Who the devil is fool enough to give up his expectations?

CHAZELLE [continuing his philippic]. You may not be, but I am! We have no chances at all. Time was when nothing was more encouraging than a civil-service career. So many men were in the army that there were not enough for the government work; the maimed and the halt and the sick ones, like Paulmier, and the near-sighted ones, all had their chance of a rapid promotion. But now, ever since the Chamber invented what they call special training, and the rules and regulations for civil-service examiners, we are worse off than common soldiers. The poorest places are at the mercy of a thousand mischances because we are now ruled by a thousand sovereigns.

BIXIOU [returning]. Are you crazy, Chazelle? Where do you find a thousand sovereigns?—not in your pocket, are they?

CHAZELLE. Count them up. There are four hundred over there at the end of the pont de la Concorde (so called because it leads to the scene of perpetual discord between the Right and Left of the Chamber); three hundred more at the end of the rue de Tournon. The court, which ought to count for the other three hundred, has seven hundred parts less power to get a man appointed to a place under government than the Emperor Napoleon had.

FLEURY. All of which signifies that in a country where there are three powers you may bet a thousand to one that a government clerk who has no influence but his own merits to advance him will remain in obscurity.

BIXIOU [looking alternately at Chazelle and Fleury]. My sons, you have yet to learn that in these days the worst state of life is the state of belonging to the State.

FLEURY. Because it has a constitutional government.

COLLEVILLE. Gentlemen, gentlemen! no politics!

BIXIOU. Fleury is right. Serving the State in these days is no longer serving a prince who knew how to punish and reward. The State now is *everybody*. Everybody of course cares for nobody. Serve everybody and you serve nobody. Nobody is interested in nobody; the government clerk lives between the two negations. The world has neither pity nor respect, neither heart nor head; everybody forgets to-morrow the service of yesterday. Now each one of you may be, like Monsieur Baudoyer, ·an administrative genius, a Chateaubriand of reports, a Bossuet of circulars, the Canalis of memorials, the gifted son of diplomatic despatches; but I tell you there is a fatal law which interferes with all administrative genius, — I mean the law of promotion by average. This average is based on the statistics of promotion and the statistics of mortality combined. It is very certain that on entering whichever section of the Civil Service you please at the age of eighteen, you can't get eighteen hundred francs a year till you reach the age of thirty. Now there's no free and independent career in which, in the course of twelve years, a young man who has gone through the grammar-school, been vaccinated, is exempt from military service, and possesses all his faculties (I don't mean transcendent ones) can't amass a capital of forty-five thousand francs in centimes, which represents a permanent income equal to our salaries, which are, after all, precarious. In twelve years a grocer can earn enough to give him ten thousand francs a year; a painter can daub a mile of canvass and be decorated with the Legion of honor, or pose as a neglected genius. A literary man becomes professor of something or other, or a journalist at a hundred francs for a thousand lines; he writes *feuilletons*, or he gets into Sainte-Pélagie for a brilliant article that offends the Jesuits, — which of course is an immense benefit to him and makes him a politician at once. Even a lazy man, who does nothing but make debts, has time to marry a widow who pays them; a priest finds time to become a bishop *in partibus.* A sober, intelligent young fellow, who begins with a small capital as a money-changer, soon buys a share in a broker's business; and, to go even lower, a petty clerk becomes a notary, a rag-picker lays by two or three thousand francs a year, and the poorest workmen often become manufacturers; whereas, in the rotatory movement of this present civilization, which mistakes perpetual division and redivision for progress, an unhappy civil-service clerk, like Chazelle for instance, is forced to dine for twenty-two sous a meal, struggles with his

tailor and bootmaker, gets into debt, and is an absolute nothing; worse than that, he becomes an idiot!
Come, gentlemen, now's the time to make a stand!
Let us all give in our resignations! Fleury, Chazelle,
fling yourselves into other employments and become
the great men you really are.

CHAZELLE [calmed down by Bixiou's allocution].
No, I thank you [general laughter].

BIXIOU.   You are wrong; in your situation I should
try to get ahead of the general secretary.

CHAZELLE [uneasily].   What has he to do with me?

BIXIOU.   You'll find out; do you suppose Baudoyer
will overlook what happened just now?

FLEURY.   Another piece of Baudoyer's spite! You've
a queer fellow to deal with in there.   Now, Monsieur
Rabourdin, — there's a man for you!   He put work on
my table to-day that you couldn't get through with in
this office in three days; well, he expects to have it
done by four o'clock to-day.   But he is not always at
my heels to hinder me from talking to my friends.

BAUDOYER [appearing at the door].   Gentlemen, you
will admit that if you have the legal right to find fault
with the chamber and the administration you must at
least do so elsewhere than in this office.   [To Fleury.]
What are you doing here, monsieur?

FLEURY [insolently].   I came to tell these gentlemen
that there was to be a general turn-out.   Du Bruel is

sent for to the ministry, and Dutocq also. Everybody is asking who will be appointed.

BAUDOYER [retiring]. It is not your affair, sir; go back to your own office, and do not disturb mine.

FLEURY [in the doorway]. It would be a shameful injustice if Rabourdin lost the place; I swear I'd leave the service. Did you find that anagram, papa Colleville?

COLLEVILLE. Yes, here it is.

FLEURY [leaning over Colleville's desk]. Capital! famous! This is just what will happen if the administration continues to play the hypocrite. [He makes a sign to the clerks that Baudoyer is listening.] If the government would frankly state its intentions without concealments of any kind, the liberals would know what they had to deal with. An administration which sets its best friends against itself, such men as those of the "Débats," Chateaubriand, and Royer-Collard, is only to be pitied!

COLLEVILLE [after consulting his colleagues]. Come, Fleury, you're a good fellow, but don't talk politics here; you don't know what harm you may do us.

FLEURY [dryly]. Well, adieu, gentlemen; I have my work to do by four o'clock.

While this idle talk had been going on, des Lupeaulx was closeted in his office with du Bruel, where, a little later, Dutocq joined them. Des Lupeaulx had heard from his valet of La Billardière's death, and wishing to please the two ministers, he wanted an obituary article to appear in the evening papers.

"Good morning, my dear du Bruel," said the semi-minister to the head-clerk as he entered, and not inviting him to sit down. "You have heard the news? La Billardière is dead. The ministers were both present when he received the last sacraments. The worthy man strongly recommended Rabourdin, saying he should die with less regret if he could know that his successor were the man who had so constantly done his work. Death is a torture which makes a man confess everything. The minister agreed the more readily because his intention and that of the Council was to reward Monsieur Rabourdin's numerous services. In fact, the Council of State needs his experience. They say that young La Billardière is to leave the division of his late father and go to the Commission of Seals; that's just the same as if the King had made him a present of a hundred thousand francs, — the place can always be sold. But I know the news will delight your division, which will thus get rid of him. Du Bruel, we must get ten or a dozen lines about the worthy late director into the papers; his Excellency will glance them over, — he reads the papers. Do you know the particulars of old La Billardière's life?"

Du Bruel made a sign in the negative.

"No?" continued des Lupeaulx. "Well then; he was mixed up in the affairs of La Vendée, and he was one of the confidants of the late King. Like Monsieur le Comte de Fontaine he always refused to hold communication with the First Consul. He was a bit of a *chouan;* born in Brittany of a parliamentary family, and ennobled by Louis XVIII. How old was he? never mind about that; just say his loyalty was untarnished, his religion enlightened, — the poor old fellow hated churches and never set foot in one, but you had better make him out a ' pious vassal.' Bring in, gracefully, that he sang the song of Simeon at the accession of Charles X. The Comte d'Artois thought very highly of La Billardière, for he co-operated in the unfortunate affair of Quiberon and took the whole responsibility on himself. You know about that, don't you? La Billardière defended the King in a printed pamphlet in reply to an impudent history of the Revolution written by a journalist; you can allude to his loyalty and devotion. But be very careful what you say; weigh your words, so that the other newspapers can't laugh at us; and bring me the article when you've written it. Were you at Rabourdin's yesterday?"

"Yes, *monseigneur*," said du Bruel, "Ah! beg pardon."

"No harm done," answered des Lupeaulx, laughing.

"Madame Rabourdin looked delightfully handsome,"

added du Bruel. "There are not two women like her in Paris. Some are as clever as she, but there's not one so gracefully witty. Many women may be even handsomer, but it would be hard to find one with such variety of beauty. Madame Rabourdin is far superior to Madame Colleville," said the vaudevillist, remembering des Lupeaulx's former affair. "Flavie owes what she is to the men about her, whereas Madame Rabourdin is all things in herself. It is wonderful too what she knows; you can't tell secrets in Latin before *her*. If I had such a wife, I know I should succeed in everything."

"You have more mind than an author ought to have," returned des Lupeaulx, with a conceited air. Then he turned round and perceived Dutocq. "Ah, good-morning, Dutocq," he said. "I sent for you to lend me your Charlet — if you have the whole complete. Madame la comtesse knows nothing of Charlet."

Du Bruel retired.

"Why do you come in without being summoned?" said des Lupeaulx, harshly, when he and Dutocq were left alone. "Is the State in danger that you must come here at ten o'clock in the morning, just as I am going to breakfast with his Excellency?"

"Perhaps it is, monsieur," said Dutocq, dryly. "If I had had the honor to see you earlier, you would probably not have been so willing to support Monsieur Rabourdin, after reading his opinion of you."

Dutocq opened his coat, took a paper from the left-hand breast-pocket and laid it on des Lupeaulx's desk, pointing to a marked passage. Then he went to the door and slipped the bolt, fearing interruption. While he was thus employed, the secretary-general read the opening sentence of the article, which was as follows:

"MONSIEUR DES LUPEAULX. A government degrades itself by openly employing such a man, whose real vocation is for police diplomacy. He is fitted to deal with the political filibusters of other cabinets, and it would be a pity therefore to employ him on our internal detective police. He is above a common spy, for he is able to understand a plan; he could skilfully carry through a dark piece of work and cover his retreat safely."

Des Lupeaulx was succinctly analyzed in five or six such paragraphs, — the essence, in fact, of the biographical portrait which we gave at the beginning of this history. As he read the first words the secretary felt that a man stronger than himself sat in judgment on him; and he at once resolved to examine the memorandum, which evidently reached far and high, without allowing Dutocq to know his secret thoughts. He therefore showed a calm, grave face when the spy returned to him. Des Lupeaulx, like lawyers, magistrates, diplomatists, and all whose work obliges them to pry into the human heart, was past being surprised at anything. Hardened in treachery and in all the tricks and wiles of hatred, he could take a stab in the back and not let his face tell of it.

"How did you get hold of this paper?"

Dutocq related his good luck; des Lupeaulx's face as he listened expressed no approbation; and the spy ended in terror an account which began triumphantly.

"Dutocq, you have put your finger between the bark and the tree," said the secretary, coldly. "If you don't want to make powerful enemies I advise you to keep this paper a profound secret; it is a work of the utmost importance and already well known to me."

So saying, des Lupeaulx dismissed Dutocq by one of those glances that are more expressive than words.

"Ha! that scoundrel of a Rabourdin has put his finger in this!" thought Dutocq, alarmed on finding himself anticipated; "he has reached the ear of the administration, while I am left out in the cold. I should n't have thought it!"

To all his other motives of aversion to Rabourdin he now added the jealousy of one man to another man of the same calling, — a most powerful ingredient in hatred.

When des Lupeaulx was left alone, he dropped into a strange meditation. What power was it of which Rabourdin was the instrument? Should he, des Lupeaulx, use this singular document to destroy him, or should he keep it as a weapon to succeed with the wife? The mystery that lay behind this paper was all darkness to des Lupeaulx, who read with something akin to terror page after page, in which the men of his acquaintance were judged with unerring wisdom. He admired Rabourdin, though stabbed to his vitals by what he said of him. The breakfast-hour suddenly cut short his meditation.

"His Excellency is waiting for you to come down," announced the minister's footman.

The minister always breakfasted with his wife and children and des Lupeaulx, without the presence of servants. The morning meal affords the only moment of privacy which public men can snatch from the current of overwhelming business. Yet in spite of the precautions they take to keep this hour for private intimacies and affections, a good many great and little people manage to infringe upon it. Business itself will, as at this moment, thrust itself in the way of their scanty comfort.

"I thought Rabourdin was a man above all ordinary petty manœuvres," began the minister; "and yet here, not ten minutes after La Billardière's death, he sends me this note by La Brière, — it is like a stage missive. Look," said his Excellency, giving des Lupeaulx a paper which he was twirling in his fingers.

Too noble in mind to think for a moment of the

shameful meaning La Billardière's death might lend to his letter, Rabourdin had not withdrawn it from La Brière's hands after the news reached him. Des Lupeaulx read as follows : —

" MONSEIGNEUR, — If twenty-three years of irreproachable services may claim a favor, I entreat your Excellency to grant me an audience this very day. My honor is involved in the matter of which I desire to speak."

"Poor man!" said des Lupeaulx, in a tone of compassion which confirmed the minister in his error. "We are alone; I advise you to see him now. You have a meeting of the Council when the Chamber rises; moreover, your Excellency has to reply to-day to the opposition; this is really the only hour when you can receive him."

Des Lupeaulx rose, called the servant, said a few words, and returned to his seat. "I have told them to bring him in at dessert," he said.

Like all other ministers under the Restoration, this particular minister was a man without youth. The charter granted by Louis XVIII. had the defect of tying the hands of the kings by compelling them to deliver the destinies of the nation into the control of the middle-aged men of the Chamber and the septuagenarians of the peerage; it robbed them of the right to lay hands on a man of statesmanlike talent

wherever they could find him, no matter how young
he was or how poverty-stricken his condition might
be. Napoleon alone was able to employ young men
as he chose, without being restrained by any consideration. After the overthrow of that mighty will,
vigor deserted power. Now the period when effemi-
nacy succeeds to vigor presents a contrast that is
far more dangerous in France than in other countries.
As a general thing, ministers who were old before
they entered office have proved second or third rate,
while those who were taken young have been an
honor to European monarchies and to the republics
whose affairs they have directed. The world still
rings with the struggle between Pitt and Napoleon,
two men who conducted the politics of their respective countries at an age when Henri de Navarre,
Richelieu, Mazarin, Colbert, Louvois, the Prince of
Orange, the Guises, Machiavelli, in short, all the best
known of our great men, coming from the ranks or
born to a throne, began to rule the State. The Convention — that model of energy — was made up in a
great measure of young heads; no sovereign can ever
forget that it was able to put fourteen armies into the
field against Europe. Its policy, fatal in the eyes of
those who cling to what is called absolute power, was
nevertheless dictated by strictly monarchical principles,
and it behaved itself like any of the great kings.

After ten or a dozen years of parliamentary struggle, having studied the science of politics until he was worn down by it, this particular minister had come to be enthroned by his party, who considered him in the light of their business man. Happily for him he was now nearer sixty than fifty years of age; had he retained even a vestige of juvenile vigor he would quickly have quenched it. But, accustomed to back and fill, retreat and return to the charge, he was able to endure being struck at, turn and turn about, by his own party, by the opposition, by the court, by the clergy, because to all such attacks he opposed the inert force of a substance which was equally soft and consistent; thus he reaped the benefits of what was really his misfortune. Harassed by a thousand questions of government, his mind, like that of an old lawyer who has tried every species of case, no longer possessed the spring which solitary minds are able to retain, nor that power of prompt decision which distinguishes men who are early accustomed to action, and young soldiers. How could it be otherwise? He had practised sophistries and quibbled instead of judging; he had criticised effects and done nothing for causes; his head was full of plans such as a political party lays upon the shoulders of a leader, — matters of private interest brought to an orator supposed to have a future, a jumble of schemes and impracticable requests. Far from coming fresh to his work, he was wearied out with marching and counter-marching, and when he finally reached the much desired height of his present position, he found himself in a thicket of thorny bushes with a thousand conflicting wills to conciliate. If the statesmen of the Restoration had been allowed to follow out their own ideas, their capacity would doubtless have been less criticised; but though their wills were often forced, their age saved them from attempting the resistance which youth opposes to intrigues, both high and low, — intrigues which vanquished Richelieu, and to which, in a lower sphere, Rabourdin was to succumb.

After the rough and tumble of their first struggles in political life these men, less old than aged, have to endure the additional wear and tear of a ministry. Thus it is that their eyes begin to weaken just as they need to have the clear-sightedness of eagles; their mind is weary when its youth and fire need to be redoubled. The minister in whom Rabourdin sought to confide was in the habit of listening to men of undoubted superiority as they explained ingenious theories of government, applicable or inapplicable to the affairs of France. Such men, by whom the difficulties of national policy were never apprehended, were in the habit of attacking this minister personally whenever a parliamentary battle or a contest with the secret follies of the court took

place, — on the eve of a struggle with the popular mind,
or on the morrow of a diplomatic discussion which divided the Council into three separate parties.   Caught
in such a predicament, a statesman naturally keeps a
yawn ready for the first sentence designed to show him
how the public service could be better managed.   At
such periods not a dinner took place among bold
schemers or financial and political lobbyists where the
opinions of the Bourse and the Bank, the secrets of
diplomacy, and the policy necessitated by the state of
affairs in Europe were not canvassed and discussed.
The minister had his own private councillors in des
Lupeaulx and his secretary, who collected and pondered
all opinions and discussions for the purpose of analyzing
and controlling the various interests proclaimed and
supported by so many clever men.   In fact, his misfortune was that of most other ministers who have passed
the prime of life ; he trimmed and shuffled under all his
difficulties, — with journalism, which at this period it
was thought advisable to repress in an underhand way
rather than fight openly ; with financial as well as labor
questions ; with the clergy as with that other question
of the public lands ; with liberalism as with the Chamber.   After manœuvring his way to power in the course
of seven years, the minister believed that he could
manage all questions of administration in the same way.
It is so natural to think we can maintain a position by

the same methods which served us to reach it that no one ventured to blame a system invented by mediocrity to please minds of its own calibre. The Restoration, like the Polish revolution, proved to nations as to princes the true value of a Man, and what will happen if that necessary man is wanting. The last and the greatest weakness of the public men of the Restoration was their honesty, in a struggle in which their adversaries employed the resources of political dishonesty, lies, and calumnies, and let loose upon them, by all subversive means, the clamor of the unintelligent masses, able only to understand revolt.

Rabourdin told himself these things. But he had made up his mind to win or lose, like a man weary of gambling who allows himself a last stake; ill-luck had given him as adversary in the game a sharper like des Lupeaulx. With all his sagacity, Rabourdin was better versed in matters of administration than in parliamentary optics, and he was far indeed from imagining how his confidence would be received; he little thought that the great work that filled his mind would seem to the minister nothing more than a theory, and that a man who held the position of a statesman would confound his reform with the schemes of political and self-interested talkers.

As the minister rose from table, thinking of François Keller, his wife detained him with the offer of a bunch of grapes, and at that moment Rabourdin was announced. Des Lupeaulx had counted on the minister's preoccupation and his desire to get away; seeing him for the moment occupied with his wife, the general-secretary went forward to meet Rabourdin; whom he petrified with his first words, said in a low tone of voice: —

"His Excellency and I know what the subject is that occupies your mind; you have nothing to fear;" then, raising his voice, he added, "neither from Dutocq nor from any one else."

"Don't feel uneasy, Rabourdin," said his Excellency, kindly, but making a movement to get away.

Rabourdin came forward respectfully, and the minister could not evade him.

"Will your Excellency permit me to see you for a moment in private?" he said, with a mysterious glance.

The minister looked at the clock and went towards the window, whither the poor man followed him.

"When may I have the honor of submitting the matter of which I spoke to your Excellency? I desire to fully explain the plan of administration to which the paper that was taken belongs —"

"Plan of administration!" exclaimed the minister, frowning, and hurriedly interrupting him. "If you have anything of that kind to communicate you must wait for the regular day when we do business together. I ought to be at the Council now; and I have an answer

to make to the Chamber on that point which the opposition raised before the session ended yesterday. Your
day is Wednesday next; I could not work yesterday,
for I had other things to attend to; political matters
are apt to interfere with purely administrative ones."

"I place my honor with all confidence in your Excellency's hands," said Rabourdin gravely, "and I
entreat you to remember that you have not allowed me
time to give you an immediate explanation of the stolen
paper — "

"Don't be uneasy," said des Lupeaulx, interposing
between the minister and Rabourdin, whom he thus interrupted; "in another week you will probably be appointed — "

The minister smiled as he thought of des Lupeaulx's
enthusiasm for Madame Rabourdin, and he glanced
knowingly at his wife. Rabourdin saw the look, and
tried to imagine its meaning; his attention was diverted
for a moment, and his Excellency took advantage of the
fact to make his escape.

"We will talk of all this, you and I," said des Lupeaulx, with whom Rabourdin, much to his surprise,
now found himself alone. "Don't be angry with Dutocq; I'll answer for his discretion."

"Madame Rabourdin is charming," said the minister's wife, wishing to say the civil thing to the head of
a bureau.

The children all gazed at Rabourdin with curiosity. The poor man had come there expecting some serious, even solemn, result, and he was like a great fish caught in the threads of a flimsy net; he struggled with himself.

" Madame la comtesse is very good," he said.

" Shall I not have the pleasure of seeing Madame here some Wednesday?" said the countess. "Pray bring her; it will give me pleasure."

"Madame Rabourdin herself receives on Wednesdays," interrupted des Lupeaulx, who knew the empty civility of an invitation to the official Wednesdays; " but since you are so kind as to wish for her, you will soon give one of your private parties, and — "

The countess rose with some irritation.

" You are the master of my ceremonies," she said to des Lupeaulx, — ambiguous words, by which she expressed the annoyance she felt with the secretary for presuming to interfere with her private parties, to which she admitted only a select few. She left the room without bowing to Rabourdin, who remained alone with des Lupeaulx; the latter was twisting in his fingers the confidential letter to the minister which Rabourdin had intrusted to La Brière. Rabourdin recognized it.

" You have never really known me," said des Lupeaulx. " Friday evening we will come to a full understanding. Just now I must go and receive callers; his Excellency saddles me with that burden when he has other matters to attend to. But I repeat, Rabourdin, don't worry yourself; you have nothing to fear."

Rabourdin walked slowly through the corridors, amazed and confounded by this singular turn of events. He had expected Dutocq to denounce him, and found he had not been mistaken ; des Lupeaulx certainly had seen the document which judged him so severely, and yet des Lupeaulx was fawning on his judge! It was all incomprehensible. Men of upright minds are often at a loss to understand complicated intrigues, and Rabourdin was lost in a maze of conjecture without being able to discover the object of the game which the secretary was playing.

" Either he has not read the part about himself, or he loves my wife."

Such were the two thoughts to which his mind arrived as he crossed the courtyard ; for the glance he had intercepted the night before between des Lupeaulx and Célestine came back to memory like a flash of lightning.

VI.

THE WORMS AT WORK.

RABOURDIN's bureau was during his absence a prey to the keenest excitement; for the relation between the head officials and the clerks in a government office is so regulated that, when a minister's messenger summons the head of a bureau to his Excellency's presence (above all at the latter's breakfast hour), there is no end to the comments that are made. The fact that the present unusual summons followed so closely on the death of Monsieur de la Billardière seemed to give special importance to the circumstance, which was made known to Monsieur Saillard, who came at once to confer with Baudoyer. Bixiou, who happened at the moment to be at work with the latter, left him to converse with his father-in-law and betook himself to the bureau Rabourdin, where the usual routine was of course interrupted.

BIXIOU [entering]. I thought I should find you at a white heat! Don't you know what's going on down below? The virtuous woman is done for! yes, done for, crushed! Terrible scene at the ministry!

DUTOCQ [looking fixedly at him]. Are you telling the truth?

Bixiou. Pray who would regret it? Not you, certainly, for you will be made under-head-clerk and du Bruel head of the bureau. Monsieur Baudoyer gets the division.

Fleury. I'll bet a hundred francs that Baudoyer will never be head of the division.

Vimeux. I'll join in the bet; will you, Monsieur Poiret?

Poiret. I retire in January.

Bixiou. Is it possible? are we to lose the sight of those shoe-ties? What will the ministry be without you? Will nobody take up the bet on my side?

Dutocq. I can't, for I know the facts. Monsieur Rabourdin is appointed. Monsieur de la Billardière requested it of the two ministers on his death-bed, blaming himself for having taken the emoluments of an office of which Rabourdin did all the work ; he felt remorse of conscience, and the ministers, to quiet him, promised to appoint Rabourdin unless higher powers intervened.

Bixiou. Gentlemen, are you all against me? seven to one, — for I know which side you'll take, Monsieur Phellion. Well, I'll bet a dinner costing five hundred francs at the Rocher de Cancale that Rabourdin does not get La Billardière's place. That will cost you only a hundred francs each, and I'm risking five hundred, — five to one against me ! Do you take it up? [Shouting into the next room.] Du Bruel, what say you?

Phellion [laying down his pen]. Monsieur, may I ask on what you base that contingent proposal?— for contingent it is. But stay, I am wrong to call it a proposal; I should say contract. A wager constitutes a contract.

Fleury. No, no; you can only apply the word "contract" to agreements that are recognized in the Code. Now the Code allows of no action for the recovery of a bet.

Dutocq. Proscribe a thing and you recognize it.

Bixiou. Good! my little man.

Poiret. Dear me!

Fleury. True! when one refuses to pay one's debts that's recognizing them.

Thuillier. You would make famous lawyers.

Poiret. I am as curious as Monsieur Phellion to know what grounds Monsieur Bixiou has for —

Bixiou [shouting across the office]. Du Bruel! Will you bet?

Du Bruel [appearing at the door]. Heavens and earth, gentlemen, I'm very busy; I have something very difficult to do; I've got to write an obituary notice of Monsieur de la Billardière. I do beg you to be quiet; you can laugh and bet afterwards.

Bixiou. That's true, du Bruel; the praise of an honest man is a very difficult thing to write. I'd rather any day draw a caricature of him.

Du Bruel. Do come and help me, Bixiou.

Bixiou [following him]. I'm willing; though I can do such things much better when eating.

Du Bruel. Well, we will go and dine together afterwards. But listen, this is what I have written [reads]: "The Church and the Monarchy are daily losing many of those who fought for them in Revolutionary times."

Bixiou. Bad, very bad; why don't you say, "Death carries on its ravages among the few surviving defenders of the monarchy and the old and faithful servants of the King, whose heart bleeds under these reiterated blows? [Du Bruel writes rapidly.] Monsieur le Baron Flamet de la Billardière died this morning of dropsy, caused by heart disease." You see, it is just as well to show there are hearts in government offices; and you ought to slip in a little flummery about the emotions of the Royalists during the Terror, — might be useful, hey! But stay, — no! the petty papers would be sure to say the emotions came more from the stomach than the heart. Better leave that out. What are you writing now?

Du Bruel [reading]. "Issuing from an old parliamentary stock in which devotion to the throne was hereditary, as was also attachment to the faith of our fathers, Monsieur de la Billardière — "

Bixiou. Better say Monsieur le Baron de la Billardière.

Du Bruel.   But he was n't baron in 1793.

Bixiou. No matter. Don't you remember that under the Empire Fouchè was telling an anecdote about the Convention, in which he had to quote Robespierre, and he said, " Robespierre called out to me, ' Duc d'Otrante, go to the Hôtel de Ville.' "   There 's a precedent for you !

Du Bruel.   Let me just write that down ; I can use it in a vaudeville. — But to go back to what we were saying.   I don't want to put " Monsieur le baron," because I am reserving his honors till the last, when they rained upon him.

Bixiou.   Oh ! very good ; that.'s theatrical, — the finale of the article.

Du Bruel [continuing].   " In appointing Monsieur de la Billardière gentleman-in-ordinary — "

Bixiou. Very ordinary !

Du Bruel.   " — of the Bedchamber, the King rewarded not only the services rendered by the Provost, who knew how to harmonize the severity of his functions with the customary urbanity of the Bourbons, but the bravery of the Vendean hero, who never bent the knee to the imperial idol. He leaves a son, who inherits his loyalty and his talents."

Bixiou.   Don't you think all that is a little too florid? I should tone down the poetry. " Imperial idol ! " " bent the knee ! " damn it, my dear fellow, writing vaudevilles has ruined your style; you can't come down to pedestrian prose. I should say, "He belonged to the small number of those who." Simplify, simplify! the man himself was a simpleton.

Du Bruel. That's vaudeville, if you like! You would make your fortune at the theatre, Bixiou."

Bixiou. What have you said about Quiberon? [Reads over du Bruel's shoulder.] Oh, that won't do! Here, this is what you must say: "He took upon himself, in a book recently published, the responsibility for all the blunders of the expedition to Quiberon, — thus proving the nature of his loyalty, which did not shrink from any sacrifice." That's clever and witty, and exalts La Billardière.

Du Bruel. At whose expense?

Bixiou [solemn as a priest in a pulpit]. Why, Hoche and Tallien, of course; don't you read history?

Du Bruel. No. I subscribed to the Baudouin series, but I've never had time to open a volume; one can't find matter for vaudevilles there.

Phellion [at the door]. We all want to know, Monsieur Bixiou, what made you think that the worthy and honorable Monsieur Rabourdin, who has so long done the work of this division for Monsieur de la Billardière, — he, who is the senior head of all the bureaus, and whom, moreover, the minister summoned as soon as he heard of the departure of the late Monsieur de la Billardière, — will not be appointed head of the division.

Bixiou. Papa Phellion, you know geography?

Phellion [bridling up]. I should say so!

Bixiou. And history?

Phellion [affecting modesty]. Possibly.

Bixiou [looking fixedly at him]. Your diamond pin is loose, it is coming out. Well, you may know all that, but you don't know the human heart; you have gone no further in the geography and history of that organ than you have in the environs of the city of Paris.

Poiret [to Vimeux]. Environs of Paris? I thought they were talking of Monsieur Rabourdin.

Bixiou. About that bet? Does the entire bureau Rabourdin bet against me?

All. Yes.

Bixiou. Du Bruel, do you count in?

Du Bruel. Of course I do. We want Rabourdin to go up a step and make room for others.

Bixiou. Well, I accept the bet, — for this reason; you can hardly understand it, but I'll tell it to you all the same. It would be right and just to appoint Monsieur Rabourdin (looking full at Dutocq), because, in that case, long and faithful service, honor, and talent would be recognized, appreciated, and properly rewarded. Such an appointment is in the best interests of the administration. [Phellion, Poiret, and Thuillier listen stupidly, with the look of those who try to peer before them in the darkness.] Well, it is just because the promotion would be so fitting, and because the man has such merit, and because the measure is so eminently wise and equitable that I bet Rabourdin will not be appointed. Yes, you'll see, that appointment will slip up, just like the invasion from Boulogne, and the march to Russia, for the success of which a great genius had gathered together all the chances. It will fail as all good and just things do fail in this low world. I am only backing the devil's game.

Du Bruel. Who do you think will be appointed?

Bixiou. The more I think about Baudoyer the more sure I feel that he unites all the opposite qualities; therefore I think he will be the next head of this division.

Dutocq. But Monsieur des Lupeaulx, who sent for me to borrow my Charlet, told me positively that Monsieur Rabourdin was appointed, and that the little La Billardière would be made Clerk of the Seals.

Bixiou. Appointed, indeed! The appointment can't be made and signed under ten days. It will certainly not be known before New-year's day. There he goes now across the courtyard; look at him, and say if the virtuous Rabourdin looks like a man in the sunshine of favor. I should say he knows he 's dismissed. [Fleury rushes to the window.] Gentlemen, adieu; I 'll go and

tell Monsieur Baudoyer that I hear from you that Rabourdin is appointed; it will make him furious, the
pious creature! Then I'll tell him of our wager, to cool
him down,—a process we call at the theatre turning
the Wheel of Fortune, don't we, du Bruel? Why do I
care who gets the place? simply because if Baudoyer
does he will make me under-head-clerk [goes out].

POIRET. Everybody says that man is clever, but as
for me, I never can understand a word he says [goes
on copying]. I listen and listen; I hear words, but I
never get at any meaning; he talks about the environs
of Paris when he discusses the human heart and [lays
down his pen and goes to the stove] declares he backs
the devil's game when it is a question of Russia and
Boulogne; now what is there so clever in that, I'd like
to know? We must first admit that the devil plays any
game at all, and then find out what game; possibly
dominoes [blows his nose].

FLEURY [interrupting]. Père Poiret is blowing his
nose; it must be eleven o'clock.

DU BRUEL. So it is! Goodness! I'm off to the secretary; he wants to read the obituary.

POIRET. What was I saying?

THUILLIER. Dominoes, — perhaps the devil plays
dominoes. [Sébastien enters to gather up the different papers and circulars for signature.]

VIMEUX. Ah! there you are, my fine young man.

Your days of hardship are nearly over; you'll get a post. Monsieur Rabourdin will be appointed. Were n't you at Madame Rabourdin's last night? Lucky fellow! they say that really superb women go there.

Sébastien. Do they? I did n't know.

Fleury. Are you blind?

Sébastien. I don't like to look at what I ought not to see.

Phellion [delighted]. Well said, young man!

Vimeux. The devil! well, you looked at Madame Rabourdin enough, any how; a charming woman.

Fleury. Pooh! thin as a rail. I saw her in the Tuileries, and I much prefer Percilliée, the ballet-mistress, Castaing's victim.

Phellion. What has an actress to do with the wife of a government official?

Dutocq. They both play comedy.

Fleury [looking askance at Dutocq]. The physical has nothing to do with the moral, and if you mean —

Dutocq. I mean nothing.

Fleury. Do you all want to know which of us will really be made head of this bureau?

All. Yes, tell us.

Fleury. Colleville.

Thuillier. Why?

Fleury. Because Madame Colleville has taken the shortest way to it — through the sacristy.

THUILLIER.   I am too much Colleville's friend not to beg you, Monsieur Fleury, to speak respectfully of his wife.

PHELLION.   Defenceless woman should never be made the subject of conversation here —

VIMEUX.   All the more because the charming Madame Colleville won't invite Fleury to her house.   He backbites her in revenge.

FLEURY.   She may not receive me on the same footing that she does Thuillier, but I go there —

THUILLIER.   When? how? — under her windows?

Though Fleury was dreaded as a bully in all the offices, he received Thuillier's speech in silence.   This meekness, which surprised the other clerks, was owing to a certain note for two hundred francs, of doubtful value, which Thuillier agreed to pass over to his sister. After this skirmish dead silence prevailed.   They all wrote steadily from one to three o'clock.   Du Bruel did not return.

About half-past three the usual preparations for departure, the brushing of hats, the changing of coats, went on in all the ministerial offices.   That precious thirty minutes thus employed served to shorten by just so much the day's labor.   At this hour the over-heated rooms cool off; the peculiar odor that hangs about the bureaus evaporates; silence is restored.   By four o'clock none but a few clerks who do their duty conscientiously remain. A minister may know who are the real workers under him if he will take the trouble to walk through the divisions after four o'clock, — a species of prying, however, that no one of his dignity would condescend to.

The various heads of divisions and bureaus usually encountered each other in the courtyards at this hour and exchanged opinions on the events of the day. On this occasion they departed by twos and threes, most of them agreeing in favor of Rabourdin; while the old stagers, like Monsieur Clergeot, shook their heads and said, *Habent sua sidera lites.* Saillard and Baudoyer were politely avoided, for nobody knew what to say to them about La Billardière's death, it being fully understood that Baudoyer wanted the place, though it was certainly not due to him.

When Saillard and his son-in-law had gone a certain distance from the ministry the former broke silence and said : "Things look badly for you, my poor Baudoyer."

"I can't understand," replied the other, "what Elisabeth was dreaming of when she sent Godard in such a hurry to get a passport for Falleix ; Godard tells me she hired a post-chaise by the advice of my uncle Mitral, and that Falleix has already started for his own part of the country."

"Some matter connected with our business," suggested Saillard.

"Our most pressing business just now is to look after Monsieur de la Billardière's place," returned Baudoyer, crossly.

They were just then near the entrance of the Palais-Royal on the rue Saint-Honoré. Dutocq came up, bowing, and joined them.

"Monsieur," he said to Baudoyer, "if I can be useful to you in any way under the circumstances in which you find yourself, pray command me, for I am not less devoted to your interests than Monsieur Godard."

"Such an assurance is at least consoling," replied Baudoyer; "it makes me aware that I have the confidence of honest men."

"If you would kindly employ your influence to get me placed in your division, taking Bixiou as head of the bureau and me as under-head-clerk, you will secure the future of two men who are ready to do anything for your advancement."

"Are you making fun of us, monsieur?" asked Saillard, staring at him stupidly.

"Far be it from me to do that," said Dutocq. "I have just come from the printing-office of the ministerial journal (where I carried from the general-secretary an obituary notice of Monsieur de la Billardière), and I there read an article which will appear to-night about you, which has given me the highest opinion of your character and talents. If it is necessary to crush

Rabourdin I'm in a position to give him the final blow; please to remember that."

Dutocq disappeared.

"May I be shot if I understand a single word of it," said Saillard, looking at Baudoyer, whose little eyes were expressive of stupid bewilderment. "I must buy the newspaper to-night."

When the two reached home and entered the salon on the ground-floor, they found a large fire lighted, and Madame Saillard, Elisabeth, Monsieur Gaudron and the curate of Saint-Paul's sitting by it. The curate turned at once to Monsieur Baudoyer, to whom Elisabeth made a sign which he failed to understand.

"Monsieur," said the curate, "I have lost no time in coming in person to thank you for the magnificent gift with which you have adorned my poor church. I dared not run in debt to buy that beautiful monstrance, worthy of a cathedral. You, who are one of our most pious and faithful parishioners, must have keenly felt the bareness of the high altar. I am on my way to see Monseigneur the coadjutor, and he will, I am sure, send you his own thanks later."

"I have done nothing as yet —" began Baudoyer.

"Monsieur le curé," interposed his wife, cutting him short. "I see I am forced to betray the whole secret. Monsieur Baudoyer hopes to complete the gift by sending you a dais for the coming Fête-Dieu. But the purchase must depend on the state of our finances, and our finances depend on my husband's promotion."

"God will reward those who honor him," said Monsieur Gaudron, preparing, with the curate, to take leave.

"But will you not," said Saillard to the two ecclesiastics, "do us the honor to take pot luck with us?"

"You can stay, my dear vicar," said the curate to Gaudron; "you know I am engaged to dine with the curate of Saint-Roch, who, by the bye, is to bury Monsieur de la Billardière to-morrow."

"Monsieur le curé de Saint-Roch might say a word for us," began Baudoyer. His wife pulled the skirt of his coat violently.

"Do hold your tongue, Baudoyer," she said, leading him aside and whispering in his ear. "You have given a monstrance to the church, that cost five thousand francs. I'll explain it all later."

The miserly Baudoyer made a sulky grimace, and continued gloomy and cross for the rest of the day.

"What did you busy yourself about Falleix's passport for? Why do you meddle in other people's affairs?" he presently asked her.

"I must say, I think Falleix's affairs are as much ours as his," returned Elisabeth, dryly, glancing at her husband to make him notice Monsieur Gaudron, before whom he ought to be silent.

"Certainly, certainly," said old Saillard, thinking of his co-partnership.

"I hope you reached the newspaper office in time?" remarked Elisabeth to Monsieur Gaudron, as she helped him to soup.

"Yes, my dear lady," answered the vicar; "when the editor read the little article I gave him, written by the secretary of the Grand Almoner, he made no difficulty. He took pains to insert it in a conspicuous place. I should never have thought of that; but this young journalist has a wide-awake mind. The defenders of religion can enter the lists against impiety without disadvantage at the present moment, for there is a great deal of talent in the royalist press. I have every reason to believe that success will crown your hopes. But you must remember, my dear Baudoyer, to promote Monsieur Colleville; he is an object of great interest to his Eminence; in fact, I am desired to mention him to you."

"If I am head of the division, I will make him head of one of my bureaus, if you want me to," said Baudoyer.

The matter thus referred to was explained after dinner, when the ministerial organ (bought and sent up by the porter) proved to contain among its Paris news the following articles, called items : —

"Monsieur le Baron de la Billardière died this morning, after a long and painful illness. The king loses a devoted servant, the Church a most pious son. Monsieur de la Billardière's end has fitly crowned a noble life, consecrated in dark and troublous times to perilous missions, and of late years to arduous civic duties. Monsieur de la Billardière was provost of a department, where his force of character triumphed over all the obstacles that rebellion arrayed against him. He subsequently accepted the difficult post of director of a division (in which his great acquirements were not less useful than the truly French affability of his manners) for the express purpose of conciliating the serious interests that arise under its administration. No rewards have ever been more truly deserved than those by which the King, Louis XVIII., and his present Majesty took pleasure in crowning a loyalty which never faltered under the usurper. This old family still survives in the person of a single heir to the excellent man whose death now afflicts so many warm friends. His Majesty has already graciously made known that Monsieur Benjamin de la Billardière will be included among the gentlemen-in-ordinary of the Bedchamber.

"The numerous friends who have not already received their notification of this sad event are hereby informed that the funeral will take place to-morrow at four o'clock, in the church of Saint-Roch. The memorial address will be delivered by Monsieur l'Abbé Fontanon."

"Monsieur Isidore-Charles-Tréville-Baudoyer, representing one of the oldest bourgeois families of Paris, and head of a bureau in the late Monsieur de la Billardière's division, has lately recalled the old traditions of piety and devotion which formerly distinguished these great families, so jealous for the honor and glory of religion, and so faithful in preserving its monuments. The church of Saint-Paul has long needed a monstrance in keeping with the magnificence of that basilica, itself due to the Company of Jesus. Neither the vestry nor the curate were rich enough to decorate the altar. Monsieur Baudoyer has bestowed upon the parish a monstrance that many persons have seen and admired at Monsieur Gohier's, the king's jeweller. Thanks to the piety of this gentleman, who did not shrink from the immensity of the price, the church of Saint-Paul possesses to-day a masterpiece of the jeweller's art designed by Monsieur de Sommervieux. It gives us pleasure to make known this fact, which proves how powerless the declamations of liberalism have been on the mind of the Parisian bourgeoisie. The upper ranks of that body have at all times been royalist, and they prove it when occasion offers."

" The price was five thousand francs," said the Abbè Gaudron ; " but as the payment was in cash, the court jeweller reduced the amount."

" ' Representing one of the oldest bourgeois families of Paris ! ' " Saillard was saying to himself ; " there it is printed, — in the official paper, too ! "

" Dear Monsieur Gaudron," said Madame Baudoyer, " please help my father to compose a little speech that he could slip into the countess's ear when he takes her the monthly stipend, — a single sentence that would cover all ! I must leave you. I am obliged to go out with my uncle Mitral. Would you believe it? I was unable to find my uncle Bidault at home this afternoon. Oh, what a dog-kennel he lives in ! But Monsieur Mitral, who knows his ways, says he does all his business between eight o'clock in the morning and midday, and that after that hour he can be found only at a certain café called the Café Thémis, — a singular name.

"Is justice done there?" said the abbé, laughing.

"Do you ask why he goes to a café at the corner of the rue Dauphine and the quai des Augustins? They say he plays dominoes there every night with his friend Monsieur Gobseck. I don't wish to go to such a place alone; my uncle Mitral will take me there and bring me back."

At this instant Mitral showed his yellow face, surmounted by a wig which looked as though it might be made of hay, and made a sign to his niece to come at once, and not keep a carriage waiting at two francs an hour. Madame Baudoyer rose and went away without giving any explanation to her husband or father.

"Heaven has given you in that woman," said Monsieur Gaudron to Baudoyer when Elisabeth had disappeared, "a perfect treasure of prudence and virtue, a model of wisdom, a Christian who gives sure signs of possessing the Divine spirit. Religion alone is able to form such perfect characters. To-morrow I shall say a mass for the success of your good cause. It is all-important, for the sake of the monarchy and of religion itself that you should receive this appointment. Monsieur Rabourdin is a liberal; he subscribes to the 'Journal des Débats,' a dangerous newspaper, which made war on Monsieur le Comte de Villèle to please the wounded vanity of Monsieur de Chateaubriand. His Eminence will read the newspaper to-night, if only to see what is said of his poor friend Monsieur de la Billardière; and Monseigneur the coadjutor will speak of you to the King. As for Monsieur le curé, I know him well. When I think of what you have now done for his dear church, I feel sure he will not forget you in his prayers; more than that, he is dining at this moment with the coadjutor at the house of the curate of Saint-Roch."

These words made Saillard and Baudoyer begin to perceive that Elisabeth had not been idle ever since Godard informed her of Monsieur de la Billardière's decease.

"Isn't she clever, that Elisabeth of mine?" cried Saillard, comprehending more clearly than Monsieur l'abbé the rapid undermining, like the path of a mole, which his daughter had undertaken.

"She sent Godard to Rabourdin's door to find out what newspaper he takes," said Gaudron; "and I mentioned the name to the secretary of his Eminence, — for we live at a crisis when the Church and Throne must keep themselves informed as to who are their friends and who their enemies."

"For the last five days I have been trying to find the right thing to say to his Excellency's wife," said Saillard.

"All Paris will read that," cried Baudoyer, whose eyes were still riveted on the paper.

"Your eulogy costs us four thousand eight hundred francs, son-in-law!" exclaimed Madame Saillard.

"You have adorned the house of God," said the Abbé Gaudron.

"We might have got salvation without doing that," she returned. "But if Baudoyer gets the place, which is worth eight thousand more, the sacrifice is not so great. If he does n't get it! hey, papa," she added, looking at her husband, "how we shall have bled!—"

"Well, never mind," said Saillard, enthusiastically, "we can always make it up through Falleix, who is going to extend his business and use his brother, whom he has made a stockbroker on purpose. Elisabeth might have told us, I think, why Falleix went off in such a hurry. But let's invent my little speech. This is what I thought of: 'Madame, if you would say a word to his Excellency—'"

"'If you would *deign*,'" said Gaudron; "add the word 'deign,' it is more respectful. But you ought to know, first of all, whether Madame la Dauphine will grant you her protection, and then you could suggest to Madame la comtesse the idea of co-operating with the wishes of her Royal Highness."

"You ought to designate the vacant post," said Baudoyer.

"'Madame la comtesse,'" began Saillard, rising, and bowing to his wife, with an agreeable smile.

"Goodness! Saillard; how ridiculous you look. Take care, my man, you 'll make the woman laugh."

"'Madame la comtesse,'" resumed Saillard. "Is that better, wife?"

"Yes, my duck."

"'The place of the late worthy Monsieur de la Billardière is vacant; my son-in-law, Monsieur Baudoyer —'"

"'Man of talent and extreme piety,'" prompted Gaudron.

"Write it down, Baudoyer," cried old Saillard, "write that sentence down."

Baudoyer proceeded to take a pen and wrote, without a blush, his own praises, precisely as Nathan or Canalis might have reviewed one of their own books.

"'Madame la comtesse' — Don't you see, mother?" said Saillard to his wife; "I am supposing you to be the minister's wife."

"Do you take me for a fool?" she answered sharply. "I know that."

"'The place of the late worthy Monsieur de la Billardière is vacant; my son-in-law, Monsieur Baudoyer, a man of consummate talent and extreme piety —'" After looking at Monsieur Gaudron, who was reflecting, he added, "'will be very glad if he gets it.' That's not bad; it's brief and it says the whole thing."

" But do wait, Saillard ; don't you see that Monsieur l'abbé is turning it over in his mind?" said Madame Saillard ; " don't disturb him."

" ' Will be very thankful if you would deign to interest yourself in his behalf,'" resumed Gaudron. " ' And in saying a word to his Excellency you will particularly please Madame la Dauphine, by whom he has the honor and the happiness to be protected.' "

" Ah! Monsieur Gaudron, that sentence is worth more than the monstrance ; I don't regret the four thousand eight hundred — Besides, Baudoyer, my lad, you 'll pay them, won't you? Have you written it all down? "

" I shall make you repeat it, father, morning and evening," said Madame Saillard. " Yes, that 's a good speech. How lucky you are, Monsieur Gaudron, to know so much. That 's what it is to be brought up in a seminary ; they learn there how to speak to God and his saints."

" He is as good as he is learned," said Baudoyer, pressing the priest's hands. " Did you write that article? " he added, pointing to the newspaper.

" No," answered Gaudron, " it was written by the secretary of his Eminence, a young abbé who is under obligations to me, and who takes an interest in Monsieur Colleville ; he was educated at my expense."

" A good deed is always rewarded," said Baudoyer.

While these four personages were sitting down to

their game of boston, Elisabeth and her uncle Mitral reached the Café Thémis, with much discourse as they drove along about a matter which Elisabeth's keen perceptions told her was the most powerful lever that could be used to force the minister's hand in the affair of her husband's appointment. Uncle Mitral, a former sheriff's officer, crafty, clever at sharp practice, and full of expedients and judicial precautions, believed the honor of his family to be involved in the appointment of his nephew. His avarice had long led him to estimate the contents of old Gigonnet's strong-box, for he knew very well they would go in the end to benefit his nephew Baudoyer; and it was therefore important that the latter should obtain a position which would be in keeping with the combined fortunes of the Saillards and old Gigonnet, which would finally devolve on the Baudoyers' little daughter; and what an heiress she would be with an income of a hundred thousand francs! to what social position might she not aspire with that fortune? He adopted all the ideas of his niece Elisabeth and thoroughly understood them. He had helped in sending off Falleix expeditiously, explaining to him the advantage of taking post horses. After which, while eating his dinner, he reflected that it would be as well to give a twist of his own to the clever plan invented by Elisabeth.

When they reached the Café Thémis he told his niece that he alone could manage Gigonnet in the matter they both had in view, and he made her wait in the hackney-coach and bide her time to come forward at the right moment. Elisabeth saw through the window-panes the two faces of Gobseck and Gigonnet (her uncle Bidault), which stood out in relief against the yellow wood-work of the old café, like two cameo heads, cold and impassible, in the rigid attitude that their gravity gave them. The two Parisian misers were surrounded by a number of other old faces, on which " thirty per cent discount " was written in circular wrinkles that started from the nose and turned round the glacial cheek-bones. These remarkable physiognomies brightened up on seeing Mitral, and their eyes gleamed with tigerish curiosity.

" Hey, hey ! it is papa Mitral ! " cried one of them, named Chaboisseau, a little old man who discounted for a publisher.

" Bless me, so it is ! " said another, a broker named Métivier, " ha, that 's an old monkey well up in his tricks."

" And you," retorted Mitral, " you are an old crow who knows all about carcasses."

" True," said the stern Gobseck.

" What are you here for? Have you come to seize friend Métivier? " asked Gigonnet, pointing to the broker, who had the bluff face of a porter.

" Your great-niece Elisabeth is out there, papa Gigonnet," whispered Mitral.

"What! some misfortune?" said Bidault. The old man drew his eyebrows together and assumed a tender look like that of an executioner when about to go to work officially. In spite of his Roman virtue he must have been touched, for his red nose lost somewhat of its color.

"Well, suppose it is misfortune, won't you help Saillard's daughter? — a girl who has knitted your stockings for the last thirty years!" cried Mitral.

"If there's good security I don't say I won't," replied Gigonnet. "Falleix is in with them. Falleix has just set up his brother as a broker, and he is doing as much business as the Brézacs; and what with? his mind, perhaps! Saillard is no simpleton."

"He knows the value of money," put in Chaboisseau.

That remark, uttered among those old men, would have made an artist and thinker shudder as they all nodded their heads.

"But it is none of my business," resumed Bidault-Gigonnet. "I'm not bound to care for my neighbors' misfortunes. My principle is never to be off my guard with friends or relatives; you can't perish except through weakness. Apply to Gobseck; he is softer."

The usurers all applauded these doctrines with a shake of their metallic heads. An onlooker would have fancied he heard the creaking of ill-oiled machinery.

"Come, Gigonnet, show a little feeling," said Chaboisseau, "they 've knit your stockings for thirty years."

"That counts for something," remarked Gobseck.

"Are you all alone? Is it safe to speak?" said Mitral, looking carefully about him. "I come about a good piece of business."

"If it is good, why do you come to us?" said Gigonnet, sharply, interrupting Mitral.

"A fellow who was gentleman of the Bedchamber," went on Mitral, "a former *chouan*,—what 's his name? — La Billardière is dead."

"True," said Gobseck.

"And our nephew is giving monstrances to a church," snarled Gigonnet.

"He is not such a fool as to give them, he sells them, old man," said Mitral, proudly. "He wants La Billardière's place, and in order to get it, we must seize —"

"*Seize!* you 'll never be anything but a sheriff's officer," put in Métivier, striking Mitral amicably on the shoulder; "I like that, I do!"

"Seize Monsieur Clément des Lupeaulx in our clutches," continued Mitral; "Elisabeth has discovered how to do it, and he is —"

"Elisabeth;" cried Gigonnet, interrupting again; "dear little creature! she takes after her grandfather, my poor brother! he never had his equal! Ah, you should have seen him buying up old furniture; what tact! what shrewdness! What does Elisabeth want?"

"Hey, hey!" cried Mitral, "you 've got back your bowels of compassion, papa Gigonnet! That phenomenon has a cause."

"Always a child," said Gobseck to Gigonnet, "you are too quick on the trigger."

"Come, Gobseck and Gigonnet, listen to me; you want to keep well with des Lupeaulx, don't you? You 've not forgotten how you plucked him in that affair about the king's debts, and you are afraid he 'll ask you to return him some of his feathers," said Mitral.

"Shall we tell him the whole thing?" asked Gobseck, whispering to Gigonnet.

"Mitral is one of us; he would n't play a shabby trick on his former customers," replied Gigonnet. "You see, Mitral," he went on, speaking to the ex-sheriff in a low voice, "we three have just bought up all those debts, the payment of which depends on the decision of the liquidation committee.

"How much will you lose?" asked Mitral.

"Nothing," said Gobseck.

"Nobody knows we are in it," added Gigonnet; "Samanon screens us."

"Come, listen to me, Gigonnet; it is cold, and your niece is waiting outside. You 'll understand what I want in two words. You must at once, between you, send two hundred and fifty thousand francs (without interest) into the country after Falleix, who has gone post-haste, with a courier in advance of him."

"Is it possible!" said Gobseck.

"What for?" cried Gigonnet, "and where to?"

"To des Lupeaulx's magnificent country-seat," replied Mitral. "Falleix knows the country, for he was born there; and he is going to buy up land all round the secretary's miserable hovel, with the two hundred and fifty thousand francs I speak of, — good land, well worth the price. There are only nine days before us for drawing up and recording the notarial deeds (bear that in mind). With the addition of this land, des Lupeaulx's present miserable property would pay taxes to the amount of one thousand francs, the sum necessary to make a man eligible to the Chamber. *Ergo*, with it des Lupeaulx goes into the electoral college, becomes eligible, count, and whatever he pleases. You know the deputy who has slipped out and left a vacancy, don't you?"

The two misers nodded.

"Des Lupeaulx would cut off a leg to get elected in his place," continued Mitral; "but he must have the title-deeds of the property in his own name, and then mortgage them back to us for the amount of the purchase-money. Ah! now you begin to see what I am after! First of all, we must make sure of Baudoyer's appointment, and des Lupeaulx will get it for us on these terms; after that is settled we will hand him back to you. Falleix is now canvassing the electoral vote. Don't you perceive that you have Lupeaulx completely in your power until after the election? — for Falleix's friends are a large majority. Now do you see what I mean, papa Gigonnet?"

"It 's a clever game," said Métivier.

"We 'll do it," said Gigonnet; "you agree, don't you, Gobseck? Falleix can give us security and put mortgages on the property in my name; we 'll go and see des Lupeaulx when all is ready."

"We 're robbed," said Gobseck.

"Ha, ha!" laughed Mitral, "I 'd like to know the robber!"

"Nobody can rob us but ourselves," answered Gigonnet. "I told you we were doing a good thing in buying up all des Lupeaulx's paper from his creditors at sixty per cent discount."

"Take this mortgage on his estate and you 'll hold him tighter still through the interest," answered Mitral.

"Possibly," said Gobseck.

After exchanging a shrewd look with Gobseck, Gigonnet went to the door of the café.

"Elisabeth! follow it up, my dear," he said to his niece. "We hold your man securely; but don't neglect accessories. You have begun well, clever woman! go on as you began and you'll have your uncle's esteem," and he grasped her hand, gayly.

"But," said Mitral, "Métivier and Chaboisseau heard it all, and they may play us a trick and tell the matter to some opposition journal which would catch the ball on its way and counteract the effect of the ministerial article. You must go alone, my dear; I dare not let those two cormorants out of my sight." So saying he re-entered the café.

The next day the numerous subscribers to a certain liberal journal read, among the Paris items, the following article, inserted authoritatively by Chaboisseau and Métivier, share-holders in the said journal, brokers for publishers, printers, and paper-makers, whose behests no editor dared refuse : —

"Yesterday a ministerial journal plainly indicated as the probable successor of Monsieur le Baron de la Billardière, Monsieur Baudoyer, one of the worthiest citizens of a populous quarter, where his benevolence is scarcely less known than the piety on which the ministerial organ laid so much stress. Why was that sheet silent as to his talents? Did it reflect that in boasting of the bourgeoise nobility of Monsieur Baudoyer — which, certainly, is a nobility as good as any other — it was pointing out a reason for the exclusion of the candidate? A gratuitous piece of perfidy! an attempt to kill with a caress! To appoint Monsieur Baudoyer is to do honor to the virtues, the talents of the middle classes, of whom we shall ever be the supporters, though their cause seems at

times a lost one. This appointment, we repeat, will be an
act of justice and good policy; consequently we may be sure
it will not be made."

On the morrow, Friday, the usual day for the dinner
given by Madame Rabourdin, whom des Lupeaulx had
left at midnight, radiant in beauty, on the staircase
of the Bouffons, arm in arm with Madame de Camps
(Madame Firmiani had lately married), the old roué
awoke with his thoughts of vengeance calmed, or
rather refreshed, and his mind full of a last glance
exchanged with Célestine.

"I'll make sure of Rabourdin's support by forgiving
him now, — I'll get even with him later. If he has n't
this place for the time being I should have to give up
a woman who is capable of becoming a most precious
instrument in the pursuit of high political fortune.
She understands everything; shrinks from nothing,
from no idea whatever! — and besides, I can't know
before his Excellency what new scheme of administration Rabourdin has invented. No, my dear des
Lupeaulx, the thing in hand is to win all now for your
Célestine. You may make as many faces as you please,
Madame la comtesse, but you will invite Madame Rabourdin to your next select party."

Des Lupeaulx was one of those men who to satisfy
a passion are quite able to put away revenge in some

dark corner of their minds. His course was taken; he was resolved to get Rabourdin appointed.

"I will prove to you, my dear fellow, that I deserve a good place in your galley," thought he as he seated himself in his study and began to unfold a newspaper.

He knew so well what the ministerial organ would contain that he rarely took the trouble to read it, but on this occasion he did open it to look at the article on La Billardière, recollecting with amusement the dilemma in which du Bruel had put him by bringing him the night before Bixiou's mischievous amendments to the obituary. He was laughing to himself as he reread the biography of the late Comte de Fontaine, dead a few months earlier, which he had hastily substituted for that of La Billardière, when his eyes were dazzled by the name of Baudoyer. He read with fury the article which pledged the minister, and then he rang violently for Dutocq, to send him at once to the editor. But what was his astonishment on reading the reply of the opposition paper! The situation was evidently serious. He knew the game, and he saw that the man who was shuffling his cards for him was a Greek of the first order. To dictate in this way through two opposing newspapers in one evening, and to begin the fight by forestalling the intentions of the minister was a daring game! He recognized the pen of a liberal editor, and resolved to question him that night at the opera. Dutocq appeared.

"Read that," said des Lupeaulx, handing him the two journals, and continuing to run his eye over others to see if Baudoyer had pulled any further wires. "Go to the office and ask who has dared to thus compromise the minister."

"It was not Monsieur Baudoyer himself," answered Dutocq, "for he never left the ministry yesterday. I need not go and inquire; for when I took your article to the newspaper office I met a young abbé who brought in a letter from the Grand Almoner, before which you yourself would have had to bow."

"Dutocq, you have a grudge against Monsieur Rabourdin, and it is n't right; for he has twice saved you from being turned out. However, we are not masters of our own feelings; we sometimes hate our benefactors. Only, remember this; if you show the slightest treachery to Rabourdin, without my permission, it will be your ruin. As to that newspaper, let the Grand Almoner subscribe as largely as we do, if he wants its services. Here we are at the end of the year; the matter of subscriptions will come up for discussion, and I shall have something to say on that head. As to La Billardière's place, there is only one way to settle the matter; and that is to appoint Rabourdin this very day."

"Gentlemen," said Dutocq, returning to the clerks' office and addressing his colleagues. "I don't know if

Bixiou has the art of looking into futurity, but if you have not read the ministerial journal I advise you to study the article about Baudoyer; then, as Monsieur Fleury takes the opposition sheet, you can see the reply. Monsieur Rabourdin certainly has talent, but a man who in these days gives a six-thousand-franc monstrance to the Church has a devilish deal more talent than he."

Bixiou [entering]. What say you, gentlemen, to the First Epistle to the Corinthians in our pious ministerial journal, and the reply Epistle to the Ministers in the opposition sheet? How does Monsieur Rabourdin feel now, du Bruel?

Du Bruel [rushing in]. I don't know. [He drags Bixiou back into his cabinet, and says in a low voice] My good fellow, your way of helping people is like that of the hangman who jumps upon a victim's shoulders to break his neck. You got me into a scrape with des Lupeaulx, which my folly in ever trusting you richly deserved. A fine thing indeed, that article on La Billardière. I sha'n't forget the trick! Why, the very first sentence was as good as telling the King he was superannuated and it was time for him to die. And as to that Quiberon bit, it said plainly that the King was a — What a fool I was!

Bixiou [laughing]. Bless my heart! are you getting angry? Can't a fellow joke any more?

Du Bruel. Joke! joke indeed. When you want to be made head-clerk somebody shall joke with you, my dear fellow.

Bixiou [in a bullying tone]. Angry, are we?

Du Bruel. Yes!

Bixiou [dryly]. So much the worse for you.

Du Bruel [uneasy]. You would n't pardon such a thing yourself, I know.

Bixiou [in a wheedling tone]. To a friend? indeed I would. [They hear Fleury's voice.] There's Fleury cursing Baudoyer. Hey, how well the thing has been managed! Baudoyer will get the appointment. [Confidentially] After all, so much the better. Du Bruel, just keep your eye on the consequences. Rabourdin would be a mean-spirited creature to stay under Baudoyer; he will send in his resignation, and that will give us two places. You can be head of the bureau and take me for under-head-clerk. We will make vaudevilles together, and I'll fag at your work in the office.

Du Bruel [smiling]. Dear me, I never thought of that. Poor Rabourdin! I shall be sorry for him, though.

Bixiou. That shows how much you love him! [Changing his tone] Ah, well, I don't pity him any longer. He's rich; his wife gives parties and does n't ask me, — me, who go everywhere! Well, good-bye, my dear fellow, good-bye, and don't owe me a grudge!

[He goes out through the clerks' office.] Adieu, gentlemen; did n't I tell you yesterday that a man who has nothing but virtues and talents will always be poor, even though he has a pretty wife?

HENRY. You are so rich, you!

BIXIOU. Not bad, my Cincinnatus! But you 'll give me that dinner at the Rocher de Cancale.

POIRET. It is absolutely impossible for me to understand Monsieur Bixiou.

PHELLION [with an elegiac air]. Monsieur Rabourdin so seldom reads the newspapers that it might perhaps be serviceable to deprive ourselves momentarily by taking them in to him. [Fleury hands over his paper, Vimeux the office sheet, and Phellion departs with them.]

At that moment des Lupeaulx, coming leisurely downstairs to breakfast with the minister, was asking himself whether, before playing a trump card for the husband, it might not be prudent to probe the wife's heart and make sure of a reward for his devotion. He was feeling about for the small amount of heart that he possessed, when, at a turn of the staircase, he encountered his lawyer, who said to him, smiling, "Just a word, Monseigneur," in the tone of familiarity assumed by men who know they are indispensable.

"What is it, my dear Desroches?" exclaimed the politician. "Has anything happened?"

"I have come to tell you that all your notes and debts have been bought up by Gobseck and Gigonnet, under the name of a certain Samanon."

"Men whom I helped to make their millions!"

"Listen," whispered the lawyer. "Gigonnet (really named Bidault) is the uncle of Saillard, your cashier; and Saillard is father-in-law to a certain Baudoyer, who thinks he has a right to the vacant place in your ministry. Don't you think I have done right to come and tell you?"

"Thank you," said des Lupeaulx, nodding to the lawyer with a shrewd look.

"One stroke of your pen will buy them off," said Desroches, leaving him.

"What an immense sacrifice!" muttered des Lupeaulx. "It would be impossible to explain it to a woman," thought he. "Is Célestine worth more than the clearing off of my debts? — that is the question. I'll go and see her this morning."

So the beautiful Madame Rabourdin was to be, within an hour, the arbiter of her husband's fate, and no power on earth could warn her of the importance of her replies, or give her the least hint to guard her conduct and compose her voice. Moreover, in addition to her mischances, she believed herself certain of success, never dreaming that Rabourdin was undermined in all directions by the secret sapping of the mollusks.

"Well, Monseigneur," said des Lupeaulx, entering the little salon where they breakfasted, "have you seen the articles on Baudoyer?"

"For God's sake, my dear friend," replied the minister, "don't talk of those appointments just now; let me have an hour's peace! They cracked my ears last night with that monstrance. The only way to save Rabourdin is to bring his appointment before the Council, unless I submit to having my hand forced. It is enough to disgust a man with the public service. I must purchase the right to keep that excellent Rabourdin by promoting a certain Colleville!"

"Why not make over the management of this pretty little comedy to me, and rid yourself of the worry of it? I'll amuse you every morning with an account of the game of chess I should play with the Grand Almoner," said des Lupeaulx.

"Very good," said the minister, "settle it with the head examiner. But you know perfectly well that nothing is more likely to strike the king's mind than just those reasons the opposition journal has chosen to put forth. Good heavens! fancy managing a ministry with such men as Baudoyer under me!"

"An imbecile bigot," said des Lupeaulx, "and as utterly incapable as —"

"— as La Billardière," added the minister.

"But La Billardière had the manners of a gentleman-in-ordinary," replied des Lupeaulx. " Madame," he continued, addressing the countess, " it is now an absolute necessity to invite Madame Rabourdin to your next private party. I must assure you she is the intimate friend of Madame de Camps; they were at the Opera together last night. I first met her at the hôtel Firmiani. Besides, you will see that she is not of a kind to compromise a salon."

" Invite Madame Rabourdin, my dear," said the minister, " and pray let us talk of something else."

15

VII.

SCENES FROM DOMESTIC LIFE.

PARISIAN households are literally eaten up with the desire to be in keeping with the luxury that surrounds them on all sides, and few there are who have the wisdom to let their external situation conform to their internal revenue. But this vice may perhaps denote a truly French patriotism, which seeks to maintain the supremacy of the nation in the matter of dress. France reigns through clothes over the whole of Europe; and every one must feel the importance of retaining a commercial sceptre that makes fashion in France what the navy is to England. This patriotic ardor which leads a nation to sacrifice everything to appearances — to the *paroistre*, as d'Aubigné said in the days of Henri IV. — is the cause of those vast secret labors which employ the whole of a Parisian woman's morning, when she wishes, as Madame Rabourdin wished, to keep up on twelve thousand francs a year the style that many a family with thirty thousand does not indulge in. Consequently, every Friday, — the day of her dinner-parties, — Madame Rabourdin helped the chambermaid to do the rooms; for the cook went early to market, and the man-servant was cleaning the silver, folding the napkins, and polishing the glasses. The ill-advised individual who might happen, through an oversight of the porter, to enter Madame Rabourdin's establishment about eleven o'clock in the morning would have found her in the midst of a disorder the reverse of picturesque, wrapped in a dressing-gown, her hair ill-dressed, and her feet in old slippers, attending to the lamps, arranging the flowers, or cooking in haste an extremely unpoetic breakfast. The visitor to whom the mysteries of Parisian life were unknown would certainly have learned for the rest of his life not to set foot in these greenrooms at the wrong moment; a woman caught at her matin mysteries would ever after point him out as a man capable of the blackest crimes; or she would talk of his stupidity and indiscretion in a manner to ruin him. The true Parisian woman, indulgent to all curiosity that she can put to profit, is implacable to that which makes her lose her prestige. Such a domiciliary invasion may be called, not only (as they say in the police reports) an attack on privacy, but a burglary, a robbery of all that is most precious, namely, *credit*. A woman is quite willing to let herself be surprised half-dressed, with her hair about her shoulders. If her hair is all her own she scores one; but she will never allow herself to be seen

" doing " her own rooms, or she loses her *paroistre*, — that precious *seeming-to-be!*

Madame Rabourdin was in full tide of preparation for her Friday dinner, standing in the midst of provisions the cook had just fished from the vast ocean of the markets, when Monsieur des Lupeaulx made his way stealthily in. The general-secretary was certainly the last man Madame Rabourdin expected to see, and so, when she heard his boots creaking in the ante-chamber, she exclaimed, impatiently, " The hair-dresser already !" — an exclamation as little agreeable to des Lupeaulx as the sight of des Lupeaulx was agreeable to her. She immediately escaped into her bedroom, where chaos reigned ; a jumble of furniture to be put out of sight, with other heterogeneous articles of more or rather less elegance, — a domestic carnival, in short. The bold des Lupeaulx followed the handsome fugitive, so piquant did she seem to him in her dishabille. There is something indescribably alluring to the eye in a portion of flesh seen through an hiatus in the under-garment, more attractive far than when it rises gracefully above the circular curve of the velvet bodice, to the vanishing line of the prettiest swan's-neck that ever lover kissed before a ball. When the eye dwells on a woman in full dress making exhibition of her magnificent white shoulders, do we not fancy that we see the elegant dessert of a grand dinner? But the glance that glides through the disarray of muslins rumpled in sleep enjoys, as it were, a feast of stolen fruit glowing between the leaves on a garden wall.

"Stop! wait!" cried the pretty Parisian, bolting the door of the disordered room.

She rang for Thérèse, called for her daughter, the cook, and the man-servant, wishing she possessed the whistle of the machinist at the Opera. Her call, however, answered the same purpose. In a moment, another phenomenon! the salon assumed a piquant morning look, quite in keeping with the becoming toilet hastily got together by the fugitive; we say it to her glory, for she was evidently a clever woman, in this at least.

"You!" she said, coming forward, "at this hour? What has happened?"

"Very serious things," answered des Lupeaulx. "You and I must understand each other now."

Célestine looked at the man behind his glasses, and understood the matter.

"My principal vice," she said, "is oddity. For instance, I do not mix up affections with politics; let us talk politics, — business, if you will, — the rest can come later. However, it is not really oddity nor a whim that forbids me to mingle ill-assorted colors and put together things that have no affinity, and compels me to avoid discords; it is my natural instinct as an artist. We women have politics of our own."

Already the tones of her voice and the charm of her manners were producing their effect on the secretary and metamorphosing his roughness into sentimental courtesy; she had recalled him to his obligations as a lover. A clever pretty woman makes an atmosphere about her in which the nerves relax and the feelings soften.

"You are ignorant of what is happening," said des Lupeaulx, harshly, for he still thought it best to make a show of harshness. "Read that."

He gave the two newspapers to the graceful woman, having drawn a line in red ink round each of the famous articles.

"Good heavens!" she exclaimed, "but this is dreadful! Who is this Baudoyer?"

"A donkey," answered des Lupeaulx; "but, as you see, he uses means, — he gives monstrances; he succeeds, thanks to some clever hand that pulls the wires."

The thought of her debts crossed Madame Rabourdin's mind and blurred her sight, as if two lightning flashes had blinded her eyes at the same moment; her ears hummed under the pressure of the blood that began to beat in her arteries; she remained for a moment quite bewildered, gazing at a window which she did not see.

"But you are faithful to us?" she said at last, with

a winning glance at des Lupeaulx, as if to attach him
to her.

"That is as it may be," he replied, answering her
glance with an interrogative look which made the
poor woman blush.

"If you demand caution-money you may lose all,"
she said, laughing; "I thought you more magnanimous
than you are. And you, you thought me less a person
than I am, — a sort of school-girl."

"You have misunderstood me," he said, with a covert
smile; "I meant that I could not assist a man who
plays against me just as l'Étourdi played against
Mascarille."

"What can you mean?"

"This will prove to you whether I am magnanimous
or not."

He gave Madame Rabourdin the memorandum stolen
by Dutocq, pointing out to her the passage in which her
husband had so ably analyzed him.

"Read that."

Célestine recognized the handwriting, read the paper,
and turned pale under the blow.

"All the ministries, the whole service is treated in
the same way," said des Lupeaulx.

"Happily," she said, "you alone possess this document. I cannot explain it, even to myself."

"The man who stole it is not such a fool as to let

me have it without keeping a copy for himself; he is too great a liar to admit it, and too clever in his business to give it up. I did not even ask him for it."

"Who is he?"

"Your chief clerk."

"Dutocq! People are always punished through their kindnesses! But," she added, "he is only a dog who wants a bone."

"Do you know what the other side offer me, poor devil of a general-secretary?"

"What?"

"I owe thirty thousand and odd miserable francs,— you will despise me because it is n't more, but here, I grant you, I am insignificant. Well, Baudoyer's uncle has bought up my debts, and is, doubtless, ready to give me a receipt for them if Baudoyer is appointed."

"But all that is monstrous."

"Not at all; it is monarchical and religious, for the Grand Almoner is concerned in it. Baudoyer himself must appoint Colleville in return for ecclesiastical assistance."

"What shall you do?"

"What will you bid me do?" he said, with charming grace, holding out his hand.

Célestine no longer thought him ugly, nor old, nor white and chilling as a hoar-frost, nor indeed anything that was odious and offensive, but she did not give him her hand. At night, in her salon, she would have let him take it a hundred times, but here, alone and in the morning, the action seemed too like a promise that might lead her far.

"And they say that statesmen have no hearts!" she cried enthusiastically, trying to hide the harshness of her refusal under the grace of her words. "The thought used to terrify me," she added, assuming an innocent, ingenuous air.

"What a calumny!" cried des Lupeaulx. "Only this week one of the stiffest of diplomatists, a man who has been in the service ever since he came to manhood, has married the daughter of an actress, and has introduced her at the most iron-bound court in Europe as to quarterings of nobility."

"You will continue to support us?"

"I am to draw up your husband's appointment — But no cheating, remember."

She gave him her hand to kiss, and tapped him on the cheek as she did so. "You are mine!" she said.

Des Lupeaulx admired the expression.

[That night, at the Opera, the old coxscomb related the incident as follows: "A woman who did not want to tell a man she would be his, — an acknowledgment a well-bred woman never allows herself to make,— changed the words into 'You are mine.' Don't you think the evasion charming?"]

"But you must be my ally," he answered. "Now listen, your husband has spoken to the minister of a plan for the reform of the administration; the paper I have shown you is a part of that plan. I want to know what it is. Find out, and tell me to-night."

"I will," she answered, wholly unaware of the important nature of the errand which brought des Lupeaulx to the house that morning.

"Madame, the hair-dresser."

"At last!" thought Célestine. "I don't see how I should have got out of it if he had delayed much longer."

"You do not know to what lengths my devotion can go," said des Lupeaulx, rising. "You shall be invited to the first select party given by his Excellency's wife."

"Ah, you are an angel!" she cried. "And I see now how much you love me; you love me intelligently."

"To-night, dear child" he said, "I shall find out at the Opera what journalists are conspiring for Baudoyer, and we will measure swords together."

"Yes, but you must dine with us, will you not? I have taken pains to get the things you like best—"

"All that is so like love," said des Lupeaulx to himself as he went downstairs, "that I am willing to be deceived in that way for a long time. Well, if she *is* tricking me I shall know it. I'll set the cleverest of all traps before the appointment is fairly signed, and I'll read her heart. Ah! my little cats, I know you!

for, after all, women are just what we men are. Twenty-eight years old, virtuous, and living here in the rue Duphot! — a rare piece of luck and worth cultivating," thought the elderly butterfly as he fluttered down the staircase.

" Good heavens! that man, without his glasses, must look funny enough in a dressing-gown! " thought Célestine, " but the harpoon is in his back and he'll tow me where I want to go; I am sure now of that invitation. He has played his part in my comedy."

When, at five o'clock in the afternoon, Rabourdin came home to dress for dinner, his wife presided at his toilet and presently laid before him the fatal memorandum which, like the slipper in the Arabian Nights, the luckless man was fated to meet at every turn.

" Who gave you that? " he asked, thunderstruck.

" Monsieur des Lupeaulx."

" So he has been here! " cried Rabourdin, with a look which would certainly have made a guilty woman turn pale, but which Célestine received with unruffled brow and a laughing eye.

" And he is coming back to dinner," she said. "Why that startled air? "

" My dear," replied Rabourdin, "I have mortally offended des Lupeaulx; such men never forgive, and yet he fawns upon me! Do you think I don't see why? "

"The man seems to me," she said, "to have good taste; you can't expect me to blame him. I really don't know anything more flattering to a woman than to please a worn-out palate. After—"

"A truce to nonsense, Célestine. Spare a much-tried man. I cannot get an audience of the minister, and my honor is at stake."

"Good heavens, no! Dutocq can have the promise of a good place as soon as you are named head of the division."

"Ah! I see what you are about, dear child," said Rabourdin; "but the game you are playing is just as dishonorable as the real thing that is going on around us. A lie is a lie, and an honest woman—"

"Let me use the weapons employed against us."

"Célestine, the more that man des Lupeaulx feels he is foolishly caught in a trap, the more bitter he will be against me."

"What if I get him dismissed altogether?"

Rabourdin looked at his wife in amazement.

"I am thinking only of your advancement; it was high time, my poor husband," continued Célestine. "But you are mistaking the dog for the game," she added, after a pause. "In a few days des Lupeaulx will have accomplished all that I want of him. While you are trying to speak to the minister, and before you can even see him on business, I shall have seen

him and spoken with him. You are worn out in
trying to bring that plan of your brain to birth, — a
plan which you have been hiding from me; but you
will find that in three months your wife has accomplished more than you have done in six years. Come,
tell me this fine scheme of yours."

Rabourdin, continuing to shave, cautioned his wife
not to say a word about his work, and after assuring her
that to confide a single idea to des Lupeaulx would be
to put the cat near the milk-jug, he began an explanation of his labors.

"Why did n't you tell me this before, Rabourdin?"
said Célestine, cutting her husband short at his fifth
sentence. "You might have saved yourself a world
of trouble. I can understand that a man should be
blinded by an idea for a moment, but to nurse it up
for six or seven years, that 's a thing I cannot comprehend! You want to reduce the budget, — a vulgar and commonplace idea! The budget ought, on
the contrary, to reach two thousand millions. Then,
indeed, France would be great. If you want a new
system let it be one of loans, as Monsieur de Nucingen
keeps saying. The poorest of all treasuries is the one
with a surplus that it never uses; the mission of a
minister of finance is to fling gold out of the windows.
It will come back to him through the cellars; and you,
you want to hoard it! The thing to do is to increase

the offices and all government employments, instead of reducing them! So far from lessening the public debt, you ought to increase the creditors. If the Bourbons want to reign in peace, let them seek creditors in the towns and villages, and place their loans there; above all, they ought not to let foreigners draw interest away from France; some day an alien nation might ask us for the capital. Whereas if capital and interest are held only in France, neither France nor credit can perish. That's what saved England. Your plan is the tradesman's plan. An ambitious public man should produce some bold scheme, — he should make himself another Law, without Law's fatal ill-luck; he ought to exhibit the power of credit, and show that we should reduce, not principal, but interest, as they do in England."

"Come, come, Célestine," said Rabourdin; "mix up ideas as much as you please, and make fun of them, — I'm accustomed to that; but don't criticise a work of which you know nothing as yet."

"Do I need," she asked, "to know a scheme the essence of which is to govern France with a civil service of six thousand men instead of twenty thousand? My dear friend, even allowing it were the plan of a man of genius, a king of France who attempted to carry it out would get himself dethroned. You can keep down a feudal aristocracy by levelling a few heads, but you can't subdue a hydra with thousands.

And is it with the present ministers — between ourselves, a wretched crew — that you expect to carry out your reform? No, no; change the monetary system if you will, but do not meddle with men, with little men; they cry out too much, whereas gold is dumb."

"But, Célestine, if you will talk, and put wit before argument, we shall never understand each other."

"Understand!   I understand what that paper, in which you have analyzed the capacities of the men in office, will lead to," she replied, paying no attention to what her husband said. "Good heavens! you have sharpened the axe to cut off your own head. Holy Virgin! why did n't you consult me?   I could have at least prevented you from committing anything to writing, or, at any rate, if you insisted on putting it to paper, I would have written it down myself, and it should never have left this house. Good God! to think that he never told me! That's what men are! capable of sleeping with the wife of their bosom for seven years, and keeping a secret from her! Hiding their thoughts from a poor woman for seven years! — doubting her devotion!"

"But," cried Rabourdin, provoked, "for eleven years and more I have been unable to discuss anything with you because you insist on cutting me short and substituting your ideas for mine. You know nothing at all about my scheme."

"Nothing! I know all."

"Then tell it to me!" cried Rabourdin, angry for the first time since his marriage.

"There! it is half-past six o'clock; finish shaving, and dress at once," she cried hastily, after the fashion of women when pressed on a point they are not ready to talk of. "I must go; we'll adjourn the discussion, for I don't want to be nervous on a reception-day. Good heavens! the poor soul!" she thought, as she left the room, "it *is* hard to be in labor for seven years and bring forth a dead child! And not trust his wife!"

She went back into the room.

"If you had listened to me you would never have interceded to keep your chief clerk; he stole that abominable paper, and has, no doubt, kept a fac-simile of it. Adieu, man of genius!"

Then she noticed the almost tragic expression of her husband's grief; she felt she had gone too far, and ran to him, seized him just as he was, all lathered with soap-suds, and kissed him tenderly.

"Dear Xavier, don't be vexed," she said. "To-night, after the people are gone, we will study your plan; you shall speak at your ease, — I will listen just as long as you wish me to. Is n't that nice of me? What do I want better than to be the wife of Mohammed?"

She began to laugh; and Rabourdin laughed too, for
the soapsuds were clinging to Célestine's lips, and her
voice had the tones of the purest and most steadfast
affection.

"Go and dress, dear child; and above all, don't say
a word of this to des Lupeaulx. Swear you will not.
That is the only punishment that I impose — "

"*Impose!*" she cried. "Then I won't swear anything.".

"Come, come, Célestine, I said in jest a really serious
thing."

"To-night," she said, "I mean your general-secretary
to know whom I am really intending to attack; he has
given me the means."

"Attack whom?"

"The minister," she answered, drawing herself up.
"We are to be invited to his wife's private parties."

In spite of his Célestine's loving caresses, Rabourdin,
as he finished dressing, could not prevent certain painful
thoughts from clouding his brow.

"Will she ever appreciate me? he said to himself.
"She does not even understand that she is the sole in-
centive of my whole work. How wrong-headed, and yet
how excellent a mind! — If I had not married I might
now have been high in office and rich. I could have
saved half my salary; my savings well-invested would
have given me to-day ten thousand francs a year out-

side of my office, and I might then have become, through a good marriage — Yes, that is all true," he exclaimed, interrupting himself, " but I have Célestine and my two children." The man flung himself back upon his happiness. To the best of married lives there come moments of regret. He entered the salon and looked around him. " There are not two women in Paris who understand making life pleasant as she does. To keep such a home as this on twelve thousand francs a year ! " he thought, looking at the flower-stands bright with bloom, and thinking of the social enjoyments that were about to gratify his vanity. " She was made to be the wife of a minister. When I think of his Excellency's wife, and how little she helps him ! the good woman is a comfortable middle-class dowdy, and when she goes to the palace or into society — " He pinched his lips together. Very busy men are apt to have very ignorant notions about household matters, and you can make them believe that a hundred thousand francs afford little or that twelve thousand afford all.

Though impatiently expected, and in spite of the flattering dishes prepared for the palate of the gourmet-emeritus, des Lupeaulx did not come to dinner ; in fact he came in very late, about midnight, an hour when a company dwindles and conversations become intimate and confidential. Andoche Finot, the journalist, was one of the few remaining guests.

"I now know all," said des Lupeaulx, when he was comfortably seated on a sofa at the corner of the fire-place, a cup of tea in his hand and Madame Rabourdin standing before him with a plate of sandwiches and some slices of a cake very appropriately called "leaden cake." "Finot, my dear and witty friend, you can render a great service to our gracious queen by letting loose a few dogs upon the men we were talking of. You have against you," he said to Rabourdin, lowering his voice so as to be heard only by the three persons whom he addressed, "a set of usurers and priests — money and the church. The article in the liberal journal was instigated by an old money-lender to whom the paper was under obligations; but the young fellow who wrote it cares nothing about it. The paper is about to change hands, and in three days more will be on our side. The royalist opposition,— for we have, thanks to Monsieur de Chateaubriand, a royalist opposition, that is to say, royalists who have gone over to the liberals, — however, there's no need to discuss political matters now, — these assassins of Charles X. have promised me to support your appointment at the price of our acquiescence in one of their amendments. All my batteries are manned. If they threaten us with Baudoyer we shall say to the clerical phalanx, ' Such and such a paper and such and such men will attack your measures and the whole press will be against you' (for even the ministerial journals which I influence will be deaf and dumb, won't they, Finot?). 'Appoint Rabourdin, a faithful servant, and public opinion is with you — '"

"Hi, hi!" laughed Finot.

"So, there's no need to be uneasy," said des Lupeaulx. "I have arranged it all to-night; the Grand Almoner must yield."

"I would rather have had less hope, and you to dinner," whispered Célestine, looking at him with a vexed air which might very well pass for an expression of wounded love.

"This must win my pardon," he returned, giving her an invitation to the ministry for the following Tuesday.

Célestine opened the letter, and a flush of pleasure came into her face. No enjoyment can be compared to that of gratified vanity.

"You know what the countess's Tuesdays are," said des Lupeaulx, with a confidential air. "To the usual ministerial parties they are what the 'Petit-Château' is to a court ball. You will be at the heart of power! You will see there the Comtesse Féraud, who is still in favor notwithstanding Louis XVIII.'s death, Delphine de Nucingen, Madame de Listomère, the Marquise d'Espard, and your dear Firmiani; I have had her invited to give you her support in case the other women attempt to black-ball you. I long to see you in the midst of them."

Célestine threw up her head like a thoroughbred before the race, and re-read the invitation just as Baudoyer and Saillard had re-read the articles about themselves in the newspapers, without being able to quaff enough of it.

"*There* first, and *next* at the Tuileries," she said to des Lupeaulx, who was startled by the words and by the attitude of the speaker, so expressive were they of ambition and security.

"Can it be that I am only a stepping-stone?" he asked himself. He rose, and went into Madame Rabourdin's bedroom, where she followed him, understanding from a motion of his head that he wished to speak to her privately.

"Well, your husband's plan," he said; "what of it?"

"Bah! the useless nonsense of an honest man!" she replied. "He wants to suppress fifteen thousand offices and do the work with five or six thousand. You never heard of such nonsense; I will let you read the whole document when copied; it is written in perfect good faith. His analysis of the officials was prompted only by his honesty and rectitude, — poor dear man!"

Des Lupeaulx was all the more reassured by the genuine laugh which accompanied these jesting and contemptuous words, because he was a judge of lying and knew that Célestine spoke in good faith.

"But still, what is at the bottom of it all?" he asked.

"Well, he wants to do away with the land-tax and substitute taxes on consumption."

"Why it is over a year since François Keller and Nucingen proposed some such plan, and the minister himself is thinking of a reduction of the land-tax."

"There!" exclaimed Célestine, "I told him there was nothing new in his scheme."

"No; but he is on the same ground with the best financier of the epoch, — the Napoleon of finance. Something may come of it. Your husband must surely have some special ideas in his method of putting the scheme into practice."

"No, it is all commonplace," she said, with a disdainful curl of her lip. "Just think of governing France with five or six thousand offices, when what is really needed is that everybody in France should be personally enlisted in the support of the government."

Des Lupeaulx seemed satisfied that Rabourdin, to whom in his own mind he had granted remarkable talents, was really a man of mediocrity.

"Are you quite sure of the appointment? You don't want a bit of feminine advice?" she said.

"You women are greater adepts than we in refined treachery," he said, nodding.

"Well, then, say *Baudoyer* to the court and clergy,

to divert suspicion and put them to sleep, and then, at the last moment, write *Rabourdin.*"

"There are some women who say *yes* as long as they need a man, and *no* when he has played his part," returned des Lupeaulx, significantly.

"I know they do," she answered, laughing; "but they are very foolish, for in politics everything recommences. Such proceedings may do with fools, but you are a man of sense. In my opinion the greatest folly any one can commit is to quarrel with a clever man."

"You are mistaken," said des Lupeaulx, "for such a man pardons. The real danger is with the petty spiteful natures who have nothing to do but study revenge, —I spend my life among them."

When all the guests were gone, Rabourdin came into his wife's room, and after asking for her strict attention, he explained his plan and made her see that it did not cut down the revenue but on the contrary increased it; he showed her in what ways the public funds were employed, and how the State could increase tenfold the circulation of money by putting its own, in the proportion of a third, or a quarter, into the expenditures which would be sustained by private or local interests. He finally proved to her plainly that his plan was not mere theory, but a system teeming with methods of execution. Célestine, brightly enthusiastic, sprang into her husband's arms and sat upon his knee in the chimney-corner.

"At last I find the husband of my dreams!" she cried. "My ignorance of your real merit has saved you from des Lupeaulx's claws. I calumniated you to him gloriously and in good faith."

The man wept with joy. His day of triumph had come at last. Having labored for years to satisfy his wife, he found himself a great man in the eyes of his sole public.

"To one who knows how good you are, how tender, how equable in temper, how loving, you are tenfold greater still. But," she added, "a man of genius is always more or less a child; and you are a child, a dearly beloved child," she said, caressing him. Then she drew the invitation from that particular spot where women put what they sacredly hide, and showed it to him.

"Here is what I wanted," she said; "Des Lupeaulx has put me face to face with the minister, and were he a man of iron, his Excellency shall be made for a time to bend the knee to me."

The next day Célestine began her preparations for entrance into the inner circle of the ministry. It was her day of triumph, her own! Never courtesan took such pains with herself as this honest woman bestowed upon her person. No dressmaker was ever so tor-

mented as hers. Madame Rabourdin forgot nothing.
She went herself to the stable where she hired carriages, and chose a coupé that was neither old, nor
bourgeois, nor showy. Her footman, like the footmen
of great houses, had the dress and appearance of a
master. About ten on the evening of the eventful
Tuesday, she left home in a charming full mourning attire. Her hair was dressed with jet grapes of
exquisite workmanship, — an ornament costing three
thousand francs, made by Fossin for an Englishwoman
who had left Paris before it was finished. The leaves
were of stamped iron-work, as light as the vine-leaves
themselves, and the artist had not forgotten the graceful tendrils, which twined in the wearer's curls just as,
in nature, they catch upon the branches. The brace-
lets, necklace, and earrings were all what is called
Berlin iron-work; but these delicate arabesques were
made in Vienna, and seemed to have been fashioned
by the fairies who, the stories tell us, are condemned
by a jealous Carabosse to collect the eyes of ants,
or weave a fabric so diaphanous that a nutshell can
contain it. Madame Rabourdin's graceful figure, made
more slender still by the black draperies, was shown
to advantage by a carefully cut dress, the two sides of
which met at the shoulders in a single strap without
sleeves. At every motion she seemed, like a butterfly, to
be about to leave her covering; but the gown held firmly

on by means of some contrivance of the wonderful dress-maker. The robe was of *mousseline de laine* — a material which the manufacturers had not yet sent to the Paris markets; a delightful stuff which some months later was to have a wild success, a success which went further and lasted longer than most French fashions. The actual economy of *mousseline de laine,* which needs no washing, has since injured the sale of cotton fabrics enough to revolutionize the Rouen manufactories. Célestine's little feet, covered with fine silk stockings and turk-satin shoes (for silk-satin is inadmissible in deep mourning) were of elegant proportions. Thus dressed, she was very handsome. Her complexion, beautified by a bran-bath, was softly radiant. Her eyes, suffused with the light of hope, and sparkling with intelligence, justified her claims to the superiority which des Lupeaulx, proud and happy on this occasion, asserted for her.

She entered the room well (women will understand the meaning of that expression), bowed gracefully to the minister's wife, with a happy mixture of deference and of self-respect, and gave no offence by a certain reliance on her own dignity; for every beautiful woman has the right to seem a queen. With the minister himself she took the pretty air of sauciness which women may properly allow themselves with men, even when they are grand dukes. She reconnoitred the field, as it were, while taking her seat, and saw that she was in the midst of one of those select parties of few persons, where the women eye and appraise each other, and every word said echoes in all ears; where every glance is a stab, and conversation a duel with witnesses; where all that is commonplace seems commoner still, and where every form of merit or distinction is silently accepted as though it were the natural level of all present. Rabourdin betook himself to the adjoining salon in which a few persons were playing cards; and there he planted himself on exhibition, as it were, which proved that he was not without social intelligence.

"My dear," said the Marquise d'Espard to the Comtesse Féraud, Louis XVIII.'s last mistress, "Paris is certainly unique. It produces — whence and how, who knows? — women like this person, who seems ready to will and to do anything."

"She really does will, and does do everything," put in des Lupeaulx, puffed up with satisfaction.

At this moment the wily Madame Rabourdin was courting the minister's wife. Carefully coached the evening before by des Lupeaulx, who knew all the countess's weak spots, she was flattering her without seeming to do so. Every now and then she kept silence; for des Lupeaulx, in love as he was, knew her defects, and said to her the night before, "Be careful not to talk too much," — words which were really an immense proof of attachment. Bertrand Barrère left behind him this sublime axiom: "Never interrupt a woman when dancing to give her advice," to which we may add (to make this chapter of the female code complete), "Never blame a woman for scattering her pearls."

The conversation became general. From time to time Madame Rabourdin joined in, just as a well-trained cat puts a velvet paw on her mistress's laces with the claws carefully drawn in. The minister, in matters of the heart, had few emotions. There was not another statesman under the Restoration who had so completely done with gallantry as he; even the opposition papers, the "Miroir," "Pandora," and "Figaro," could not find a single throbbing artery with which to reproach him. Madame Rabourdin knew this, but she knew also that ghosts return to old castles, and she had taken it into her head to make the minister jealous of the happiness which des Lupeaulx was appearing to enjoy. The latter's throat literally gurgled with the name of his divinity. To launch his supposed mistress successfully, he was endeavoring to persuade the Marquise d'Espard, Madame de Nucingen, and the countess, in an eight-ear conversation, that they had better admit Madame Rabourdin to their coalition; and Madame de Camps was supporting him.

At the end of an hour the minister's vanity was greatly tickled ; Madame Rabourdin's cleverness pleased him, and she had won his wife, who, delighted with the siren, invited her to come to all her receptions whenever she pleased.

" For your husband, my dear," she said, " will soon be director ; the minister intends to unite the two divisions and place them under one director ; you will then be one of us, you know."

His Excellency carried off Madame Rabourdin on his arm to show her a certain room, which was then quite celebrated because the opposition journals blamed him for decorating it extravagantly ; and together they laughed over the absurdities of journalism.

" Madame, you really must give the countess and myself the pleasure of seeing you here often."

And he went on with a round of ministerial compliments.

" But, Monseigneur," she replied, with one of those glances which women hold in reserve, " it seems to me that that depends on you."

" How so? "

" You alone can give me the right to come here."

" Pray explain."

" No ; I said to myself before I came that I would certainly not have the bad taste to seem a petitioner."

" No, no, speak freely. Places asked in this way

are never out of place," said the minister, laughing; for there is no jest too silly to amuse a solemn man.

"Well, then, I must tell you plainly that the wife of the head of a bureau is out of place here; a director's wife is not."

"That point need not be considered," said the minister, "your husband is indispensable to the administration; he is already appointed."

"Is that a veritable fact?"

"Would you like to see the papers in my study? They are drawn up."

"Then," she said, pausing in a corner where she was alone with the minister, whose eager attentions were now very marked, "let me tell you that I can make you a return."

She was on the point of revealing her husband's plan, when des Lupeaulx, who had glided noiselessly up to them, uttered an angry sound, which meant that he did not wish to appear to have overheard what, in fact, he had been listening to. The minister gave an ill-tempered look at the old beau, who, impatient to win his reward, had hurried, beyond all precedent, the preliminary work of the appointment. He had carried the papers to his Excellency that evening, and desired to take himself, on the morrow, the news of the appointment to her whom he was now endeavoring to exhibit as his mistress. Just then the minister's valet approached des Lupeaulx in a mysterious manner, and told him that his own servant wished him to deliver to him at once a letter of the utmost importance.

The general-secretary went up to a lamp and read a note thus worded: —

Contrary to my custom, I am waiting in your ante-chamber to see you; you have not a moment to lose if you wish to come to terms with

Your obedient servant,

GOBSECK.

The secretary shuddered when he saw the signature, which we regret we cannot give in fac-simile, for it would be valuable to those who like to guess character from what may be called the physiognomy of signature. If ever a hieroglyphic sign expressed an animal, it was assuredly this written name, in which the first and the final letter approached each other like the voracious jaws of a shark, — insatiable, always open, seeking whom to devour, both strong and weak. As for the wording of the note, the spirit of usury alone could have inspired a sentence so imperative, so insolently curt and cruel, which said all and revealed nothing. Those who had never heard of Gobseck would have felt, on reading words which compelled him to whom they were addressed to obey, yet gave no order, the presence of the implacable money-lender of the rue des Grès. Like a dog called to heel by the huntsman,

des Lupeaulx left his present quest and went immediately to his own rooms, thinking of his hazardous position. Imagine a general to whom an aide-de-camp
rides up and says : "The enemy with thirty thousand
fresh troops is attacking on our right flank."

A very few words will serve to explain this sudden
arrival of Gigonnet and Gobseck on the field of battle,
— for des Lupeaulx found them both waiting. At eight
o'clock that evening, Martin Falleix, returning on the
wings of the wind, — thanks to three francs to the post-
boys and a courier in advance, — had brought back
with him the deeds of the property signed the night
before. Taken at once to the Café Thémis by Mitral,
these securities passed into the hands of the two usurers, who hastened (though on foot) to the ministry. It
was past eleven o'clock. Des Lupeaulx trembled when
he saw those sinister faces, emitting a simultaneous look
as direct as a pistol shot and as brilliant as the flash
itself.

"What is it, my masters?" he said.

The two extortioners continued cold and motionless.
Gigonnet silently pointed to the documents in his hand,
and then at the servant.

"Come into my study," said des Lupeaulx, dismiss-
ing his valet by a sign.

"You understand French very well," remarked
Gigonnet, approvingly.

"Have you come here to torment a man who enabled each of you to make a couple of hundred thousand francs?"

"And who will help us to make more, I hope," said Gigonnet.

"Some new affair?" asked des Lupeaulx. "If you want me to help you, consider that I recollect the past."

"So do we," answered Gigonnet.

"My debts must be paid," said des Lupeaulx, disdainfully, so as not to seem worsted at the outset.

"True," said Gobseck.

"Let us come to the point, my son," said Gigonnet. "Don't stiffen your chin in your cravat; with us all that is useless. Take these deeds and read them."

The two usurers took a mental inventory of des Lupeaulx's study while he read with amazement and stupefaction a deed of purchase which seemed wafted to him from the clouds by angels.

"Don't you think you have a pair of intelligent business agents in Gobseck and me?" asked Gigonnet.

"But tell me, to what do I owe such able co-operation? said des Lupeaulx, suspicious and uneasy.

"We knew eight days ago a fact that without us you would not have known till to-morrow morning. The president of the chamber of commerce, a deputy, as you know, feels himself obliged to resign."

Des Lupeaulx's eyes dilated, and were as big as daisies.

"Your minister has been tricking you about this event," said the concise Gobseck.

"You master me," said the general-secretary, bowing with an air of profound respect, bordering however, on sarcasm.

"True," said Gobseck.

"Can you mean to strangle me?"

"Possibly."

"Well, then, begin your work, executioners," said the secretary, smiling.

"You will see," resumed Gigonnet, "that the sum total of your debts is added to the sum loaned by us for the purchase of the property; we have bought them up."

"Here are the deeds," said Gobseck, taking from the pocket of his greenish overcoat a number of legal papers.

"You have three years in which to pay off the whole sum," said Gigonnet.

"But," said des Lupeaulx, frightened at such kindness, and also by so apparently fantastic an arrangement. "What do you want of me?"

"La Billardière's place for Baudoyer," said Gigonnet, quickly.

"That's a small matter, though it will be next to

impossible for me to do it," said des Lupeaulx. "I have just tied my hands."

" Bite the cords with your teeth," said Gigonnet.

" They are sharp," added Gobseck.

" Is that all?" asked des Lupeaulx.

" We keep the title-deeds of the property till the debts are paid," said Gigonnet, putting one of the papers before des Lupeaulx; " and if the matter of the appointment is not satisfactorily arranged within six days our names will be substituted in place of yours."

" You are deep," cried the secretary.

" Exactly," said Gobseck.

" And this is all?" exclaimed des Lupeaulx.

" All," said Gobseck.

" You agree?" asked Gigonnet.

Des Lupeaulx nodded his head.

" Well, then, sign this power of attorney. Within two days Baudoyer is to be nominated; within six your debts will be cleared off, and —"

" And what?" asked des Lupeaulx.

" We guarantee —"

" Guarantee! — what?" said the secretary, more and more astonished.

" Your election to the Chamber," said Gigonnet, rising on his heels. " We have secured a majority of fifty-two farmers' and mechanics' votes, which will be thrown precisely as those who lend you this money dictate."

Des Lupeaulx wrung Gigonnet's hand.

"It is only such as we who never misunderstand each other," he said; "this is what I call doing business. I'll make you a return gift."

"Right," said Gobseck.

"What is it?" asked Gigonnet.

"The cross of the Legion of honor for your imbecile of a nephew."

"Good," said Gigonnet, "I see you know him well."

The pair took leave of des Lupeaulx, who conducted them to the staircase.

"They must be secret envoys from foreign powers," whispered the footmen to each other.

Once in the street, the two usurers looked at each other under a street lamp and laughed.

"He will owe us nine thousand francs interest a year," said Gigonnet; "that property does n't bring him in five."

"He is under our thumb for a long time," said Gobseck.

"He'll build; he'll commit extravagancies," continued Gigonnet; "Falleix will get his land."

"His interest is only to be made deputy; the old fox laughs at the rest," said Gobseck.

"Hey! hey!"

"Hi! hi!"

These dry little exclamations served as a laugh to the two old men, who took their way back (always on foot) to the Café Thémis.

Des Lupeaulx returned to the salon and found Madame Rabourdin sailing with the wind of success, and very charming; while his Excellency, usually so gloomy, showed a smooth and gracious countenance.

"She performs miracles," thought des Lupeaulx. "What a wonderfully clever woman! I must get to the bottom of her heart."

"Your little lady is decidedly handsome," said the Marquise to the secretary; " now if she only had your name."

"Yes, her defect is that she is the daughter of an auctioneer. She will fail for want of birth," replied des Lupeaulx, with a cold manner that contrasted strangely with the ardor of his remarks about Madame Rabourdin not half an hour earlier.

The marquise looked at him fixedly.

"The glance you gave them did not escape me," she said, motioning towards the minister and Madame Rabourdin; " it pierced the mask of your spectacles. How amusing you both are, to quarrel over that bone!"

As the marquise turned to leave the room the minister joined her and escorted her to the door.

"Well," said des Lupeaulx to Madame Rabourdin, "what do you think of his Excellency?"

"He is charming. We must know these poor ministers to appreciate them," she added, slightly raising her voice so as to be heard by his Excellency's wife. "The newspapers and the opposition calumnies are so misleading about men in politics that we are all more or less influenced by them; but such prejudices turn to the advantage of statesmen when we come to know them personally.

"He is very good-looking," said des Lupeaulx.

"Yes, and I assure you he is quite lovable," she said, heartily.

"Dear child," said des Lupeaulx, with a genial, caressing manner; "you have actually done the impossible."

"What is that?"

"Resuscitated the dead. I did not think that man had a heart; ask his wife. But he may have just enough for a passing fancy. Therefore profit by it. Come this way, and don't be surprised." He led Madame Rabourdin into the boudoir, placed her on a sofa, and sat down beside her. "You are very sly," he said, "and I like you the better for it. Between ourselves, you are a clever woman. Des Lupeaulx served to bring you into this house, and that is all you wanted of him, is n't it? Now when a woman decides

to love a man for what she can get out of him it is
better to take a sexagenarian Excellency than a quad-
ragenarian secretary; there's more profit and less
annoyance. I'm a man with spectacles, grizzled hair,
worn out with dissipation, — a fine lover, truly! I tell
myself all this again and again. It must be admitted,
of course, that I can sometimes be useful, but never
agreeable. Is n't that so? A man must be a fool if he
cannot reason about himself. You can safely admit
the truth and let me see to the depths of your heart;
we are partners, not lovers. If I show some tenderness at times, you are too superior a woman to pay any
attention to such follies; you will forgive me, — you
are not a school-girl, or a bourgeoise of the rue Saint-
Denis. Bah! you and I are too well brought up for
that. There's the Marquise d'Espard who has just
left the room; this is precisely what she thinks and
does. She and I came to an understanding two years
ago [the coxscomb!], and now she has only to write
me a line and say, 'My dear des Lupeaulx, you will
oblige me by doing such or such a thing,' and it is done
at once. We are engaged at this very moment in getting a commission of lunacy on her husband. Ah! you
women, you can get what you want by the bestowal of
a few favors. Well, then, my dear child, bewitch the
minister. I'll help you; it is my interest to do so.
Yes, I wish he had a woman who could influence him;

he would n't escape me, — for he does escape me quite often, and the reason is that I hold him only through his intellect. Now if I were one with a pretty woman who was also intimate with him, I should hold him by his weaknesses, and that is much the firmest grip. Therefore, let us be friends, you and I, and share the advantages of the conquest you are making."

Madame Rabourdin listened in amazement to this singular profession of rascality. The apparent artlessness of this political swindler prevented her from suspecting a trick.

"Do you believe he really thinks of me?" she asked, falling into the trap.

"I know it; I am certain of it."

"Is it true that Rabourdin's appointment is signed?"

"I gave him the papers this morning. But it is not enough that your husband should be made director; he must be Master of petitions."

"Yes," she said.

"Well, then, go back to the salon and coquette a little more with his Excellency."

"It is true," she said, "that I never fully understood you till to-night. There is nothing commonplace about *you.*"

"We will be two old friends," said des Lupeaulx, "and suppress all tender nonsense and tormenting love; we will take things as they did under the

Regency. Ah! they had plenty of wit and wisdom in those days!"

"You are really strong; you deserve my admiration," she said, smiling, and holding out her hand to him, "one does more for one's friend, you know, than for one's — "

She left him without finishing her sentence.

"Dear creature!" thought des Lupeaulx, as he saw her approach the minister, "des Lupeaulx has no longer the slightest remorse in turning against you. To-morrow evening when you offer me a cup of tea, you will be offering me a thing I no longer care for. All is over. Ah! when a man is forty years of age women may take pains to catch him, but they won't love him."

He looked himself over in a mirror, admitting honestly that though he did very well as a politician he was a wreck on the shores of Cythera. At the same moment Madame Rabourdin was gathering herself together for a becoming exit. She wished to make a last graceful impression on the minds of all, and she succeeded. Contrary to the usual custom in society, every one cried out as soon as she was gone, "What a charming woman!" and the minister himself took her to the outer door.

"I am quite sure you will think of me to-morrow," he said, alluding to the appointment.

"There are so few high functionaries who have agreeable wives," remarked his Excellency on re-entering the room, "that I am very well satisfied with our new acquisition."

"Don't you think her a little overpowering?" said des Lupeaulx with a piqued air.

The women present all exchanged expressive glances; the rivalry between the minister and his secretary amused them and instigated one of those pretty little comedies which Parisian women play so well. They excited and led on his Excellency and des Lupeaulx by a series of comments on Madame Rabourdin: one thought her too studied in manner, too eager to appear clever; another compared the graces of the middle classes with the manners of high life, while des Lupeaulx defended his pretended mistress as we all defend an enemy in society.

"Do her justice, ladies," he said; "is it not extraordinary that the daughter of an auctioneer should appear as well as she does? See where she came from, and what she is. She will end in the Tuileries; that is what she intends, — she told me so."

"Suppose she is the daughter of an auctioneer," said the Comtesse Féraud, smiling, "that will not hinder her husband's rise to power."

"Not in these days, you mean," said the minister's wife, tightening her lips.

" Madame," said his Excellency to the countess, sternly, " such sentiments and such speeches lead to revolutions; unhappily, the court and the great world do not restrain them. You would hardly believe, however, how the injudicious conduct of the aristocracy in this respect displeases certain clear-sighted personages at the palace. If I were a great lord, instead of being, as I am, a mere country gentleman who seems to be placed where he is to transact your business for you, the monarchy would not be as insecure as I now think it. What becomes of a throne which does not bestow dignity on those who administer its government? We are far indeed from the days when a king could make men great at will, — such men as Louvois, Colbert, Richelieu, Jeannin, Villeroy, Sully, — Sully, in his origin, was no greater than I. I speak to you thus because we are here in private among ourselves. I should be very paltry indeed if I were personally offended by such speeches. After all, it is for us and not for others to make us great."

" You are appointed, dear," cried Célestine, pressing her husband's hand as they drove away. " If it had not been for des Lupeaulx I should have explained your scheme to his Excellency. But I will do it next Tuesday, and it will help the further matter of making you Master of petitions."

In the life of every woman there comes a day when she shines in all her glory ; a day which gives her an unfading recollection to which she recurs with happiness all her life.   As Madame Rabourdin took off one by one the ornaments of her apparel, she thought over the events of this evening, and marked the day among the triumphs and glories of her life, — all her beauties had been seen and envied, she had been praised and flattered by the minister's wife, delighted thus to make the other women jealous of her ; but, above. all, her grace and vanities had shone to the profit of conjugal love.   Her husband was appointed.

"Did you think I looked well to-night?" she said to him, joyously.

At the same instant Mitral, waiting at the Café Thémis, saw the two usurers returning, but was unable to perceive the slightest indications of the result on their impassible faces.

"What of it?" he said, when they were all seated at table.

"Same as ever," replied Gigonnet, rubbing his hands, "victory with gold."

"True," said Gobseck.

Mitral took a cabriolet and went straight to the Saillards and Baudoyers, who were still playing boston at a late hour.   No one was present but the Abbé

Gaudron. Falleix, half-dead with the fatigue of his journey, had gone to bed.

" You will be appointed, nephew," said Mitral; " and there's a surprise in store for you."

" What is it? " asked Saillard.

" The cross of the Legion of honor?" cried Mitral.

"God protects those who guard his altars," said Gaudron.

Thus the Te Deum was sung with equal joy and confidence in both camps.

VIII.

FORWARD, MOLLUSKS!

THE next day, Wednesday, Monsieur Rabourdin was
to transact business with the minister, for he had filled
the late La Billardière's place since the beginning of the
latter's illness. On such days the clerks came punctually, the servants were specially attentive, there was
always a certain excitement in the offices on these sign-
ing-days, — and why, nobody ever knew. On this occasion the three servants were at their post, flattering
themselves they should get a few fees ; for a rumor of
Rabourdin's nomination had spread through the ministry the night before, thanks to Dutocq. Uncle Antoine
and Laurent had donned their full uniform, when, at a
quarter to eight, des Lupeaulx's servant came in with a
letter, which he begged Antoine to give secretly to Dutocq, saying that the general-secretary had ordered him
to deliver it without fail at Monsieur Dutocq's house by
seven o'clock.

"I'm sure I don't know how it happened," he said,
"but I overslept myself. I've only just waked up, and
he'd play the devil's tattoo on me if he knew the letter

hadn't gone. I know a famous secret, Antoine; but don't say anything about it to the clerks if I tell you; promise? He would send me off if he knew I had said a single word; he told me so."

"What's inside the letter?" asked Antoine, eying it.

"Nothing; I looked this way — see."

He made the letter gape open, and showed Antoine that there was nothing but blank paper to be seen.

"This is going to be a great day for you, Laurent," went on the secretary's man. "You are to have a new director. Economy must be the order of the day, for they are going to unite the two divisions under one director — you fellows will have to look out!"

"Yes, nine clerks are put on the retired list," said Dutocq, who came in at the moment; "how did you hear that?"

Antoine gave him the letter, and he had no sooner opened it than he rushed headlong downstairs in the direction of the secretary's office.

The bureaus Rabourdin and Baudoyer, after idling and gossiping since the death of Monsieur de la Billardière, were now recovering their usual official look and the *dolce far niente* habits of a government office. Nevertheless, the approaching end of the year did cause rather more application among the clerks, just as porters and servants become at that season more unctuously civil. They all came punctually, for one thing; more remained after four o'clock than was usual at other times. It was not forgotten that fees and gratuities depend on the last impressions made upon the minds of masters. The news of the union of the two divisions, that of La Billardière and that of Clergeot, under one director, had spread through the various offices. The number of the clerks to be retired was known, but all were in ignorance of the names. It was taken for granted that Poiret would not be replaced, and that would be a retrenchment. Little La Billardière had already departed. Two new supernumeraries had made their appearance, and, alarming circumstance! they were both sons of deputies. The news told about in the offices the night before, just as the clerks were dispersing, agitated all minds, and for the first half-hour after arrival in the morning they stood around the stoves and talked it over. But earlier than that, Dutocq, as we have seen, had rushed to des Lupeaulx on receiving his note, and found him dressing. Without laying down his razor, the general-secretary cast upon his subordinate the glance of a general issuing an order.

"Are we alone?" he asked.

"Yes, monsieur."

"Very good. March on Rabourdin; forward! steady! Of course you kept a copy of that paper?"

"Yes."

"You understand me? *Inde iræ!* There must be

a general hue and cry raised against him. Find some way to start a clamor—"

"I could get a man to make a caricature, but I have n't five hundred francs to pay for it."

" Who would make it?"

" Bixiou."

" He shall have a thousand and be under-head-clerk to Colleville, who will arrange with him; tell him so."

" But he would n't believe it on nothing more than my word."

" Are you trying to make me compromise myself? Either do the thing or let it alone; do you hear me? "

" If Monsieur Baudoyer were director—"

" Well, he will be. Go now, and make haste; you have no time to lose. Go down the back-stairs; I don't want people to know you have just seen me."

While Dutocq was returning to the clerks' office and asking himself how he could best incite a clamor against his chief without compromising himself, Bixiou rushed to the Rabourdin office for a word of greeting. Believing that he had lost his bet the incorrigible joker thought it amusing to pretend that he had won it.

Bixiou [mimicking Phellion's voice]. Gentlemen, I salute you with a collective how d' ye do, and I appoint Sunday next for the dinner at the Rocher de Cancale. But a serious question presents itself. Is that dinner to include the clerks who are dismissed?

POIRET. And those who retire?

BIXIOU. Not that I care, for it is n't I who pay. [General stupefaction.] Baudoyer is appointed. I think I already hear him calling Laurent [mimicking Baudoyer], "Laurent! lock up my hair-shirt, and my scourge." [They all roar with laughter.] Yes, yes, he laughs well who laughs last. Gentlemen, there's a great deal in that anagram of Colleville's. *Xavier Rabourdin, chef de bureau — D'abord rêva bureaux, e-u fin riche.* If I were named *Charles X., par la grâce de Dieu roi de France et de Navarre,* I should tremble in my shoes at the fate those letters anagrammatize.

THUILLIER. Look here! are you making fun?

BIXIOU. No, I am not. Rabourdin resigns in a rage at finding Baudoyer appointed director.

VIMEUX [entering]. Nonsense, no such thing! Antoine (to whom I have just been paying forty francs that I owed him) tells me that Monsieur and Madame Rabourdin were at the minister's private party last night and stayed till midnight. His Excellency escorted Madame Rabourdin to the staircase. It seems she was divinely dressed. In short, it is quite certain that Rabourdin is to be director. Riffé, the secretary's copying clerk, told me he sat up all the night before to draw the papers; it is no longer a secret. Monsieur Clergeot is retired. After thirty years' service that's no misfortune. Monsieur Cochin, who is rich —

BIXIOU.   By cochineal.

VIMEUX.   Yes, cochineal; he's a partner in the house of Matifat, rue des Lombards.   Well, he is retired; so is Poiret.   Neither is to be replaced.   So much is certain; the rest is all conjecture.   The appointment of Monsieur Rabourdin is to be announced this morning; they are afraid of intrigues.

BIXIOU.   What intrigues?

FLEURY.   Baudoyer's, confound him! 'The priests uphold him; here's another article in the liberal journal, — only half a dozen lines, but they are queer [reads]:

"Certain persons spoke last night in the lobby of the Opera-house of the return of Monsieur de Chateaubriand to the ministry, basing their opinion on the choice made of Monsieur Rabourdin (the protegé of the friends of the noble viscount) to fill the office for which Monsieur Baudoyer was first selected. The clerical party is not likely to withdraw unless in deference to the great writer."

Blackguards!

DUTOCQ [entering, having heard the whole discussion]. Blackguards! Who? Rabourdin? Then you know the news?

FLEURY [rolling his eyes savagely].   Rabourdin a blackguard! Are you mad, Dutocq? do you want a ball in your brains to give them weight?

DUTOCQ.   I said nothing against Monsieur Rabourdin; only it has just been told to me in confidence that he has written a paper denouncing all the clerks and officials, and full of facts about their lives; in short, the reason why his friends support him is because he has written this paper against the administration, in which we are all exposed —

PHELLION [in a loud voice]. Monsieur Rabourdin is incapable of —

BIXIOU. Very proper in you to say so. Tell me, Dutocq [they whisper together and then go into the corridor].

BIXIOU. What has happened?

DUTOCQ. Do you remember what I said to you about that caricature?

BIXIOU. Yes, what then?

DUTOCQ. Make it, and you shall be under-head-clerk with a famous fee. The fact is, my dear fellow, there's dissension among the powers that be. The minister is pledged to Rabourdin, but if he does n't appoint Baudoyer he offends the priests and their party. You see, the King, the Dauphin and the Dauphine, the clergy, and lastly the court, all want Baudoyer; the minister wants Rabourdin.

BIXIOU. Good!

DUTOCQ. To ease the matter off, the minister, who sees he must give way, wants to strangle the difficulty. We must find some good reason for getting rid of Rabourdin. Now somebody has lately unearthed a paper of his, exposing the present system of administration and wanting to reform it ; and that paper is going the rounds, — at least, this is how I understand the matter. Make the drawing we talked of ; in so doing you 'll play the game of all the big people, and help the minister, the court, the clergy, — in short, everybody ; and you 'll get your appointment. Now do you understand me?

BIXIOU. I don't understand how you came to know all that ; perhaps you are inventing it.

DUTOCQ. Do you want me to let you see what Rabourdin wrote about you?

BIXIOU. Yes.

DUTOCQ. Then come home with me ; for I must put the document into safe keeping.

BIXIOU. You go first alone. [Re-enters the bureau Rabourdin.] What Dutocq told you is really all true, word of honor ! It seems that Monsieur Rabourdin has written and sent in very unflattering descriptions of the clerks whom he wants to " reform." That 's the real reason why his secret friends wish him appointed. Well, well ; we live in days when nothing astonishes me [flings his cloak about him like Talma, and declaims] : —

> " Thou who hast seen the fall of grand, illustrious heads,
>   Why thus amazed, insensate that thou art,"

to find a man like Rabourdin employing such means?

Baudoyer is too much of a fool to know how to use them. Accept my congratulations, gentlemen; either way you are under a most illustrious chief [goes off].

POIRET. I shall leave this ministry without ever comprehending a single word that gentleman utters. What does he mean with his " heads that fall"?

FLEURY. "Heads that fell?" why, think of the four sergeants of Rochelle, Ney, Berton, Caron, the brothers Faucher, and the massacres.

PHELLION. He asserts very flippantly things that he only guesses at.

FLEURY. Say at once that he lies; in his mouth truth itself turns to corrosion.

PHELLION. Your language is unparliamentary and lacks the courtesy and consideration which are due to a colleague.

VIMEUX. It seems to me that if what he says is false, the proper name for it is calumny, defamation of character; and such a slanderer deserves a thrashing.

FLEURY [getting hot]. If the government offices are public places, the matter ought to be taken into the police-courts.

PHELLION [wishing to avert a quarrel, tries to turn the conversation]. Gentlemen, might I ask you to keep quiet? I am writing a little treatise on moral philosophy, and I am just at the heart of it.

FLEURY [interrupting]. What are you saying about it, Monsieur Phellion?

PHELLION [reading]. " *Question.* — What is the soul of man?

" *Answer.* — A spiritual substance which thinks and reasons."

THUILLIER. Spiritual substance! you might as well talk about immaterial stone.

POIRET. Don't interrupt; let him go on.

PHELLION [continuing]. " *Quest.* — Whence comes the soul?

" *Ans.* — From God, who created it of a nature one and indivisible; the destructibility thereof is, consequently, not conceivable, and he hath said — "

POIRET [amazed]. God said?

PHELLION. Yes, monsieur; tradition authorizes the statement.

FLEURY [to Poiret]. Come, don't interrupt, yourself.

PHELLION [resuming]. " — and he hath said that he created it immortal; in other words, the soul can never die.

" *Quest.* — What are the uses of the soul?

" *Ans.* — To comprehend, to will, to remember; these constitute understanding, volition, memory.

" *Quest.* — What are the uses of the understanding?

" *Ans.* — To know. It is the eye of the soul."

FLEURY. And the soul is the eye of what?

PHELLION [continuing]. "*Quest.* — What ought the understanding to know?

" *Ans.* — Truth.

"*Quest.* — Why does man possess volition?

" *Ans.* — To love good and hate evil.

"*Quest.* — What is good?

" *Ans.* — That which makes us happy."

VIMEUX. Heavens! do you teach that to young ladies?

PHELLION. Yes [continuing]. " *Quest.* — How many kinds of good are there?"

FLEURY. Amazingly indecorous, to say the least.

PHELLION [aggrieved]. Oh, monsieur! [Controlling himself.] But here's the answer, — that's as far as I have got [reads] : —

" *Ans.* — There are two kinds of good, — eternal good and temporal good."

POIRET [with a look of contempt]. And does that sell for anything?

PHELLION. I hope it will. It requires great application of mind to carry on a system of questions and answers ; that is why I ask you to be quiet and let me think, for the answers —

THUILLIER [interrupting]. The answers might be sold separately.

POIRET. Is that a pun?

THUILLIER. No ; a riddle.

PHELLION. I am sorry I interrupted you [he dives into his office desk]. But [to himself] at any rate, I have stopped their talking about Monsieur Rabourdin.

At this moment a scene was taking place between the minister and des Lupeaulx which decided Rabourdin's fate. The general-secretary had gone to see the minister in his private study before the breakfast-hour, to make sure that La Brière was not within hearing.

" Your Excellency is not treating me frankly — "

" He means a quarrel," thought the minister; " and all because his mistress coquetted with me last night. I did not think you so juvenile, my dear friend," he said aloud.

" Friend?" said the general-secretary, " that is what I want to find out."

The minister looked haughtily at des Lupeaulx.

" We are alone," continued the secretary, " and we can come to an understanding. The deputy of the arrondissement in which my estate is situated — "

"So it is really an estate!" said the minister, laughing, to hide his surprise.

"Increased by a recent purchase of two hundred thousand francs' worth of adjacent property," replied des Lupeaulx, carelessly. " You knew of the deputy's approaching resignation at least ten days ago, and you did not tell me of it. You were perhaps not bound to do so, but you knew very well that I am most anxious to take my seat in the Centre.   Has it occurred to you that I might fling myself back on the ' Doctrine' ?— which, let me tell you, will destroy the administration and the monarchy both if you continue to allow the party of representative government to be recruited from men of talent whom you ignore. Don't you know that in every nation there are fifty to sixty, not more, dangerous heads, whose schemes are in proportion to their ambition? The secret of knowing how to govern is to know those heads well, and either to chop them off or buy them. I don't know how much talent I have, but I know that I have ambition; and you are committing a serious blunder when you set aside a man who wishes you well. The anointed head dazzles for the time being, but what next?— Why, a war of words; discussions will spring up once more and grow embittered, envenomed. Then, for your own sake, I advise you not to find me at the Left Centre.   In spite of your prefect's manœuvres (instructions for which no doubt went from here confidentially) I am secure of a majority. The time has come for you and me to understand each other. After a breeze like this people sometimes become closer friends than ever. I must be made count and receive the grand cordon of the Legion of honor as a reward for my public services.   However, I care less for those things just now than I do for something else in which you are more personally concerned. You have not yet appointed Rabourdin, and I have news this morning which tends to show that most persons will be better satisfied if you appoint Baudoyer."

"Appoint Baudoyer!" echoed the minister. "Do you know him?"

"Yes," said des Lupeaulx; "but suppose he proves incapable, as he will, you can then get rid of him by asking those who protect him to employ him elsewhere. You will thus get back an important office to give to friends; it may come in at the right moment to facilitate some compromise."

"But I have pledged it to Rabourdin."

"That may be; and I don't ask you to make the change this very day. I know the danger of saying yes and no within twenty-four hours. But postpone the appointment, and don't sign the papers till the day after to-morrow; by that time you may find it impossible to retain Rabourdin, — in fact, in all probability, he will send you his resignation — "

"His resignation?"

"Yes."

"Why?"

"He is the tool of a secret power in whose interests he has carried on a system of espionage in all the ministries, and the thing has been discovered by mere accident. He has written a paper of some kind, giving short histories of all the officials. Everybody is talking of it; the clerks are furious. For heaven's sake, don't transact business with him to-day; let me find some means for you to avoid it. Ask an audience of the King; I am sure you will find great satisfaction there if you concede the point about Baudoyer; and you can obtain something as an equivalent. Your position will be better than ever if you are forced later to dismiss a fool whom the court party impose upon you."

"What has made you turn against Rabourdin?"

"Would you forgive Monsieur de Chateaubriand for writing an article against the ministry? Well, read that, and see how Rabourdin has treated me in his secret document," said des Lupeaulx, giving the paper to the minister. "He pretends to reorganize the government from beginning to end, — no doubt in the interests of some secret society of which, as yet, we know nothing. I shall continue to be his friend for the sake of watching him; by that means I may render the government such signal service that they will have to make me count; for the peerage is the only thing I really care for. I want you fully to understand that I am not seeking office or anything else that would cause me to stand in your way; I am simply aiming for the peerage, which will enable me to marry a banker's daughter with an income of a couple of hundred thousand francs. And so, allow me to render you a few signal services which will make the King feel that I have saved the throne. I

have long said that Liberalism would never offer us a
pitched battle. It has given up conspiracies, Carbona-
roism, and revolts with weapons; it is now sapping and
mining, and the day is coming when it will be able to
say, 'Out of that and let me in!' Do you think I
have been courting Rabourdin's wife for my own pleasure? No, but I got much information from her. So
now, let us agree on two things; first, the postponement
of the appointment; second, your *sincere* support of my
election. You shall find at the end of the session that
I have amply repaid you."

For all answer, the minister took the appointment
papers and placed them in des Lupeaulx's hand.

"I will go and tell Rabourdin," added des Lupeaulx,
"that you cannot transact business with him till
Saturday."

The minister replied with an assenting gesture. The
secretary despatched his man with a message to Rabourdin that the minister could not work with him until
Saturday, on which day the Chamber was occupied with
private bills, and his Excellency had more time at his
disposal.

Just at this moment Saillard, having brought the
monthly stipend, was slipping his little speech into the
ear of the minister's wife, who drew herself up and
answered with dignity that she did not meddle in political matters, and besides, she had heard that Monsieur

Rabourdin was already appointed. Saillard, terrified, rushed up to Baudoyer's office, where he found Dutocq, Godard, and Bixiou in a state of exasperation difficult to describe; for they were reading the terrible paper on the administration in which they were all discussed.

BIXIOU [with his finger on a paragraph]. Here *you* are, père Saillard. Listen [reads] : —

" *Saillard.* — The office of cashier to be suppressed in all the ministries; their accounts to be kept in future at the Treasury. Saillard is rich and does not need a pension."

Do you want to hear about your son-in-law? [Turns over the leaves.] Here he is [reads] : —

" *Baudoyer.* — Utterly incapable. To be thanked and dismissed. Rich; does not need a pension."

And here 's for Godard [reads] : —

" *Godard.* — Should be dismissed; pension one-third of his present salary."

In short, here we all are. Listen to what I am [reads]: " An artist who might be employed by the civil list, at the Opera, or the Menus-Plaisirs, or the Muséum. Great deal of capacity, little self-respect, no application, — a restless spirit." Ha! I 'll give you a touch of the artist, Monsieur Rabourdin!

SAILLARD. Suppress cashiers! Why, the man 's a monster?

Bixiou. Let us see what he says of our mysterious Desroys. [Turns over the pages; reads.]

" *Desroys.* — Dangerous; because he cannot be shaken in principles that are subversive of monarchial power. He is the son of a *Conventionel*, and he admires the Convention. He may become a very mischievous journalist."

Baudoyer. The police are not worse spies!

Godard. I shall go to the general-secretary and lay a complaint in form; we must all resign in a body if such a man as that is put over us.

Dutocq. Gentlemen, listen to me; let us be prudent. If you rise at once in a body, we may all be accused of rancor and revenge. No, let the thing work, let the rumor spread quietly. When the whole ministry is aroused your remonstrances will meet with general approval.

Bixiou. Dutocq believes in the principles of the grand air composed by the sublime Rossini for Basilio, — which goes to show, by the bye, that the great composer was also a great politician. I shall leave my card on Monsieur Rabourdin to-morrow morning, inscribed thus: " *Bixiou;* no self-respect, no application, restless mind."

Godard. A good idea, gentlemen. Let us all leave our cards to-morrow on Rabourdin inscribed in the same way.

Dutocq [leading Bixiou apart]. Come, you 'll agree to make that caricature now, won't you?

Bixiou. I see plainly, my dear fellow, that you knew all about this affair ten days ago [looks him in the eye]. Am I to be under-head-clerk?

Dutocq. On my word of honor, yes, and a thousand-franc fee beside, just as I told you. You don't know what a service you 'll be rendering to powerful personages.

Bixiou. You know them?

Dutocq. Yes.

Bixiou. Well, then I want to speak with them.

Dutocq [dryly]. You can make the caricature or not, and you can be under-head-clerk or not, — as you please.

Bixiou. At any rate, let me see that thousand francs.

Dutocq. You shall have them when you bring the drawing.

Bixiou. Forward, march! that lampoon shall go from end to end of the bureaus to-morrow morning. Let us go and torment the Rabourdins. [Then speaking to Saillard, Godard, and Baudoyer, who were talking together in a low voice.] We are going to stir up the neighbors. [Goes with Dutocq into the Rabourdin bureau. Fleury, Thuillier, and Vimeux are there, talking excitedly.] What's the matter, gentlemen? All that I told you turns out to be true; you can go and see for yourselves the work of this infamous informer; for it is in the hands of the virtuous, honest, estimable, upright, and pious Baudoyer, who is indeed utterly incapable of doing any such thing. Your chief has got every one of you under the guillotine. Go and see; follow the crowd; money returned if you are not satisfied; execution GRATIS! The appointments are postponed. All the bureaus are in arms; Rabourdin has been informed that the minister will not work with him. Come, be off; go and see for yourselves.

They all depart except Phellion and Poiret, who are left alone. The former loved Rabourdin too well to look for proof that might injure a man he was determined not to judge; the other had only five days more to remain in the office, and cared nothing either way. Just then Sébastien came down to collect the papers for signature. He was a good deal surprised, though he did not show it, to find the office deserted.

PHELLION. My young friend [he rose, a rare thing], do you know what is going on? what scandals are rife about Monsieur Rabourdin whom you love, and [bending to whisper in Sébastien's ear] whom I love as much as I respect him. They say he has committed the imprudence to leave a paper containing comments on the officials lying about in the office— [Phellion stopped short, caught the young man in his strong arms, seeing that he turned pale and was near fainting, and placed him on a chair.] "A key, Monsieur Poiret, to put down his back; have you a key?"

Poiret. I have the key of my domicile.

[Old Poiret junior promptly inserted the said key between Sébastien's shoulders, while Phellion gave him some water to drink. The poor lad no sooner opened his eyes than he began to weep. He laid his head on Phellion's desk, and all his limbs were as limp as if struck by lightning; while his sobs were so heartrending, so genuine, that for the first time in his life Poiret's feelings were stirred by the sufferings of another.]

Phellion [speaking firmly]. ·Come, come, my young friend; courage! In times of trial we must show courage. You are a man. What is the matter? What has happened to distress you so terribly?

Sébastien [sobbing]. It is I who have ruined Monsieur Rabourdin. I left that paper lying about when I copied it. I have killed my benefactor; I shall die myself. Such a noble man!—a man who ought to be minister!

Poiret [blowing his nose]. Then it is true he wrote the report.

Sébastien [still sobbing]. But it was to — there, I was going to tell his secrets! Ah! that wretch of a Dutocq; it was he who stole the paper.

His tears and sobs recommenced and made so much

noise that Rabourdin came up to see what was the matter. He found the young fellow almost fainting in the arms of Poiret and Phellion.

RABOURDIN. What is the matter, gentlemen?

SÉBASTIEN [struggling to his feet and then falling on his knees before Rabourdin]. I have ruined you, monsieur. That memorandum, — Dutocq, the monster, he must have taken it.

RABOURDIN [calmly]. I knew that already [he lifts Sébastien]. You are a child, my young friend. [Speaks to Phellion.] Where are the other gentlemen?

PHELLION. Monsieur, they have gone into Monsieur Baudoyer's office to see a paper which it is said —

RABOURDIN [interrupting him]. Enough. [Goes out, taking Sébastien with him. Poiret and Phellion look at each other in amazement, and do not know what to say.]

POIRET [to Phellion]. Monsieur Rabourdin! —

PHELLION [to Poiret]. Monsieur Rabourdin! —

POIRET. Well, I never! Monsieur Rabourdin!

PHELLION. But did you notice how calm and dignified he was?

POIRET [with a sly look that was more like a grimace]. I should n't be surprised if there were something under it all.

PHELLION. A man of honor; pure and spotless.

POIRET. Who is?

PHELLION. Monsieur Poiret, you think as I think about Dutocq; surely you understand me?

POIRET [nodding his head three times and answering with a shrewd look]. Yes. [The other clerks return.]

FLEURY. A great shock; I still don't believe the thing. Monsieur Rabourdin, a king among men! If such men are spies, it is enough to disgust one with virtue. I have always put Rabourdin among Plutarch's heroes.

VIMEUX. It is all true.

POIRET [reflecting that he had only five days more to stay in the office]. But gentlemen, what do you say about the man who stole that paper, who spied upon Rabourdin? [Dutocq left the room.]

FLEURY. I say he is a Judas Iscariot. Who is he?

PHELLION [significantly]. He is not here at *this moment.*

VIMEUX [enlightened]. It is Dutocq!

PHELLION. I have no proof of it, gentlemen. While you were gone, that young man, Monsieur de la Roche, nearly fainted here. See his tears on my desk!

POIRET. We held him fainting in our arms. — My key, the key of my domicile! — dear, dear! it is down his back. [Poiret goes hastily out.]

VIMEUX. The minister refused to transact business with Rabourdin to-day; and Monsieur Saillard, to whom the secretary said a few words, came to tell

Monsieur Baudoyer to apply for the cross of the Legion of honor, — there is one to be granted, you know, on New-year's day, to all the heads of divisions. It is quite clear what it all means. Monsieur Rabourdin is sacrificed by the very persons who employed him. Bixiou says so. We were all to be turned out, except Sébastien and Phellion.

Du Bruel [entering]. Well, gentlemen, is it true?

Thuillier. To the last word.

Du Bruel [putting his hat on again]. Good-bye. [Hurries out.]

Thuillier. He may rush as much as he pleases to his Duc de Rhétoré and Duc de Maufrigneuse, but Colleville is to be our under-head-clerk, that's certain.

Phellion. Du Bruel always seemed to be attached to Monsieur Rabourdin.

Poiret [returning]. I have had a world of trouble to get back my key. That boy is crying still, and Monsieur Rabourdin has disappeared. [Dutocq and Bixiou enter.]

Bixiou. Ha, gentlemen! strange things are going on in your bureau. Du Bruel! I want you. [Looks into the adjoining room.] Gone?

Thuillier. Full speed.

Bixiou. What about Rabourdin?

Fleury. Distilled, evaporated, melted! Such a man, the king of men, that he —

Poiret [to Dutocq]. That little Sébastien, in his trouble, said that you, Monsieur Dutocq, had taken the paper from him ten days ago.

Bixiou [looking at Dutocq]. You must clear yourself of *that*, my good friend. [All the clerks look fixedly at Dutocq.]

Dutocq. Where's the little viper who copied it?

Bixiou. Copied it? How did you know he copied it? Ha! ha! it is only the diamond that cuts the diamond. [Dutocq leaves the room.]

Poiret. Would you listen to me, Monsieur Bixiou? I have only five days and a half to stay in this office, and I do wish that once, only once, I might have the pleasure of understanding what you mean. Do me the honor to explain what diamonds have to do with these present circumstances.

Bixiou. I meant, papa, — for I'm willing for once to bring my intellect down to the level of yours, — that just as the diamond alone can cut the diamond, so it is only one inquisitive man who can defeat another inquisitive man.

Fleury. "Inquisitive man" stands for "spy."

Poiret. I don't understand.

Bixiou. Very well; try again some other time.

Monsieur Rabourdin, after taking Sébastien to his room, had gone straight to the minister; but the

minister was at the Chamber of Deputies. Rabourdin
went at once to the Chamber, where he wrote a note
to his Excellency, who was at that moment in the
tribune engaged in a hot discussion. Rabourdin waited,
not in the conference hall, but in the courtyard, where,
in spite of the cold, he resolved to remain and inter-
cept his Excellency as he got into his carriage. The
usher of the Chamber had told him that the minister
was in the thick of a controversy raised by the nineteen
members of the extreme Left, and that the session
was likely to be stormy. Rabourdin walked to and
fro in the courtyard of the palace for five mortal
hours, a prey to feverish agitation. At half-past six
o'clock the session broke up, and the members filed
out. The minister's *chasseur* came up to find the
coachman.

"Hi, Jean!" he called out to him; "Monseigneur
has gone with the minister of war; they are going to
see the King, and after that they dine together, and
we are to fetch him at ten o'clock. There 's a Council
this evening."

Rabourdin walked slowly home, in a state of despond-
ency not difficult to imagine. It was seven o'clock,
and he had barely time to dress.

"Well, you are appointed?" cried his wife, joyously,
as he entered the salon.

Rabourdin raised his head with a grievous motion of

distress and answered, " I fear I shall never again set foot in the ministry."

" What?" said his wife, quivering with sudden anxiety.

" My memorandum on the officials is known in all the offices; and I have not been able to see the minister."

Célestine's eyes were opened to a sudden vision in which the devil, with one of his infernal flashes, showed her the meaning of her last conversation with des Lupeaulx.

" If I had behaved like a low woman," she thought, " we should have had the place."

She looked at Rabourdin with grief in her heart. A sad silence fell between them, and dinner was eaten in the midst of gloomy meditations.

" And it is my Wednesday," she said at last.

" All is not lost, dear Célestine," said Rabourdin, laying a kiss on his wife's forehead; " perhaps to-morrow I shall be able to see the minister and explain every-thing. Sébastien sat up all last night to finish the writ-ing; the papers are copied and collated; I shall place them on the minister's desk and beg him to read them through. La Brière will help me. A man is never condemned without a hearing."

" I am curious to see if Monsieur des Lupeaulx will come here to-night."

" He? Of course he will come," said Rabourdin;

"there's something of the tiger in him; he likes to lick the blood of the wounds he has given."

"My poor husband," said his wife, taking his hand, "I don't see how it is that a man who could conceive so noble a reform did not also see that it ought not to be communicated to a single person. It is one of those ideas that a man should keep in his own mind, for he alone can apply them. A statesman must do in our political sphere as Napoleon did in his; he stooped, twisted, crawled. Yes, Bonaparte crawled! To be made commander-in-chief of the Army of Italy he married Barrère's mistress. You should have waited, got yourself elected deputy, followed the politics of a party, sometimes down in the depths, at other times on the crest of the wave, and you should have taken, like Monsieur de Villèle, the Italian motto ' *Col tempo*,' in other words, ' All things are given to him who knows how to wait.' That great orator worked for seven years to get into power; he began in 1814 by protesting against the Charter when he was the same age that you are now. Here's your fault; you have allowed yourself to be kept subordinate, when you were born to rule."

The entrance of the painter Schinner imposed silence on the wife and husband, but these words made the latter thoughtful.

"Dear friend," said the painter, grasping Rabourdin's hand, "the support of artists is a useless thing enough, but let me say under these circumstances that we are all faithful to you. I have just read the evening papers. Baudoyer is appointed director and receives the cross of the Legion of honor — "

" I have been longer in the department, I have served twenty-four years," said Rabourdin with a smile.

" I know Monsieur le Comte de Sérizy, the minister of State, pretty well, and if he can help you, I will go and see him," said Schinner.

The salon soon filled with persons who knew nothing of the government proceedings. Du Bruel did not appear. Madame Rabourdin was gayer and more graceful than ever, like the charger wounded in battle, that still finds strength to carry his master from the field.

" She is very courageous," said a few women who knew the truth, and who were charmingly attentive to her, understanding her misfortunes.

" But she certainly did a great deal to attract des Lupeaulx," said the Baronne du Châtelet to the Vicomtesse de Fontaine.

" Do you think " — began the vicomtesse.

" If so," interrupted Madame de Camps, in defence of her friend, " Monsieur Rabourdin would at least have had the cross."

About eleven o'clock des Lupeaulx appeared ; and we can only describe him by saying that his spectacles were sad and his eyes joyous ; the glasses, however, obscured the glances so successfully that only a physiognomist would have seen the diabolical expression which they wore. He went up to Rabourdin and pressed the hand which the latter could not avoid giving him.

Then he approached Madame Rabourdin.

" We have much to say to each other," he remarked as he seated himself beside the beautiful woman, who received him admirably.

" Ah !" he continued, giving her a side glance, " you are grand indeed ; I find you just what I expected, glorious under defeat. Do you know that it is a very rare thing to find a superior woman who answers to the expectations formed of her. So defeat does n't dishearten you? You are right; we shall triumph in the end," he whispered in her ear. " Your fate is always in your own hands, — so long, I mean, as your ally is a man who adores you. We will hold counsel together."

" But is Baudoyer appointed?" she asked.

" Yes," said the secretary.

" Does he get the cross?"

" Not yet; but he will have it later."

" Amazing !"

" Ah ! you don't understand political exigencies."

During this evening, which seemed interminable to Madame Rabourdin, another scene was occurring in the place Royale, — one of those comedies which are played in seven Parisian salons whenever there is a change of ministry. The Saillards' salon was crowded. Monsieur and Madame Transon arrived at eight o'clock; Madame Transon kissed Madame Baudoyer, *née* Saillard. Monsieur Bataille, captain of the National Guard, came with his wife and the curate of Saint Paul's.

"Monsieur Baudoyer," said Madame Transon, "I wish to be the first to congratulate you; they have done justice to your talents. You have indeed earned your promotion."

"Here you are, director," said Monsieur Transon, rubbing his hands, "and the appointment is very flattering to this neighborhood."

"And we can truly say it came to pass without any intriguing," said the worthy Saillard. "We are none of us political intriguers; *we* don't go to select parties at the ministry."

Uncle Mitral rubbed his nose and grinned as he glanced at his niece Elisabeth, the woman whose hand had pulled the wires, who was talking with Gigonnet. Falleix, honest fellow, did not know what to make of the stupid blindness of Saillard and Baudoyer Messieurs Dutocq, Bixiou, du Bruel, Godard, and Colleville (the latter appointed head of the bureau) entered.

"What a crew!" whispered Bixiou to du Bruel. "I could make a fine caricature of them in the shapes of fishes, — dorys, flounders, sharks, and snappers, all dancing a saraband!"

"Monsieur," said Colleville, "I come to offer you my congratulations ; or rather we congratulate ourselves in having such a man placed over us ; and we desire to assure you of the zeal with which we shall co-operate in your labors. Allow me to say that this event affords a signal proof of the truth of my axiom that a man's destiny lies in the letters of his name. I may say that I knew of this appointment and of your other honors before I heard of them; for I spent the night in anagrammatizing your name as follows [proudly] : *Isidore C. T. Baudoyer, — Director, decorated by us* (his Majesty the King, of course).

Baudoyer bowed and remarked piously that names were given in baptism.

Monsieur and Madame Baudoyer, senior, father and mother of the new director, were there to enjoy the glory of their son and daughter-in-law. Uncle Gigonnet-Bidault, who had dined at the house, had a restless, fidgety look in his eye which frightened Bixiou.

"There 's a queer one," said the latter to du Bruel, calling his attention to Gigonnet, "who would do in a vaudeville. I wonder if he could be bought. Such an old scarecrow is just the thing for a sign over the Two

Baboons. And what a coat! I did think there was nobody but Poiret who could show the like of that after ten years' public exposure to the inclemencies of Parisian weather."

" Baudoyer is magnificent," said du Bruel.

" Dazzling," answered Bixiou.

" Gentlemen," said Baudoyer, " let me present you to my own uncle, Monsieur Mitral, and to my great-uncle through my wife, Monsieur Bidault.

Gigonnet and Mitral gave a glance at the three clerks so penetrating, so glittering with gleams of gold, that the two scoffers were sobered at.once.

" Hein?" said Bixiou, when they were safely under the arcades in the place Royale; " did you examine those uncles? — two copies of Shylock. I 'll bet their money is lent in the market at a hundred per cent per week. They lend on pawn; and sell most that they lay hold of, coats, gold lace, cheese, men, women, and children; they are a conglomeration of Arabs, Jews, Genoese, Genevese, Greeks, Lombards, and Parisians, suckled by a wolf and born of a Turkish woman."

" I believe you," said Godard. " Uncle Mitral used to be a sheriff's officer."

" That settles it," said du Bruel.

" I 'm off to see the proof of my caricature," said Bixiou; " but I should like to study the state of things in Rabourdin's salon to-night. You are lucky to be able to go there, du Bruel."

" I ! " said the vaudevillist, " what should I do there? My face does n't lend itself to condolences. And it is very vulgar in these days to go and see people who are down."

IX.

THE RESIGNATION.

By midnight Madame Rabourdin's salon was deserted; only two or three guests remained with des Lupeaulx and the master and mistress of the house. When Schinner and Monsieur and Madame de Camps had likewise departed, des Lupeaulx rose with a mysterious air, stood with his back to the fireplace and looked alternately at the husband and wife.

"My friends," he said, "nothing is really lost, for the minister and I are faithful to you. Dutocq simply chose between two powers the one he thought strongest. He has served the court and the Grand Almoner; he has betrayed me. But that is in the order of things; a politician never complains of treachery. Nevertheless, Baudoyer will be dismissed as incapable in a few months; no doubt his protectors will find him a place, — in the prefecture of police, perhaps, — for the clergy will not desert him."

From this point des Lupeaulx went on with a long tirade about the Grand Almoner and the dangers the government ran in relying upon the church and upon the Jesuits. We need not, we think, point out to the intelligent reader that the court and the Grand Almoner, to whom the liberal journals attributed an enormous influence over the administration, had little really to do with Monsieur Baudoyer's appointment. Such petty intrigues die in the upper sphere of great self-interests. If a few words in favor of Baudoyer were obtained by the importunity of the curate of Saint-Paul's and the Abbé Gaudron, they would have been withdrawn immediately at a suggestion from the minister. The occult power of the Congregation of Jesus (admissible certainly as confronting the bold society of the " Doctrine," entitled " Help yourself and heaven will help you,") was formidable only through the imaginary force conferred on it by subordinate powers who perpetually threatened each other with its evils. The liberal scandal-mongers delighted in representing the Grand Almoner and the whole Jesuitical Chapter as political, administrative, civil, and military giants. Fear creates bugbears. At this crisis Baudoyer firmly believed in the said Chapter, little aware that the only Jesuits who had put him where he now was sat by his own fireside, and in the Café Thémis playing dominoes.

At certain epochs in history certain powers appear, to whom all evils are attributed, though at the same time their genius is denied; they form an efficient argument in the mouth of fools. Just as Monsieur de

Talleyrand was supposed to hail all events of whatever kind with a *bon mot*, so in these days of the Restoration the clerical party had the credit of doing and undoing everything. Unfortunately, it did and undid nothing. Its influence was not wielded by a Cardinal Richelieu or a Cardinal Mazarin; it was in the hands of a species of Cardinal de Fleury, who, timid for over five years, turned bold for one day, injudiciously bold. Later on, the "Doctrine" did more, with impunity, at Saint-Merri, than Charles X. pretended to do in July, 1830. If the section on the censorship so foolishly introduced into the new charter had been omitted, journalism also would have had its Saint-Merri. The younger Branch could have legally carried out Charles X.'s plan.

"Remain where you are, head of a bureau under Baudoyer," went on des Lupeaulx. "Have the nerve to do this; make yourself a true politician; put ideas and generous impulses aside; attend only to your functions; don't say a word to your new director; don't help him with a suggestion; and do nothing yourself without his order. In three months Baudoyer will be out of the ministry, either dismissed, or stranded on some other administrative shore. They may attach him to the king's household. Twice in my life I have been set aside as you are, and overwhelmed by an avalanche of folly; I have quietly waited and let it pass."

"Yes," said Rabourdin, "but you were not calumniated; your honor was not assailed, compromised — "

"Ha, ha, ha!" cried des Lupeaulx, interrupting him with a burst of Homeric laughter. "Why, that's the daily bread of every remarkable man in this glorious kingdom of France! And there are but two ways to meet such calumny, — either yield to it, pack up, and go plant cabbages in the country; or else rise above it, march on, fearless, and don't turn your head."

"For me, there is but one way of untying the noose which treachery and the work of spies have fastened round my throat," replied Rabourdin. "I must explain the matter at once to his Excellency, and if you are as sincerely attached to me as you say you are, you will put me face to face with him to-morrow."

"You mean that you wish to explain to him your plan for the reform of the service?"

Rabourdin bowed.

"Well, then, trust the papers with me, — your memoranda, all the documents. I promise you that he shall sit up all night and examine them."

"Let us go to him, then!" cried Rabourdin, eagerly; "six years' toil certainly deserves two or three hours attention from the king's minister, who will be forced to recognize, if he does not applaud, such perseverance."

Compelled by Rabourdin's tenacity to take a straightforward path, without ambush or angle where his treachery could hide itself, des Lupeaulx hesitated for a single instant, and looked at Madame Rabourdin, while he inwardly asked himself, "Which shall I permit to triumph, my hatred for him, or my fancy for her?"

"You have no confidence in my honor," he said, after a pause. "I see that you will always be to me the author of your *secret analysis*. Adieu, madame."

Madame Rabourdin bowed coldly. Célestine and Xavier returned at once to their own rooms without a word; both were overcome by their misfortune. The wife thought of the dreadful situation in which she stood toward her husband. The husband, resolving slowly not to remain at the ministry but to send in his resignation at once, was lost in a sea of reflections; the crisis for him meant a total change of life and the necessity of starting on a new career. All night he sat before his fire, taking no notice of Célestine, who came in several times on tiptoe, in her night-dress.

"I must go once more to the ministry, to bring away my papers, and show Baudoyer the routine of the business," he said to himself at last. "I had better write my resignation now."

He turned to his table and began to write, thinking over each clause of the letter, which was as follows: —

MONSEIGNEUR, — I have the honor to inclose to your Excellency my resignation. I venture to hope that you still remember hearing me say that I left my honor in your hands, and that everything, for me, depended on my being able to give you an immediate explanation.

This explanation I have vainly sought to give. To-day it would, perhaps, be useless; for a fragment of my work relating to the administration, stolen and misused, has gone the rounds of the offices and is misinterpreted by hatred; in consequence, I find myself compelled to resign, under the tacit condemnation of my superiors.

Your Excellency may have thought, on the morning when I first sought to speak with you, that my purpose was to ask for my promotion, when, in fact, I was thinking only of the glory and usefulness of your ministry and of the public good. It is all-important, I think, to correct that impression.

Then followed the usual epistolary formulas.

It was half-past seven in the morning when the man consummated the sacrifice of his ideas; he burned everything, the toil of years. Fatigued by the pressure of thought, overcome by mental suffering, he fell asleep with his head on the back of his armchair. He was wakened by a curious sensation, and found his hands covered with his wife's tears and saw her kneeling before him. Célestine had read the resignation. She could measure the depth of his fall. They were now to be reduced to live on four thousand francs a year; and that day she had counted up her debts, — they amounted to something like thirty-two thousand francs! The most ignoble of all wretchedness had come upon them. And that noble man who had trusted her was ignorant that she had abused the fortune he had confided to her care. She was sobbing at his feet, beautiful as the Magdalen.

"My cup is full," cried Xavier, in his terror. "I am dishonored at the ministry, and dishonored — "

The light of her pure honor flashed from Célestine's eyes; she sprang up like a startled horse and cast a fulminating glance at Rabourdin.

"I! *I!*" she said, on two sublime tones. "Am I a base wife? If I were, you would have been appointed. But," she added, mournfully, "it is easier to believe that than to believe what is the truth."

"Then what is it?" said Rabourdin.

"All in three words," she said; "I owe thirty thousand francs."

Rabourdin caught his wife to his heart with a gesture of almost frantic joy, and seated her on his knee.

"Take comfort, dear," he said, in a tone of voice so adorably kind that the bitterness of her grief was changed to something inexpressibly tender. "I too have made mistakes; I have worked uselessly for my country when I thought I was being useful to her. But now I mean to take another path. If I had sold groceries we should now be millionnaires. Well, let us be grocers. You are only twenty-eight, dear angel; in ten years you shall recover the luxury that you love, which we must needs renounce for a short time. I, too, dear heart, am not a base or common husband. We will sell our farm; its value has increased of late. That and the sale of our furniture will pay my debts."

My debts! Célestine embraced her husband a thousand times in the single kiss with which she thanked him for that generous word.

"We shall still have a hundred thousand francs to put into business. Before the month is out I shall find some favorable opening. If luck gave a Martin Falleix to a Saillard, why should we despair? Wait breakfast for me. I am going now to the ministry, but I shall come back with my neck free of the yoke."

Célestine clasped her husband in her arms with a force men do not possess, even in their passionate moments; for women are stronger through emotion than men through power. She wept and laughed and sobbed in turns.

When Rabourdin left the house at eight o'clock, the porter gave him the satirical cards suggested by Bixiou. Nevertheless, he went to the ministry, where he found Sébastien waiting near the door to entreat him not to enter any of the bureaus, because an infamous caricature of him was making the round of the offices.

"If you wish to soften the pain of my downfall," he said to the lad, "bring me that drawing; I am now taking my resignation to Ernest de la Brière myself, that it may not be altered or distorted while passing through the routine channels. I have my own reasons for wishing to see that caricature."

When Rabourdin came back to the courtyard, after making sure that his letter would go straight into the minister's hands, he found Sébastien in tears, with a copy of the lithograph, which the lad reluctantly handed over to him.

"It is very clever," said Rabourdin, showing a serene brow to his companion, though the crown of thorns was on it all the same.

He entered the bureaus with a calm air, and went at once into Baudoyer's section to ask him to come to the office of the head of the division and receive instructions as to the business which that incapable being was henceforth to direct.

"Tell Monsieur Baudoyer that there must be no delay," he added, in the hearing of all the clerks; "my resignation is already in the minister's hands, and I do not wish to stay here longer than is necessary."

Seeing Bixiou, Rabourdin went straight up to him, showed him the lithograph, and said, to the great astonishment of all present, —

"Was I not right in saying you were an artist? Still, it is a pity you directed the point of your pencil against a man who cannot be judged in this way, nor indeed by the bureaus at all; — but everything is laughed at in France, even God."

Then he took Baudoyer into the office of the late La Billardière. At the door he found Phellion and Sébastien, the only two who, under his great disaster, dared to remain openly faithful to the fallen man. Rabourdin noticed that Phellion's eyes were moist, and he could not refrain from wringing his hand.

"Monsieur," said the good man, "if we can serve you in any way, make use of us."

Monsieur Rabourdin shut himself up in the late chief's office with Monsieur Baudoyer, and Phellion helped him to show the new incumbent all the administrative difficulties of his new position. At each separate affair which Rabourdin carefully explained, Baudoyer's little eyes grew as big as saucers.

"Farewell, monsieur," said Rabourdin at last, with a manner that was half-solemn, half-satirical.

Sébastien meanwhile had made up a package of papers and letters belonging to his chief and had carried them away in a hackney coach. Rabourdin passed through the grand courtyard, while all the clerks were watching from the windows, and waited there a moment to see if the minister would send him any message. His Excellency was dumb. Phellion courageously escorted the fallen man to his home, expressing his feelings of respectful admiration; then he returned to the

office, and took up his work, satisfied with his own conduct in rendering these funeral honors to neglected and
misjudged administrative talent.

BIXIOU [seeing Phellion re-enter]. *Victrix causa
diis placuit, sed victa Catoni.*

PHELLION. Yes, monsieur.

POIRET. What does that mean?

FLEURY. That priests rejoice, and Monsieur Rabourdin has the respect of men of honor.

DUTOCQ [annoyed]. You did n't say that yesterday.

FLEURY. If you address me you 'll have my hand in
your face. It is known for certain that you filched
those papers from Monsieur Rabourdin. [Dutocq leaves
the office.] Oh, yes, go and complain to your Monsieur
des Lupeaulx, spy!

BIXIOU [laughing and grimacing like a monkey]. I
am curious to know how the division will get along.
Monsieur Rabourdin is so remarkable a man that he
must have had some special views in that work of his.
Well, the minister loses a fine mind. [Rubs his hands.]

LAURENT [entering]. Monsieur Fleury is requested
to go to the secretary's office.

ALL THE CLERKS. "Done for!"

FLEURY [leaving the room]. I don't care; I am offered a place as responsible editor. I shall have all my
time to myself to lounge the streets or do amusing work
in a newspaper office.

Bixiou. Dutocq has already made them cut off the head of that poor Desroys.

Colleville [entering joyously]. Gentlemen, I am appointed head of this bureau.

Thuillier. Ah, my friend, if it were I myself, I could n't be better pleased.

Bixiou. His wife has managed it [laughter].

Poiret. Will any one tell me the meaning of all that is happening here this day?

Bixiou. Do you really want to know? Then listen. The antechamber to the administration is henceforth a chamber, the court is a boudoir, the best way to get in is through the cellar, and the bed is more than ever a cross-cut.

Poiret. Monsieur Bixiou, may I entreat you, explain?

Bixiou. I'll paraphrase my opinion. To be anything at all you must begin by being everything. It is quite certain that a reform of the service is needed; for on my word of honor, the State robs the poor officials as much as the officials rob the State in the matter of hours. But why is it that we idle as we do? because they pay us too little; and the reason of that is we are too many for the work, and your late chief, the virtuous Rabourdin, saw all this plainly. That great administrator, — for he was that, gentlemen, — saw what the thing is coming to, the thing that these idiots call the "working of our admirable institutions." The chamber

will want before long to administrate, and the administrators will want to legislate. The government will try
to administrate and the administrators will want to
govern, and so it will go on. Laws will come to be
mere regulations, and ordinances will be thought laws.
God made this epoch of the world for those who like to
laugh. I live in a state of jovial admiration of the spec-
tacle which the greatest joker of modern times, Louis
XVIII., bequeathed to us [general stupefaction]. Gentlemen, if France, the country with the best civil service
in Europe, is managed thus, what do you suppose the
other countries are like? Poor unhappy nations ! I ask
myself how they can possibly get along without two
Chambers, without the liberty of the press, without reports, without circulars even, without an army of clerks?
Dear, dear, how do you suppose they have armies and
navies? how can they exist at all without political discussions? Can they even be called nations, or governments?   It is said (mere traveller's tales) that these
strange peoples claim to have a policy, to wield a certain influence ; but that 's absurd ! how can they when
they have n't " progress " or " new lights " ? They can't
stir up ideas, they have n't an independent forum ;
they are still in the twilight of barbarism. There are
no people in the world but the French people who
have ideas. Can you understand, Monsieur Poiret
[Poiret jumped as if he had been shot], how a nation

can do without heads of divisions, general-secretaries and directors, and all this splendid array of officials, the glory of France and of the Emperor Napoleon, — who had his own good reasons for creating a myriad of offices? I don't see how those nations have the audacity to live at all. There's Austria, which has less than a hundred clerks in her war ministry, while the salaries and pensions of ours amount to a third of our whole budget, a thing that was unheard of before the Revolution. I sum up all I've been saying in one single remark, namely, that the Academy of Inscriptions and Belles-lettres, which seems to have very little to do, had better offer a prize for the ablest answer to the following question: Which is the best organized State; the one that does many things with few officials, or the one that does next to nothing with an army of them?

Poiret. Is that your last word?

Bixiou. Yes, sir! whether English, French, German or Italian, — I let you off the other languages.

Poiret [lifting his hands to heaven]. Gracious goodness! and they call you a witty man!

Bixiou. Have n't you understood me yet?

Phellion. Your last observation was full of excellent sense.

Bixiou. Just as full as the budget itself, and like the budget again, as complicated as it looks simple; and I set it as a warning, a beacon, at the edge of this hole, this gulf, this volcano, called, in the language of the "Constitutionel," "the political horizon."

POIRET. I should much prefer a comprehensible explanation.

BIXIOU. Hurrah for Rabourdin! there's my explanation; that's my opinion. Are you satisfied?

COLLEVILLE [gravely]. Monsieur Rabourdin had but one defect.

POIRET. What was it?

COLLEVILLE. That of being a statesman instead of a subordinate official.

PHELLION [standing before Bixiou]. Monsieur! why did you, who understand Monsieur Rabourdin so well, why did you make that inf — that odi — that hideous caricature?

BIXIOU. Do you forget our bet? don't you know I was backing the devil's game, and that your bureau owes me a dinner at the Rocher de Cancale?

POIRET [much put-out]. Then it is a settled thing that I am to leave this government office without ever understanding a sentence, or a single word uttered by Monsieur Bixiou.

BIXIOU. It is your own fault; ask these gentlemen. Gentlemen, have you understood the meaning of my observations? and were those observations just, and brilliant?

ALL. Alas, yes!

Minard. And the proof is that I shall send in my resignation. I shall plunge into industrial avocations.

Bixiou. What! have you managed to invent a mechanical corset, or a baby's bottle, or a fire engine, or chimneys that consume no fuel, or ovens which cook cutlets with three sheets of paper?

Minard [departing]. Adieu, I shall keep my secret.

Bixiou. Well, young Poiret junior, you see, — all these gentlemen understand me.

Poiret [crest-fallen]. Monsieur Bixiou, would you do me the honor to come down for once to my level and speak in a language I can understand?

Bixiou [winking at the rest]. Willingly. [Takes Poiret by the button of his frock-coat.] Before you leave this office forever perhaps you would be glad to know what you are —

Poiret [quickly]. An honest man, monsieur.

Bixiou [shrugging his shoulders]. — to be able to define, explain, and analyze precisely what a government clerk is? Do you know what he is?

Poiret. I think I do.

Bixiou [twisting the button]. I doubt it.

Poiret. He is a man paid by government to do work.

Bixiou. Oh! then a soldier is a government clerk?

Poiret [puzzled]. Why, no.

Bixiou. But he is paid by the government to do

work, to mount guard and show off at reviews. You may perhaps tell me that he longs to get out of his place, — that he works too hard and fingers too little metal, except that of his musket.

Poiret [his eyes wide open]. Monsieur, a government clerk is, logically speaking, a man who needs the salary to maintain himself, and is not free to get out of his place; for he doesn't know how to do anything but copy papers.

Bixiou. Ah! now we are coming to a solution. So the bureau is the clerk's shell, husk, pod. No clerk without a bureau, no bureau without a clerk. But what do you make, then, of a custom-house officer? [Poiret shuffles his feet and tries to edge away; Bixiou twists off one button and catches him by another.] He is, from the bureaucratic point of view, a neutral being. The excise-man is only half a clerk; he is on the confines between civil and military service; neither altogether soldier nor altogether clerk — Here, here, where are you going? [Twists the button.] Where does the government clerk proper end? That's a serious question. Is a prefect a clerk?"

Poiret [hesitating.] He is a functionary.

Bixiou. But you don't mean that a functionary is not a clerk? that's an absurdity.

Poiret [weary and looking round for escape]. I think Monsieur Godard wants to say something.

GODARD. The clerk is the order, the functionary the species.

BIXIOU [laughing]. I should n't have thought you capable of that distinction, my brave subordinate.

POIRET [trying to get away]. Incomprehensible!

BIXIOU. La, la, papa, don't step on your tether. If you stand still and listen, we shall come to an understanding before long. Now, here's an axiom which I bequeath to this bureau and to all bureaus: Where the clerk ends, the functionary begins; where the functionary ends, the statesman rises. There are very few statesmen among the prefects. The prefect is therefore a neutral being among the higher species. He comes between the statesman and the clerk, just as the custom-house officer stands between the civil and the military. Let us continue to clear up these important points. [Poiret turns crimson with distress.] Suppose we formulate the whole matter in a maxim worthy of Larochefoucault: Officials with salaries of twenty thousand francs are not clerks. From which we may deduce mathematically this corollary: The statesman first looms up in the sphere of high salaries; and also this second and not less logical and important corollary: Directors-general may be statesmen. Perhaps it is in that sense that more than one deputy says in his heart, "It is a fine thing to be a director-general." But in the interests of our noble French language and of the Academy —"

Poiret [magnetized by the fixity of Bixiou's eye]. The French language! the Academy!

Bixiou [twisting off the second button and seizing another]. Yes, in the interests of our noble tongue, it is proper to observe that although the head of a bureau, strictly speaking, may be called a clerk, the head of a division must be called a bureaucrat. These gentlemen [turning to the clerks and privately showing them the third button off Poiret's coat] will appreciate this delicate shade of meaning. And so, papa Poiret, don't you see it is clear that the government clerk comes to a final end at the head of a division? Now that question once settled, there is no longer any uncertainty; the government clerk who has hitherto seemed undefinable is defined.

Poiret. Yes, that appears to me beyond a doubt.

Bixiou. Nevertheless, do me the kindness to answer the following question: A judge being irremovable, and consequently debarred from being, according to your subtle distinction, a functionary, and receiving a salary which is not the equivalent of the work he does, is he to be included in the class of clerks?

Poiret [gazing at the cornice]. Monsieur, I don't follow you.

Bixiou [getting off the fourth button]. I wanted to prove to you, monsieur, that nothing is simple; but above all — and what I am going to say is intended for philosophers — I wish (if you 'll allow me to misquote a saying of Louis XVIII.), — I wish to make you see that definitions lead to muddles.

POIRET [wiping his forehead]. Excuse me, I am sick at my stomach [tries to button his coat]. Ah! you have cut off all my buttons!

BIXIOU. But the point is, *do you understand me?*

POIRET [angrily]. Yes, monsieur, I do; I understand that you have been playing me a shameful trick and twisting off my buttons while I have been standing here unconscious of it.

BIXIOU [solemnly]. Old man, you are mistaken! I wished to stamp upon your brain the clearest possible image of constitutional government [all the clerks look at Bixiou; Poiret, stupefied, gazes at him uneasily], and also to keep my word to you. In so doing I employed the parabolical method of savages. Listen and comprehend: While the ministers start discussions in the Chambers that are just about as useful and as conclusive as the one we are engaged in, the administration cuts the buttons off the tax-payers.

ALL. Bravo, Bixiou!

POIRET [who comprehends]. I don't regret my buttons.

BIXIOU. I shall follow Minard's example; I won't pocket such a paltry salary as mine any longer; I shall deprive the government of my co-operation. [Departs amid general laughter.]

Another scene was taking place in the minister's reception-room, more instructive than the one we have just related, because it shows how great ideas are allowed to perish in the higher regions of State affairs, and in what way statesmen console themselves.

Des Lupeaulx was presenting the new director, Monsieur Baudoyer, to the minister. A number of persons were assembled in the salon, — two or three ministerial deputies, a few men of influence, and Monsieur Clergeot (whose division was now merged with La Billardière's under Baudoyer's direction), to whom the minister was promising an honorable pension. After a few general remarks, the great event of the day was brought up.

A Deputy. So you lose Rabourdin?

Des Lupeaulx. He has resigned.

Clergeot. They say he wanted to reform the administration.

The Minister [looking at the deputies]. Salaries are not really in proportion to the exigencies of the civil service.

De la Brière. According to Monsieur Rabourdin, one hundred clerks with a salary of twelve thousand francs would do better and quicker work than a thousand clerks at twelve hundred.

Clergeot. Perhaps he is right.

The Minister. But what is to be done? The machine is built in that way. Must we take it to pieces and remake it? No one would have the courage to attempt that in face of the Chamber, and the foolish outcries of the Opposition, and the fierce denunciations of the press. It follows that there will happen, one of these days, some damaging " solution of continuity " between the government and the administration.

A DEPUTY. In what way?

THE MINISTER. In many ways. A minister will want to serve the public good, and will not be allowed to do so. You will create interminable delays between things and their results. You may perhaps render the theft of a penny actually impossible, but you cannot prevent the buying and selling of influence, the collusions of self-interest. The day will come when nothing will be conceded without secret stipulations, which may never see the light. Moreover, the clerks, one and all, from the least to the greatest, are acquiring opinions of their own ; they will soon be no longer the hands of a brain, the scribes of governmental thought ; the Opposition even now tends towards giving them a right to judge the government and to talk and vote against it.

BAUDOYER [in a low voice, but meaning to be heard]. Monseigneur is really fine.

DES LUPEAULX. Of course bureaucracy has its defects. I myself think it slow and insolent ; it hampers ministerial action, stifles projects, and arrests progress. But, after all, French administration is amazingly useful.

Baudoyer. Certainly!

Des Lupeaulx. If only to maintain the paper and stamp industries! Suppose it is rather fussy and provoking, like all good housekeepers, — it can at any moment render an account of its disbursements. Where is the merchant who would not gladly give five per cent of his entire capital if he could insure himself against *leakage?*

The Deputy [a manufacturer]. The manufacturing interests of all nations would joyfully unite against that evil genius of theirs called leakage.

Des Lupeaulx. After all, though statistics are the childish foible of modern statesmen, who think that figures are estimates, we must cipher to estimate. Figures are, moreover, the convincing argument of societies based on self-interest and money, and that is the sort of society the Charter has given us, — in my opinion, at any rate. Nothing convinces the "intelligent masses" as much as a row of figures. All things in the long run, say the statesmen of the Left, resolve themselves into figures. Well then, let us figure [the minister here goes off into a corner with a deputy, to whom he talks in a low voice]. There are forty thousand government clerks in France. The average of their salaries is fifteen hundred francs. Multiply forty thousand by fifteen hundred and you have sixty millions. Now, in the first place, a publicist would call the attention of Russia and China (where all government officials steal), also that of Austria, the American republics, and indeed that of the whole world, to the fact that for this price France possesses the most inquisitorial, fussy, ferreting, scribbling, paper-blotting, fault-finding old housekeeper of a civil service on God's earth. Not a copper farthing of the nation's money is spent or hoarded that is not ordered by a note, proved by vouchers, produced and re-produced on balance-sheets, and receipted for when paid; orders and receipts are registered on the rolls, and checked and verified by an army of men in spectacles. If there is the slightest mistake in the form of these precious documents, the clerk is terrified, for he lives on such minutiæ. Some nations would be satisfied to get as far as this; but Napoleon went further. That great organizer appointed supreme magistrates of a court which is absolutely unique in the world. These officials pass their days in verifying money-orders, documents, rôles, registers, lists, permits, custom-house receipts, payments, taxes received, taxes spent, etc.; all of which the clerks write or copy. These stern judges push the gift of exactitude, the genius of inquisition, the sharp-sightedness of lynxes, the perspicacity of account-books to the point of going over all the additions in search of subtractions. These sublime martyrs to figures have been known to return to an army commissary, after a delay of two years, some account in which there was an error of two farthings. This is how and why it is that the French system of administration, the purest and best on the globe has rendered robbery, as his Excellency has just told you, next to impossible, and as for peculation, it is a myth. France at this present time possesses a revenue of twelve hundred millions, and she spends it. That sum enters her treasury and that sum goes out of it. She handles, therefore, two thousand four hundred millions, and all she pays for the labor of those who do the work is sixty millions, — two and a half per.cent; and for that she obtains the certainty that there is no leakage. Our political and administrative kitchen costs us sixty millions, but the gendarmerie, the courts of law, the galleys and the police cost just as much, and give no return. Moreover, we employ a body of men who could do no other work. Waste and disorder, if such there be, can only be legislative; the Chambers lead to them and render them legal. Leakage follows in the form of public works which are neither urgent nor necessary; troops re-uniformed and gold-laced over and over again; vessels sent on useless cruises; preparations for war without ever making it; paying the debts of a State, and not requiring reimbursement or insisting on security.

BAUDOYER. But such leakage has nothing to do with the subordinate officials; this bad management of national affairs concerns the statesmen who guide the ship.

THE MINISTER [who has finished his conversation]. There is a great deal of truth in what des Lupeaulx has just said; but let me tell you [to Baudoyer], Monsieur le directeur, that few men see from the standpoint of a statesman. To order expenditures of all kinds, even useless ones, does not constitute bad management. Such acts contribute to the movement of money, the stagnation of which becomes, especially in France, dangerous to the public welfare, by reason of the miserly and profoundly illogical habits of the provinces which hoard their gold.

THE DEPUTY [who listened to des Lupeaulx]. But it seems to me that if your Excellency was right just now, and if our clever friend here [takes des Lupeaulx by the arm] was not wrong, it will be difficult to come to any conclusion on the subject.

DES LUPEAULX [after looking at the minister]. No doubt something ought to be done.

DE LA BRIÈRE [timidly]. Monsieur Rabourdin seems to have judged rightly.

THE MINISTER. I will see Rabourdin.

DES LUPEAULX. The poor man made the blunder of constituting himself supreme judge of the administration and of all the officials who compose it; he wants to do away with the present state of things, and he demands that there be only three ministries.

The Minister. He must be crazy.

The Deputy. How could you represent in three ministries the heads of all the parties in the Chamber?

Baudoyer [with an air that he imagined to be shrewd]. Perhaps Monsieur Rabourdin desired to change the Constitution, which we owe to our legislative sovereign.

The Minister [thoughtful, takes La Brière's arm and leads him into the study]. I want to see that work of Rabourdin's, and as you know about it —

De la Brière. He has burned it. You allowed him to be dishonored and he has resigned from the ministry. Do not think for a moment, Monseigneur, that Rabourdin ever had the absurd thought (as des Lupeaulx tries to make it believed) to change the admirable centralization of power.

The Minister [to himself]. I have made a mistake [is silent a moment]. No matter; we shall never be lacking in plans for reform.

De la Brière. It is not ideas, but men capable of executing them that we lack.

Des Lupeaulx, that adroit advocate of abuses came into the minister's study at this moment.

" Monseigneur, I start at once for my election."

" Wait a moment," said his Excellency, leaving the

private secretary and taking des Lupeaulx by the arm into the recess of a window. "My dear friend, let me have that arrondissement, — if you will, you shall be made count and I will pay your debts. Later, if I remain in the ministry after the new Chamber is elected, I will find a way to send in your name in a batch for the peerage."

"You are a man of honor, and I accept."

This is how it came to pass that Clément Chardin des Lupeaulx, whose father was ennobled under Louis XV., and who beareth quarterly, first, argent, a wolf ravissant carrying a lamb gules; second, purpure, three mascles argent, two and one; third, paly of twelve, gules and argent; fourth, or, on a pale endorsed, three batons fleurdelisés gules; supported by four griffon's-claws jessant from the sides of the escutcheon, with the motto *En Lupus in Historia*, was able to surmount these rather satirical arms with a count's coronet.

Toward the close of the year 1830 Monsieur Rabourdin had some business on hand which required him to visit his old ministry, where the bureaus had all been in great commotion, owing to a general removal of officials, from the highest to the lowest. This revolution bore heaviest, in point of fact, upon the lackeys, who are not fond of seeing new faces. Rabourdin had come early, knowing all the ways of the place, and he thus

chanced to overhear a dialogue between the two nephews of old Antoine, who had recently retired on a
pension.

" Well, Laurent, how is your chief of division going
on ? "

"Oh, don't talk to me about him ; I can't do anything with him.   He rings me up to ask if I have seen
his handkerchief or his snuff-box.   He receives people
without making them wait; in short, he has n't a bit of
dignity.   I 'm often obliged to say to him : But, monsieur, monsieur le comte your predecessor, for the credit
of the thing, used to punch holes with his penknife in
the arms of his chair to make believe he was working.
And he makes such a mess of his room.   I find everything topsy-turvy.   He has a very small mind.   How
about your man ? "

" Mine?   Oh, I have succeeded in training him.   He
knows exactly where his letter-paper and envelopes, his
wood, and his boxes and all the rest of his things are.
The other man used to swear at me, but this one is as
meek as a lamb, — still, he has n't the grand style !
Moreover, he is n't decorated, and I don't like to serve
a chief who is n't ; he might be taken for one of us, and
that 's humiliating.   He carries the office letter-paper
home, and asked me if I could n't go there and wait at
table when there was company."

"Hey ! what a government, my dear fellow ! "

" Yes, indeed ; everybody plays low in these days."

" I hope they won't cut down our poor wages."

" I'm afraid they will. The Chambers are prying into everything. Why, they even count the sticks of wood."

" Well, it can't last long if they go on that way."

" Hush, we're caught! somebody is listening."

" Hey! it is the late Monsieur Rabourdin. Ah, monsieur, I knew your step. If you have business to transact here I am afraid you will not find any one who is aware of the respect that ought to be paid to you; Laurent and I are the only persons remaining about the place who were here in your day. Messieurs Colleville and Baudoyer did n't wear out the morocco of the chairs after you left. Heavens, no! six months later they were made Collectors of Paris.

University Press : John Wilson and Son, Cambridge.

www.ingramcontent.com/pod-product-compliance
Lightning Source LLC
Chambersburg PA
CBHW031142120726
47905CB00006B/1788